The Young Man Who Wanted To Be A Rich and Famous Writer Too

Following the Hemingway Trail

Donald Sinclair

authorHOUSE®

AuthorHouse™
1663 Liberty Drive
Bloomington, IN 47403
www.authorhouse.com
Phone: 1-800-839-8640

First published by AuthorHouse 10/20/2009

ISBN: 978-1-4490-1987-7 (e)
ISBN: 978-1-4490-1986-0 (sc)

Printed in the United States of America
Bloomington, Indiana

This book is printed on acid-free paper.

Chapter I

"Come," the Cuban—looking jailer said to Tom, "it's your turn in court."

Sitting up on his bunk, Tom pointed to his feet; he was barefoot.

"Can I go like this?" he asked.

"I don't care if you go in naked," the guard said. "Come on."

Outside the cell, a shrimp fisherman coming back from the court room, wearing khaki pants and a dark—blue t—shirt, the same as Tom's, stopped, and kicked off his canvas rubber—sole shoes.

"Use these kid," the shrimper said. "You'll look better in there. I want these back for sure."

"Thanks," Tom said, bending his toes, forcing his feet into the shoes sizes too small.

"Let's go, the court is waiting," the jailer said. He pointed to the doorway that opened into the windowless police station.

Tom, walking on the outside edges of the shoes, hobbled to the police desk where he had been booked last night. There was a different sergant at the desk now, and looking up from what he was reading, handed two sheets of paper to the jailer as he passed.

"There," the jailer said motioning to the door marked: Key West City Court.

The judge, a small Cuban with thick green—tinted eyeglasses and a maroon sports shirt buttoned up to the neck, sat reading at a low table. The jailer handed the paper sheets to another man, a clerk, who, wearing a white shirt and black tie, was sitting at the left end of the table from the judge. Behind the judge, the window blinds, tilted shut, were slapping the window. When the wind would hold the blinds out from the window, Tom could see out to a white painted house, a palm tree, and beyond a rusting tin roof, a piece of blue ocean. Everything seemed brighter, Tom thought, brighter than he remembered it. He grinned thinking it probably just looked brighter; being that out there was free and he was stuck in here.

The blinds slammed back against the window. The judge leaned over to the clerk.

"Is the policeman here yet?"

The clerk nodded. The judge nodded.

"Thomas Cohill," the clerk said in a loud voice, reading from the sheets of paper; then he handed the papers over to the judge.

"Thomas Cohill," the judge said, "you are charged with tresspassing on the property of the Rose Garden bar after hours and public drunkeness."

"Not guilty, your honor," Tom said.

The judge and the clerk both looked up at Tom at the same time.

Tom smiled.

The court room door opened and Mark Fenton, the policeman Tom worked with at a tile company part—time, came in. Behind Fenton in his auxiliary police uniform, followed Harry Woods, the Miami Herald Key West correspondent.

Tom flushed, embarrassed, at seeing Woods. Tom knew his chance to work in Key West as a reporter for the Herald had ended when that door opened; and it was in Harry Wood's face. Tom had been talking to Woods, and Woods was recommending Tom to the Herald as a replacement reporter, because Woods' wife, after fourteen months on the island, was begging Harry to be assigned back to Miami. Tom felt the loss down in his shoes.

To hide his red face, Tom looked down at the tight canvas shoes, moving the toes. There was no getting the toes in a position where they would stop hurting. To keep them from going numb, Tom kept them moving.

Looking up from the toes, Tom saw cop Fenton standing next to him. Fenton kept looking straight at the judge.

"You arrested this man?" the judge asked Fenton.

"Yes, your honor," Fenton said, clasping his hands behind his back.

Tom, over a head taller then Fenton, could see where volunteer cop was sweating down the back of his fresh grey uniform shirt.

Harry Woods, sitting behind the judge, was leafing through a notebook, keeping his eyes down.

"Officer, what lead to this man's arrest?" the judge asked quietly.

Tom started weaving back and forth while moving his cramped toes now, trying to find relief.

"As I was walking on my beat at one this morning," Fenton recited, "on Duval street, your honor, I saw the subject here coming out the gate at the Villa Garden restaurant. Your honor, it's not the gate the bar customers usally use, so I told the subject to halt where he was."

"Instead of stopping, your honor, he says, 'Go to hell, Mark,' and keeps walking. Then, your honor, I drew my service revolver and threatened to shoot if he didn't stop."

Tom looked at the judge, who was sitting calmly, his hands folded on the table in front of him, listening.

"Officer, why again did this man appear suspicious?"

"Well, your honor, you know for yourself the trouble Mister Giovanni had at his office; being robbed in his office last spring over there, when he was counting money. Well, your honor, when I saw this man coming out the gate, and being barefoot..."

"Yes," the judge said picking up the two sheets of paper, "and was this man drunk when ... you arrested him?"

"He smelt strongly of beer, your honor."

"Thank you, officer," the judge said. Looking up at Tom rocking back and forth, asked, "How old are you?"

"Twenty," your honor.

"Where are you from? Where is your home?"

"Up north, your honor; Michigan."

Tom looked down, moving his toes hard against the soreness.

"Are you a student? "

"Yes, your honor. I mean, I was. I quit the university this year."

"Are you working here?"

"Yes, your honor. At the Secord Tile company, and sometimes for Missus McDonald ... on her boat."

People in the court smiled and shuffled their feet at the mention of Missus McDonald. She was a woman in her sixties who runs a reef—fishing charter boat. Every winter, she and her husband came down from Maine to run the old boat, and after her husband died three years ago, she runs the boat alone. Everyone in Key West knows how difficult she is to get along with, and when Tom said he worked for her, everybody grinned knowingly; the judge adjusted his glasses.

"Your honor, I work with Mark here, setting tiles for Secore," Tom said , and nodded at the policeman. "He never told me he was a cop. I've worked with him three months, almost."

The policeman, hands behind his back stared at the judge.

"I'm no thief, your honor," Tom said quietly. " I came here on the way to Havana. I'm trying to save up the thirty-six buck fare to take the ferry—boat across so I can go visit the famous writer. I want to be a writer, your honor; that's why I left the university."

Nodding, the judge said: "Those are not your shoes. Where are your shoes?"

"I left them on the boat," Tom lied. I worked scrubbing the boat down until almost ten, then I had to go over to the La Concha hotel and pass out boat business cards ... in the bar. I've got to do it," Tom said, head down, looking at loaned shoes, wriggling his toes, Missus McDonald says it's part of the job ... rounding up customers for the boat."

"Did you drink?" the judge asked.

"I had a few beers with some people who said they were interested in going out tomorrow ... I mean today.

"Were you drinking beer at the Villa Gardens also?" the judge asked.

"Yes, your honor." I stayed until closing. A waitress told me to go out by the side gate and showed me. She said Mark was out on Duval street ready to arrest anybody just to prove himself on the force ... like he did last night even trying to arrest those two submarine sailors for being drunk."

"I an going to find you guilty of public drunkeness," the judge said, writing on the papers. "That will be a fine of fifteen dollars or serving fifteen days in jail."

"My money is at my room, your honor," Tom said, lying.

"Next case," the judge said.

The jailer took hold of Tom's arm.

"If you ain't going to pay the fine," he said, "you got to go back to your cell. C'mon."

Tom looked across to Harry Woods and Harry shook his head to mean he would not help; pay the money on loan.

"Come on," the jailer said when Tom stopped to look at Harry Woods.

"Cripe," Tom said in the hallway, "I'm going to lose both jobs if I'm stuck in here for fifteen days."

"That's the way it goes," the jailer said.

Tom hobbled across the floor of the police station to the lock—up on the outside edges of the shoes.

Chapter 2

High winds and rain squalls had blown in Key West for two days. The streets flooded with water up to the bumpers of cars. Walking in the blowing rain, Tom, still barefoot, his face turned away from the wind, at the same time, watched for broken glass on the sidewalk. He had just been released from city jail.

At the corner of Eaton Street, outside his apartment house, Tom saw the electric wires sagging from their poles, snapped somewhere further up the block. Palm fronds, carried aloft by the strong wind, were caught high against the wall of the wood siding of his two—story apartment house.

In the dark stairway up, Tom tried the light switch and laughed. He left a trail up the steps, water dripping from his wet pants and shirt.

Suddenly, a flashlight beam shined from the top of the staires.

"Who's trying the lightswitch down there?" Tom heard Cassie Becker's voice ask. She had the apartment across the hall from Tom.

"Hey, Cassie, how's it going?"

"Tom? Where the hell you been? Missus Cook figured you skipped town, or something. She fumed and was ready to haul your stuff out and rent the room. But I said she could wait a day or two, it wouldn't kill her moneywise.

"Thanks," Tom said stopping on the step below Cassie.

Her thin face was like a hawk's in the low light.

"Where you been all this time, Tom? In jail?"

"Right."

"I might a known. Hey, kiddo, you're soaked to the skin. God, you better go change quick."

She leaned back and shined the light on Tom's apartment door.

"Let me have the light, Cassie."

"That's right," she said handing him the flashlight, "you ain't got windows in that cub-byhole you live in."

"It's all I can afford, right now," Tom said unlocking the door.

"Come over to my room when you change, Tom. We got a bottle. We're holding what they calls down here a hurricane party.'"

Inside, shining the light on the table, he saw his writing papers and books were as he left them. He set the flashlight on the table so it shined on the ceiling, then taking off his wet clothes, he hung them on a line in the narrow kitchen. Finding a pair of briefs, a sweat shirt, and an old pair of khaki shorts, he put them on. From under the bed he slid out an old pair of moccasins and put them on.

He remembered his empty wallet and went to the kitchen and took it out of his wet pants, opened it, and set it on the sink to dry.

He could hear the blowing rain against the thin kitchen wall above the sink and he shook his head: the place was a dump, but it beat jail any day.

Pulling open the refrigerator door, he saw the ice cubes melted, the center freeze compartment dripping water down on the shelves, defrosting. There was only a half— full bottle of catsup and an empty egg carton on the bottom in the water. He moved a chair to hold the door open to dry the inside before the electricity came back on.

Emptying the water out three ice cube trays into the sink, Tom remembered the night Cassie came to the apartment asking for ice. She and her sailor boyfriend were drinking in her room and they ran out. She was friendly after that, but Tom thought she was a little too old for him. She worked as a bartender at the Lighthouse bar on Duval.

Crossing the hall, Tom found Cassie's door open; she was sitting at a table with two old guys. Through the window behind them, Tom saw the blowing rain bending a palm tree that seemed to grow out of a cluster of trash cans down in the back yard. The light from the window made everthing seem bright compared to his room, Tom thought.

"You know these two guys?" Cassie said taking the flashlight Tom held out.

"Hi," Tom said to the guy called Harold, who seemed to spend most of his time cleaning up around the trash cans.

"I'm Georgie Brooks," the other old man said. He was small, and despite his wrinkled white shirt and cheap suspenders, seemed to want to impress on you he was better than you.

"Tom Cohill," Tom said pulling a chair up and sitting,

"Georgie's a lawyer," Cassie said and took the whiskey bottle away from Harold. "There's glasses in the cupboard."

"I'm dying for a beer," Tom said.

"It's warm, but help yourself."

Tom turned in his chair and took a beer from the frige.

"I could of used a lawyer fifteen days ago," Tom said opening and taking a long drink from the can of beer.

"Cassie told me about you just getting out of jail," Brooks said. "I could of gottn you off. I know the judge."

"I couldn't think of anybody to call," Tom said.

"You should of called me," Cassie said. "I could of at least paid the fine or something."

"Look at that rain," Harold said pointing at the window. "I don't mind hurricanes as long we don't run out a drinks."

"Right," Cassie said rolling her eyes up.

"Did you get to work outside?" Brooks asked Tom. When you were in jail, did you work cutting down coconuts from the treesaround the city?"

"Yes," Tom said. "They paid us in coconuts and cigarets, but at least we were outside."

"Why do they cut down the coconuts?" Harold asked.

"So they don't clunk the cars," Tom said; then laughed, "or somebody's head."

"How come you came to Key West?" Brooks asked, pouring more whisky from the bottle.

"He wants to be a famous writer," Cassie said, "like the fella over there in Cuba: Hemingway."

"I used to see him a lot," Brooks said taking a long drink. "Back in the days when he lived here in Key West: I was county prosecutor then. I used to drink with him at Josey Russell's first Sloppy Joe's Bar."

Nodding, Tom said, "He's the most famous author alive; I want to meet him. When I earn enough I'll take the carboat to Havana.

"He called me 'Bee—Lips' in that "To Have And Have Not" book. I'm the lawyer in that Key West story," Brooks said. "I talk to Morgan in the old Sloppy Joe's on Green street, across from the Navy base. That's me, Bee—Lips."

"There ain't many jobs around," Cassie said. "You heard any openings anywhere, Tom?"

"I can set Cuban tiles for Secord again," Tom said, "If worse comes to worse." He drank from the beer can. "Missus McDonald's daughter got sick, and mother went up to Maine, so that kills the charter boat job. A shrimper told me in jail about Missus McDonald."

"That Secord," Harold said, "he's a slave driver and he's ... Canadian. Nobody likes him; he belongs up in Miami."

"When you go to Havana," Georgie Brooks said turning his glass on the table, "I'll give you a letter of intro. You take it to the Ambos Mundo, ah, the Blue Moon bar in Havana, and give it to the bar keep. He's a friend and he'll telephone the Hemingway house and tell him about you. If the big shot wants to see you, he will tell them when he will be coming to the bar'; when he's coming to town. You might have to wait around a day or two before he comes to Havana from his farm."

"I'll take you up on the introduction, when it's time, Mister Brooks," Tom said, "when the time comes."

"Hemingway asked me to come to Havana for some drinking," Brooks said. "You tell him the reason I don't is I don't want to come back in a box. He's asked me a couple times."

"I don't understand," Tom said.

"I'm going back to my room," Harold said. "I'm getting sleepy. Booze always makes me sleepy."

"You want my flashlight for the hallway?" Cassie asked.

"I got one," Harold said pulling it out his back pocket. "I'm always ready for a hurricane. I'm an old hurricane watcher." He turned on the light and went out into the dark hall.

"What's the joke about being sent home from Havana in a box?" Tom asked Brooks, then reached into the frige for another bottle of beer.

"It's not a joke," Brooks said smiling. "Josey, took time off from the bar and went to Havana for the marlin sea-son with the big guy, and he died. Josey's wife didn't want him to go. Josey had a heart attack and died right there in Cuba. His wife was mad as hell when the body was sent back.

"I can't imagine why," Cassie said.

"Well," Brooks said, "when you tell the big guy that I didn't want to come home in a box, he'll know for sure I'm the one that said it."

"What was Hemingway like?" Tom asked. "I mean back there in the thirties."

"He was rough ... sometimes," Brooks said taking a drink. "He used to write in the morning at home up to around noon then quit for lunch. Then he'd fish with Josey, or swim or do some boxing with the locals, or just drink."

"He liked boxing," Tom said lifting the beer bottle to drink. "Was he any good at sparring around?"

"Yeah," Brooks said, thinking. "he was big. Tall, about your size, but stockier. Big shoulders and arms." Brooks smiled, nodding, "I remember one loud—mouth guy who said he was a writer too ... came down here from New York ... and was saying around the bars in town how he could lick the big guy Hemingway with one hand behind his back, and all that sort of crap.

Brooks took a quick drink, and said, "Finally, I went over to Hemingway's house on Whitehead street and told him about this New York character, about his spouting—off.

"Me and Hemingway caught up the New Yorker at the Dos Hermanos lunch counter. Hemingway sits down on the stool next to the bigmouth ... I was on the other side."

Brooks pointed to the window, "It was a sunshiney day, lunch time, and everybody was walking around. You know the Dos Hermanos?"

"Yeah," Tom said, smiling, seeing Brooks getting drunker. "It's built right to the sidewalk, the stools <u>right on</u> the sidewalk.., under a umbrella thing overhead."

"This is getting good," Cassie said. "Another drink, Georgie?"

"Yes," he said, jerking the glass toward Cassie, who knew knew Brooks was drinking too much; reached his limit.

"Have another beer, Tom," she said pouring whiskey into Brooks' glass.

"In a minute," Tom said watching her pour the whiskey.

"There we were at the lunch stand," Brooks said, "the big—talker eating chili, a bowl of chili, sitting between us. Then the big guy says, 'Georgie, I'm frightened. There is a man in town from New York and he says he's going to clean my clock. He must be a literary critic.'"

"Yeah," I says to the big guy," heard about him too."

"'What would you do if you were in my shoes, Georgie?'" the big lug asks.

"Like I always do," I says to Ernie. "Left, then a right."

"By now the jerk from New York knows it's the famous writer talking," Georgie says and takes a drink, quickly. "But he ain't letting on he knows, he just keeps eating chili. Everybody else around was watching now. They knew."

"'You mean the ole one—two?'" Ernie says and swings a left hook out over the lunch counter. Then he throws a right.'"

"Well, when he's bringing back his right arm, he backhands the challenger across his face. The challenger flies off the stool backwards and lands right out in the street on his fanny. Right there in broad daylight in front of the whole town, almost. It was around lunch time."

"Hemingway must of really clouted him," Tom said.

"Yep," Brooks said leaning back in his chair. "Ole loud—mouth got it good. Everybody laughed. The guy got up spitting out chili, then takes off up Duval street like a rabbit."

Cassie laughed: "Sounds like somebody I knew, once." She took a long drink, emptying her glass. "But he ran away for another reason. Marriage."

"Another time," Brooks said, "the big guy broke a guy's jaw over at one of those fancy hotels over on the east side of the island.

"Some jerk made a crack to the famous guy's mother, or sister, I forget, over there at one of the fancy hotels. The mother or sister was visiting him here in Key West, and he goes over and fights the jerk in the driveway, "Brooks said his eyes glassey. "The driveway was made of little white stones."

Cassie poured the last of the whiskey into her and Georgie's glass, and set the empty bottle on the floor.

"When he have any time for writing? He seems to be fighting most of the time," she asked Brooks.

Then she looked at Tom; "Is that the kind of writer you want to become? Fighting with everybody? Fooey.

"No—o, Cassie," Brooks said calmly. "I'm just telling you all this to show how well he could take care of himself."

"C'mon Cassie," Tom said. "It's not that way."

"Well he does a lot of fighting," she said. "I don't care for what reasons; that's no way to live, writer or not."

Brooks drank what whiskey was left in his glass, "He would only fight when he had to, Cassandra; understand?"

"Just when he had to," Tom repeated. "Certanly."

"He used to spar a little," Brooks said to Tom, "but I was too light to fight him. He used to say I could be the world's light weight champ if I gave up lawyering."

He stood up unsteadily, holding the back of his chair. "Think I'm going to lay down in my room for a while," he said. "Be sure to see me before you go to Cuba, Tommy."

"I will," Tom nodded, as Brooks went out the door.

The rain came against the window sounding like gravel hitting the glass. The palm tree bounced wild in the wind.

"That creep," Cassie said. "Comes in the bar and talks some legal mumbo—jumbo to the owner, then drinks on the tic for it. Harold's just as bad, except he sweeps out the bar once in a while. Deadbeats, both of them."

"Don't say that," Tom said and drank off his beer. "Cassie," he said, "I don't know how to ask this now… I'm sort of short of cash and ..."

"I don't even have a dollar, honey. Honest."

"Well then," Tom said looking at the empty beer can, "can you spare a few eggs?

"Honey," Cassie said, "I told you before, that when you're hungry and need help, just help yourself to eats in the frige. If I'm out, I showed you where the key's hid." She put her thin hand on Tom's arm. "Okay?"

"Right," Tom said looking at her hand.

"You've been away from girls for a while," Cassie said softly, "haven't you, honey?"

Tom remembered the night she knocked on his door, late one night, saying her Filipino boss said he was coming by her place with a bottle after he locked up the bar. She was in her bar clothes, Toreador pants and white blouse, and seemed frightened. They were in bed when they heard the boss knocking at her door across the hall. She said he'd been after her at work all week.

Tom nodded and said, "Yeah, two weeks and the only girls I saw were when they let us out of jail to cut coconuts up and down the streets."

"Get the door, honey."

Tom stood up and closed the door and locked it.

Cassie stood up reaching for him.

"I really go for you, kiddo," she said softly.

Later, Tom woke up in the dark, Cassie sleeping. He lay with his hands behine his head. For food he would take a empty coffee can down to the shrimp boats, like he did before. One of the crew would fill it with shrimp if the boss was not around. The rent was the big problem.

The window was dark, but he could still hear the pelt of the rain.

Chapter 3

Tom was sitting at a table in the open—air sandwich shop where Duval street meets where U. S. 1 highway ends. He liked sitting, watching people go by for the price of a beer. He was not working; the bosses' stepson was killed when he crashed his Piper Cub. The boss said he had to stay up in Miami with his wife and he would call the tile crew when they would start work again. That was for days ago.

This morning, Tom counted his forty—one dollars, and was trying to make up his mind about going to Havana and meeting the famous writer. It might mean starving over there in Cuba, he thought; but he could always eat coconuts. Then, he thought, if he was weak with hunger, and staggered up to the front gate of the famous author's house, the famous writer might be mor inclined to be friendly, remembering his, the famous writer struggling in Paris as a poor artist, and they could sit down and talk as equal suffers.

Naw, Tom thought, all this pre—starvation thinking will get you nowhere. It's crazy.

Earlier today, he talked with Georgie Brooks who said the famous writer's wife, a short blond woman, was seen shopping in Key West yesterday. Some friends of Georgie, who were friends of the famous writer and his wife, had lunch with her and she told them the writer was suffering badly from the plane crash this year in Africa. His injuries were far worse than anyone knew about, but, the famous writer's wife said, they were keeping it from the public.

Tom remembered the day of the plane crash in Africa. The newspaper on the stand in the lobby of Howard Johnson's in Grosse Pointe Woods said the writer was presumed dead. Tom remembered how he stood starring at the picture of Hemingway on the front page of The Detroit Free Press, unbelieving the writer dead, until his then girl friend, Harriet Mallory, asked him what was the matter.

Telling Harriet the writer was presumed dead, Tom remembered, made him so upset the banana split he just ate nearly came up. They bought a newspaper and read the story in the car, under the dome light, how the famous writer and wife survived the first crash, and how their rescue plane, taking off, also crashed.

Another thing he remembered was a story in the newspaper where the oldest sister of the famous writer was interviewed at her home in Grosse Pointe Farms. She told the newspaper reporter she would not comment until the body was found, his death a certainty.

That was more like it, Tom remembered himself thinking when he read that news story, outloud, to Harriet. That was the same kind of fighting spirit the famous writer had, the kind of spirit that made him so admired. And here it was coming from his sister. Tom remembered thinking thinking that courage must run deep in that whole family. Tom remembered he said to Harriet that was why everybody like to read the famous writer's stories and books; everything was always under control and if you showed courage you would not lose.

That settled it, Tom thought now in Key West, sitting in the cafe, holding the glass of beer; he will go to Cuba on the next ferry—boat, starve or no starve. He wanted to see, had to see face to face, the man who lived with courage.

A skinny young man, wearing horn—rim glasses and a sport coat, and another young man carrying a large press camera, came in the cafe and sat at a table against the wall.

Tom recalled seeing the skinny guy at the Key West Citizen newspaper office, typing, when Tom had asked for a job, talking to the editor. Skinny seemed to be acting smug and superior as he typed, some glancing at Tom, the outsider, wanting to get in.

The editor at the Citizen said the only reporting job he had open was for a sports reporter. Tom told the editor he could do all kinds of reporting, but not sports, he recalled. The editor said that was too bad because he just hired a general assignment reporter at the beginning of the week and he did not need one just now.

There was another reason for disliking the bespeckled reporter besides the one for beating him out of a job and being secure having a paycheck every week. Tom got mad just thinking about it, how maybe someday, the famous writer might read the Citizen or maybe wrapping fish in the paper, and see Tom's by—line, instead of the bespeckled creep's name. Another thing that could happen too, was that Tom might be given an interview with the famous writer if he ever came over to Key West, and Tom was working on the newspaper instead of bozo.

If only that creep had waited just one more week before he asked for the newspaper job, Tom thought, things would be a world of difference. It was a tough break for Tom, but it was settled now. He had to swallow the fact he had lost. He had no way of changing life's hard knocks. Let the creep have the crummy reporting job, Tom thought. It did not matter now, he told himself, he was heading for Cuba to meet the famous writer face—to—face.

That made him feel better.

Walking down Duval toward the Post Office where he was going to buy ferryboat tickets, Tom passed the drug store newspaper racks. The headline on the Citizen blared;

HEMINGWAY WINS NOBEL PRIZE

Tom bought a newspaper and sat down on the curb to read, and at the same time, felt excited and a sense of loss at the same time. His stomach turned.

"It's about time he won something, Tom said quietly, "after all the stories he gave to literature."

At the same time, Tom had a sinking feeling; something was wrong. He could feel it.

Reading another news story related to the Prize, Tom learned the famous writer's house in Havana was over run with diplomats, friends, well—wishers, and the world press.

And there was another news story where the famous writer wife said he was not fully recovered from all the air crash injuries. She was worried, she said, about what all this constant excitement would do to him. It was hard on him.

"They got him now," Tom said, folding the newspaper, standing up off the curb. "Those people own him and there's no getting near him, especially, unknown, young writers like me. So that's that.

Back at his apartment house, Tom set the newspaper on one of the trash cans near the door before going up the stairs. Up in his room, he lay down on the bed, folded his hands behind his head and looked up at the ceiling light.

There was no sense any more of staying in Key West, he thought, closing his eyes. It will probably be a month before the congratulations to the famous writer die down, and that is a long time to hang around Key West.

On the other hand, maybe there is a chance to land a steady job, and if that happens, there might be a chance to get over to Cuba and a chance for a talk.

If he is really sick though, his little blond wife might keep all intruders away; she would just be doing her job.

No, Tom thought, the best idea is to go home. From now on there would not be much chance to talk with the famous writer without someone cutting in to congratulate him. He was just famous now. Everybody wanted to greet and congratulate him. It was not about writing anymore, it was about celebrity now. Fame. Popularity. Everybody.

It was time to head home and begin a campaign of steady writing and quit being a camp—follower, Tom thought.

Tom turned onto his right side on the bed, his face to the wall, and went to sleep, the overhead light still on. When he woke later, it was after four o'clock. He stood up, and went into the kitchen and washed his face in cold water at the sink. Then re—counting his forty—one dollars, he headed out for the bus station.

When he came back to the room with a bus ticket, he packed his story manuacripts and books in a cardboard box, then his work shirts and pants on top, then tied the box with chalkline that had been used for reef—fishing on Missus McDonald's charter boat.

Then he packed all his good clothes and pants in the small suitcase he brought with him, feeling his stomach churn.

Cassie came in when he was checking the pockets of his raincoat.

She was dressed in a pink, freshly—ironed blouse, ready for work on the late shift at the bar.

"Hey Tom, you going someplace?"

"I'm heading home," he said dropping the coat on the bed.

"What happened? Somebody die, or something? What's the rush?

"I can't do what I came here to do, Cassie. I'm going back home."

"You mean about seeing the famous writer? You can't go see him because of all the hullabaloo over that peace prize?"

"Yes," Tom said smiling. "That's about it."

"Hell, honey," Cassie said putting her hand on Tom's arm, that stuff will all blow over in a week or two… Then you can go across."

"Naw, Cassie, it's just too hard making the rent money ... and all that here In Key West.

"You lasted this long, Tom. You can last a little longer. And hell, honey, everybody has trouble making the rent money and all that."

"You're right in a way, but I've decided to go, Cassie."

"What time your bus go, honey?"

"Seven—thirty tomorrow morning," Tom said feeling both her hands holding his arm.

"Look honey, I've got to run to work now, but do me a favor and wait before you make a move. I want to talk it over with you. Maybe I can help get you a job..."

Tom shook his head, slowly, "I don't know."

"Just wait up for me tonight, honey. I'll be home right after two.

"Where's your boy friend?

"His sub is on a sonar check run over to Guantanimo," When Tom nodded, she kissed him, but when he raised his arms to hold her, she stepped back shaking her head.

"No—no," she said quickly, "I don't want to go into work with a crushed blouse. That wouldn't look good."

Tom smiled, nodding.

"See you later, hon," she said and went out the door.

Tom thought for a minute, she was going to say something to him along the lines of leaving now, you might regret it the rest of your life. You came to meet Hemingway, do it. He was pretty sure that was her two o'clock message. Fooey.

Later that evening, when it turned dark, Tom went down to shower on the shrimp docks, bringing clean briefs and soap wrapped in a towel. There is a closed—in wooden shower stall, with hot and cold water, built for the shrimpers to use, The shrimpers in jail told Tom about it.

There was no top on the shower stall, Tom could look up and see stars.

When Tom had asked about working on a shrimp boat, the shrimpers only hired experienced hands, and besides, they said, the work was too punishing for anybody in their right mind.

On the way home from showering, Tom passed a blue—painted house with a sign, "Electric Kitchen" and smiled, at that name for a restaurant. At the narrow Green Street Bar, the first Sloppy Joe's owned by Josey Russell, Tom went in for a glass of' beer. Looking out the front window that was frosted with layers of salt spray, Tom could see the shrimp boats, and beyond them, to the mouth of the harbor and the two—story oil tanks and the Coast Guard station with the grey cutter at its dock. The submarine base was there too.

Out beyond the breakwater, Tom knew about the Sand Key lighthouse, high up out of the water on steel spider—legs, and beyond that the good fishing grounds for grouper in the Marquesas' coral reefs. Mrs. McDonald had gotten him that far.

Ninety miled south in Havana, Tom knew, the famous writer was holding court. The man he had come to visit, to learn from about becomming rich and famous by writing well, was unobtainable. The whole world was at the famous writer's door. Tom would have to wait. His turn might come later ... he would just have to try again ... later.

Back in his room, Tom set the small alarm clock for six—thirty in the morning, then laid down to read E. M. Forester's "Aspects Of The Novel" until he fell asleep.

The next morning, Tom was alone; Cassie must be with her Filipino boss, Tom thought, smiling.

After making four sandwiches with the bread and balogna left in the refrigerator, wrapping them in the plastic bread bag, he put his alarm clock in the suitcase along with the sandwiches, and picking it up, along with the cardboard box, he stood looking around the room.

"I didn't have any luck here," he said out loud.

Using his elbow, he turned the light switch off.

Chapter 4

It was near noon of the first morning Tom had come home from Key West, when he came downstairs from his bed room and met his mother in the dining room. He had talked only for a short time last night with her and his father after he arrived at two o'clock.

"What did you do down there in Key West?" his mother asked from behind the dining room table, tying a pink ribbon around a box she had just wrapped in white paper. "I mean besides giving all your money to those foreigners."

"Key West is part of the United States, mother." He pointed at the gift box, smiling. "Card parties cost a lot of money too."

"You know what I mean," she said, trimming the pink ribbon with scissors. "the way you spend money in those terribly dirty places."

Tom, sailing, knew she was talking about his trip to Acapulco, when he went broke and wired home for money. His father telegrammed the money with the message: "When will you join the navy?"

"Mother, I <u>worked</u> down in Key West. I held my own, so don't start that stuff again."

His mother was dressed for a card party, dark blue dress and a string of pearls around her neck.

"You look nice," he said smiling.

She smiled back, using the scissors making the ribbon curl.

Tom stood for a moment looking out the window, feeling home again. The long front grass outside was well trimmed. At the end of the street, he could see Lake St. Clair, blue and silver, in the warm June sunshine. It was a hot day for June, more like Florida than Michigan.

"What did you accomplish down there, son?"

"You know I went to see the famous writer, mother."

"You said that about Toronto also."

"No, mother. Toronto was for a newspaper job there."

"Your famous writer started out working for that news paper in Toronto, didn't he?"

"Yes, he did mother," Tom said watching her rolling ribbon.

Tom remembered the night he arrived in Toronto, the Canadian National Exhibition was on. Walking through the displays and kiddie rides, he found the press building. In side he found only one man typing rapidly in a room filled with typewriters and desks, all empty.

Tom remembered telling the reporter who stopped his rapid typing: "I trying to get a job on The Star."

"Have you done any newspaper work?" the reporter asked patiently, looking up from his typewriter,

"I wrote for my university newspaper and. I wrote the news assignments in my journalism classes," Tom said.

The reporter bent over a ashtray, lighting a fresh cigaret from the one he was smoking.

Then, writing on a piece of yellow paper, he said, "Okay, lad, this might help you. It's to my editor. He might put you on, eh. Ask for McLeod.

"Thanks," Tom said, shaking the reporter's hand. Outside the tent, Tom opened the note and read:

Angus,

Maybe you can help this budding American with a job, who may turn out like the famous writer (who wrote for The Star. He seems to have the requirements of a good reporter — a wild imagination — which we need badly on the Globe staff.

Neil.

Tom remembered the disappointment; he did not want to work in Toronto for the Globe and Mail. It was the Star the famous writer had worked for and that was where he wanted to work also to begin his writing career. He put the note in a trash basket as he walked past it.

Tom remembered Young street in Toronto, and The Star building, and looking at the door where the famous writer passed, as a young man and unknown. Tom remembered wishing he could see the famous writer coming out the door; they might have a drink and talk writing.

"We never had a writer in the family," Tom's mother said, as if it were a disease. "Neither side. Amazing."

She turned and put her ribbons and wrapping paper in the drawer of the china cabinet in the corner.

"It's not too hard to understand, mother," Tom said quietly, "to be truthful about it, I liked the life Hemingway lived; travelling all over the world, hunting in Africa, sport fishing, going to different wars, living out West, adventureous stuff like that. And, on top of that, being known for your writing all over the world. Amazing."

"Everyone would like that, son. To live like that, but you have to be practical in life." She smiled. "Your father does more than enough travelling in his business. Too much to suit me.

"I couldn't make it as a tax lawyer, mother."

"Your father is an executive, with many clients. He has very heavy responsibilities, and has done very well; you shouldn't belittle his work, he has given us, provided for us very comfortably and provided the finest ..."

"Mother, please don't start all that stuff, again. Not today, okay?"

"Well, I don't think you should critize your father, not at all. Not after you barge in here after trapsing to those filthy places; you might of caught something deadly out there."

"Mother, I'm too tired to argue today."

"You father may approve of you living like a vagrant, but I certainly do not. I can't even hold my head up when people ask me, 'Oh, what is your son doing now?'" She looked across the table at Tom, putting her hand on her hip. "I have to say, 'He's a writer, travelling out there somewhere.' I should say he's out there doing no thing worthwhile. And I have to smile. Embarrased."

"I'm sorry you feel that way, mother."

"Why can't you be like your friends, son, settle down and get married? Maybe you and Harriet could get together."

"Someday, but not right now, mother."

He knew she was upset when she slammed the heavy china cabinet drawer using her hip, then turned quickly through the doorway to the kitchen. He followed her; she lifted the electric coffee pot from it's base on the table.

"I guess Willow finished the coffee," she said. "You haven't had any yet today, have you?"

Tom shook his head.

"Is Willow <u>still</u> ironing out there?" his mother asked emptying the coffee grounds into a bowl on the sink.

"Yes, I can hear her out in the sun room,"

"I'll have to speak to her," his mother said rinsing the coffee pot. "Every Thursday when she comes, she does that, drains the pot. I wind up making coffee for the help."

Grinning, Tom sat down at the kitchen table.

"Maybe she's just too busy, mother, to make coffee.

"Tom, what are you going to do now that you're home?" she asked turning off the water, the pot filled. "I <u>have</u> to know ... you're beginning to worry ... I'm concerned."

"I've got some plans, mother, that may work things out to everyone's satisfaction.

"Well, I hope these <u>plans</u> are not as temporary as the other ones you have dreamed—up." She was spooning coffee into the pot, counting them, moving her lips. When she snapped the lid on the pot, she said, "You know you must plan your life, your future. You can't keep running away forever," she said plugging the electric cord into the pot, then the wall socket.

Tom thought of a short story he had read, written by the famous writer, similar to the scene taking place here now, The mother in the story was talking to a young man, the now rich and famous writer, who had just returned from the First World War, confused. Tom remembered in the story, the young man was sitting at a kitchen table, like he, Tom, was doing now, watching the bacon grease go hard on his plate as he listened to his mother. She, like

Tom's mother, was talking about him, the writer, getting a job and meeting girls, and using his father's car, all very similar to what Tom's mother was saying.

That short story was a sad one. The famous writer, as a young man, was having trouble making money from fiction writing. It was the hard time the famous writer had, that gave Tom the commaradre — the close feeling — the simularity with the famous writer's life, that Tom liked. But even though he like it, he could not write about it — like the famous writer did; the famous writer had written such a complete job on the story situation that there was no sense in Tom even trying to write about it. But Tom had to ask himself how many young people, would—be writers, had gone through, a scene similar to this.

"Tom? Tom," his mother said crisply, "are you listening to me?"

"Yes, mother."

"You look so ... distant, son. Is there something bothering you. Tell me."

"I've just been thinking, mother, about what I could do that would help my writing career and that wouldn't bother you. And I think I've found the solution."

"What is it, son?"

She sat down slowly, opposite him at the table.

"Well, we both know it's just a matter of time until I get drafted, now that I'm no longer attending the university."

"You're not going to join the army?" his mother said putting both her hands flat on the table. "No—o."

"It's the best plan, mother. I want to tour Europe and by joining the army, they'll take me over there, and at the same time I'll be serving my military requirement."

"I'm not so sure about this plan," his mother said, leaning back in her chair. "Let's see what your father has to say about it. He knows about things like this."

"There's no war, mother. "It wouldn't be the same as me going to fight in a war and all that."

"Let's just wait, Tom. We'll talk it over with your father this evening at dinner. It's only right to hear what he has to say."

"I really want to go to Europe, mother. You know how much I've talked about going over there. I'd like to see Paris and all of Italy, and Spain especially."

"Like your famous writer did, I'm sure, son."

"You're right, mother," Tom said, smiling widely. "You got me on that one."

"There's something about that famous writer that I dislike. I bet his mother is not too happy about him either," Tom's mother said getting up from the table.

"An—h, don't say things like that, mother."

"I'll scramble you some eggs. Make some, toast, son."

Tom took bread from the cupboard and put it in the toaster. The light came on at the bottom of the coffee maker, so he took out a cup and filled it, then sat back down.

"Tom, I swear, but every time I look at that famous writer's picture up in you room ... that beard ... it makes me think of the devil."

"Don't say things like that, mother," Tom said to her as she brought over a plate with scrambled eggs. He reached for the toast in the toaster on the counter next to his chair. "He's nothing like that, he's an artist," Tom said eating.

"I don't know," his mother said. "I don't approve of this whole writing life you have chosen for a career, Tom."

"It'll all work out, mother. Just wait," Tom said and took a mouthfull of eggs.

"What are you going to do today, Tommy?" his mother asked putting the frying pan in the sink, trying not to show concern.

"Think I'll go over and see Harriet — at work," Tom said eating toast. "And there's a movie I want to see tonight — maybe I can borrow dad's car, later."

"Okay, I realize," Harriet said watching Tom unlock the door of his father's Buick, then pull it open. "But I don't think it's anything to worry about."

Harriet's raincoat pulled up on her legs when she sat down in the car. Tom caught a glimpse of her white thigh under her skirt when she lifted her legs into the car, then pulled the door closed.

Tom stepped around the back of the car and quickly unlocked the driver side door and climbed in.

Harriet was pulling on the seatbelt, when Tom leaned across and kissed her. Then he slid his arm over her shoulder.

"Hey, Tom," she said calmly, "people are walking outside; they'll see us." She pushed him. "Cool it."

"Harriet, you look better than ever," he said with his face against hers. "I can't help it."

He kissed her again, then slowly put his hand on her thigh, moving it slowly up.

She pushed his hand away, hard.

"Cut it out, Tom. You're acting like a sailor who just got shore leave. Cut it out. I mean it."

"Give me a break, Hare. This isn't you; you never acted this role before. What happened? What changed our— relationship?

Tom leaned back to look at her in the car.

"Things have changed," she said, "Things are different, Tom — like I said, cut it out."

"Hare, is this because I went to Key West?"

"That's part of it." She clicked on the seat belt looking at him. "What we had before — is — over."

"Is that all you are going to say?"

"Yes."

"Babe, I thought we had a — understanding — that once my writing plans takeoff, we'd get serious, and settle down."

"Well, Tom, I have to say that I have some plans now of my own. You have to accept that."

"Okay, okay. We can talk about it later," Tom said softly. "I guess I've been too much involved in my own problems; I wasn't considering you — what you want to do. That was a mistake, and I can fix it, if you give me a chance."

She sat looking out at the people walking past the car.

They did not speak until they were driving Lakeshore Road, the Grosse Pointe Yacht Club tower, lighted, showing ahead, in the dark of a lake.

"Did you like the movie?" Tom asked, finally, to break the tension.

"It was okay," Harriet quietly said facing the window.

As they turned, an arm waved from a back table in the restaurant and both of them saw it.

"There's Sandra Beauvais waving," Tom said. "I think that's Bassler Hoyt and Judy Joyce with her. I don't know that other guy between them." Harriet waved. "There's Barbra St. John with Mark Winters. Good grief, everybody."

"You feel like talking to them, Tom? That whole crowd?

"There is no room at the table," he said, trying to figure who the unknown guy could be, when the hostess, carrying a stack of menues, came up to them.

"There's about a twenty minute wait for a table," she said softly.

"Yes," Harriet said to the hostess, "we were just leaving."

Going back out the door, Tom said, "We can either go to the Pointe Bar—B—Q, or Lombardi's for pizza, whatever you want, Hare."

"A—ah, I'm not really hungry," she said in a tone that Tom sensed as a dismissal, the same tone she used on the hostess. "Maybe we'll just go to my house."

When they were driving, Tom asked her, "Who you been going out with, while I've been away?" He took a quick look at her. "Or shouldn't I ask?"

"Nobody you know," she said folding her arms, looking forward. "Since I've been working, I don't usually go out, except on week ends. I'm saving money for ski season."

When Tom turned onto the street where Harriet lived, he said, "I've got something important to tell you, Hare."

He could feel her looking at him in the dark.

"What is it?"

He turned into the circular driveway in front of her house, stopped, then shut off the engine, then the lights.

"I'm going to join the army," he said.

"You're kidding."

"No, I've decided. I talked it over with my parents tonight at dinner."

"But why? Wait until you're drafted, then go."

"I want to go to Europe," Tom said, "and if I join now, well, they're filling up a division that is assigned f or Europe...I can be a part of it."

"You are absolutely crazy, Tom."

"Call it killing two birds with one stone; I'm going to Europe and doing my military obligation at the same time."

"Quit the pragmatic bit, Tom. You're going because the famous writer spent a lot of time in Europe. Now, you think you have to go there too. You're sick, Tom; this whole writing thing is becomming an obsession with you. It's running away with your life. You're living in a dream. You're trying to live like the famous writer did."

"That's not true", Tom said. "I want to go to Europe because there is a lot over there ... for a writer."

"Stop it, Tom. That bit don't work."

"Hare, I was thinking ... you might want to come with me to Europe," he said feeling his face flush and go warm.

She opened the car door and the dome light came on. "No, Tom. No," she said holding the door as she climbed out.

"You have a new boyfriend," he said. "There's another guy, isn't there? That's why I'm getting the bum's rush."

"Yes. Yes, Yes," she said looking at him, holding open the door of the car. "1 owe you that much; I do have a boyfriend. Damn you."

"Is that why you didn't want to sit and talk with Sandra back at Howard Johnson's?" Tom said quietly. "He was sitting there, wasn't he? That's why you wanted to leave in such a hurry, wasn't it?"

"Go to hell, Tom." She lowered her head sideways to look at him in the car. "What did you expect me to do, while you're wandering off to Key West? And that was just the beginning of you're travels; now it's Europe. You expect me to sit home and wait? Well, I didn't wait."

"I guess," Tom said, "asking you to wait would be too much to ask?

"You're the one who's too much, and now you've proved it. I came out tonight because you just came home and I wanted to explain things to you. I didn't want to start arguing again, like we always do. I'm sorry, Tom, but we should't see one another any more. I mean it. What we had before is over."

"I just wanted you to wait, Hare, until I get my writing career to a paying basis, where I can earn a living on my writing.

Harriet closed the car door and ran to house front door and went in.

Tom did not follow her up to the house; he did not want a confrontation with her parents.

Driving away, he thought of the short story by the famous writer, where the main character tells his girl friend, while out on a picnic, that their romance is over. In the story the wind blows for three days.

The scenario was shown tonight in the movie he saw at the Punch & Judy.

But he realized that the story is reversed in his life; it's the girl, Harriet, that tells him their roman-ce is over. He felt himself shaking over losing Harriet; he liked her, he had liked her for a long time.

When he thought again about the reverse in the story, he told himself his life was going to be different from the famous writer's in detail— but the essentials were still there — to make them similar. Besides, the details did not matter that much. He just had to keep writing, Tom told himself. That way, if he continues to keep it up, the lifestyle of the famous will come to him eventually.

“0f all the people who I thought understood what I was doing,” Tom said outloud, “I thought she did. I thought Harriet was with me and my writing career.” He felt his legs tremble. “I guess I’m paying, now, for wanting to be a famous writer.”

Chapter 6

Tom completed basic training at Fort Riley, Kansas in September, 1955, and because of his newspaper back ground, was sent to the Army Information School at Fort Slocum, New Rochelle, New York, for training to become an army newspaper editor. New Rochelle is located just fifteen miles north of New York city.

The first Saturday the army gave passes, he rode the train into New York City, by himself.

Getting off the train in Penn Station, he walked up Seventh Avenue to Times Square, then crossed to Fifth Avenue. It was easy walking in loose civilian clothes, and he liked the freedom the slacks, white shirt and sport coat, gave his thinking again.

He found the Scribner's publishing house that had a bookstore on the street level; before going in, he studied the building and spotted the stairs at the south end of the building. Tom thought, it was up those stairs, painted black, that writing giants climbed; the famous writer and others. Tom could hardly believe that he was seeing the place the famous writer took his work to be edited and published. Looking at the steps and shaking his head, he thought the steps looked too narrow to support giants; he thought too, how great it would be to someday go up the steps with a novel he wrote under his arm.

Going inside the bookstore, he felt smug, having already read most of the better known authors of the publishing house. A salesgirl, dressed like she just left a college campus, asked if she could help him. He had a growing dislike for the college—bookish type. They wanted to be writers so they take jobs <u>close</u> to books, in bookstores and libraries, as if being close to books would help them become writers, or some way, would help them write better.

"No thanks," he said to the salesgirl, smiling. "Just browsing — sort of."

She nodded and moved to talk to another customer.

Tom began leafing though a large picture book about the Plains Indians, when he thought again of the bookstore and library book handlers; "They seem to think they can soak up writing ability — like osmosis —absorbing it though the books already written," he said out loud.

When some people turned to look at him talking to him-self; to get off the hook, he tapped the book, and added "That's a good quote."

Leaving the bookstore, Tom walked to the Forty—Fifth Street Child's for a club sandwich and ice tea. Walking again, he found a <u>New Yorker</u> magazine on a news stand and found in a listing of events for the week that the movie "All Quiet On The Western Front" was being shown at two p.m. at the Museum of Modern Art. He smiled, thinking the anti—war film would seem more appropriate now with him being in the army. He would have to walk fast to get to the museum over on Fifty—Third street, the film started in twenty minutes.

As he was walking, he thought of the apartment the famous writer and his wife kept here in the city; he had read about it in a magazine. The location was secret. He pictured the rooms filled with trophy heads, hides and mounted fish. Maybe he was near the apartment now, he thought. He pictured the famous writer's desk full of papers and books and all kind of pictures. It would really be some-thing to see, he thought, how the famous writer lives world wide.

It was fun being in New York again, this sixth or seventh time, he thought, crossing Fifty—Third street, especially after the months in dusty Kansas. He wanted to tour the Museum of Natural History again in this city that had everything. Well, he thought, he had eight weeks of classes at Fort Slocum, that was more time to spend here then he ever had before. He had heard the class from Slocum would be given a tour of the United Nations building as part of their curriculum too. It made him grin as he skipped off the curb. He was in the right place.

Going through the doors of the Modern Art Museum to the ticket line for the movie, Tom saw a familiar face, Art Baseheart — Private Baseheart — another soldier taking, the Information course. A girl with long brown hair down her back was standing with him.

Tom had talked with Baseheart once in the mess hall at Slocurn, and again in the post library. Hardheart said he was going into advertising. He had studied at Cornell and his family lived in Scarsdale, New York.

Tom heard of a restaurant chain in New York called Horn and Baseheart, but could never ask Art if it was his family business.

Art always wore expensive cordovan leather shoes with his uniform, not regulation army shoes. He was wearing them today with a tan cotton suit.

Art's brother was attending Columbia graduate school here in the city. He was working on a Master's degree in Literature, and wanted to be a writer. Art told Tom this, after Tom said he wanted to be a writer.

"Well," Art said when he saw Tom, "I guess I'm not the only one who likes classic movies."

"Yeah," Tom said grinning, "it must be. Or maybe, just that anything about the military, I find fascinating."

"Or — anti—military," Art said.

"True, true," Tom said. "I'm just a civilian doing what he has to."

Tom stood looking at the girl, who smiled.

"This is Pam," Art said. "Pamela French. Tom… ah, I forgot the last…

"Cohill."

"Hi," Pam said, opening her eyes wide.

"What have you been up to?" Art asked. "We did a tour of Abercrombie and Fitch's tennis racquet supply for Pam."

Tom smiled.

"I've been inspecting the city's bookstores," Tom said. "We infantry men have to keep our minds in shape."

"Are you here by yourself?" Pam asked.

"Yeah," Tom said, glancing across the lobby to avoid her wide brown eyes, then down at Art's cordovan shoes, feeling that she was really asking why he was by himself.

Pam took hold of Art's arm, and looking at Tom, said, "After the movie, maybe you'd like to come with us, if you don't have other plans. You could meet my room mate. She's very nice."

"Sure, he'll come," Art said. "Right?"

"Yeah," Tom said. "I usually stay at the old Chelsea Hotel on Twenty—Third street, the old haunt of Tom Wolfe and Henry James according to the brass plaque outside the door. But the place is a little run down, now."

"Come with us," Pam said. "We'd like you to come."

"Sounds great," Tom said, nodding.

After the movie, they rode uptown on the subway, getting off at 116th Street to walk to Baseheart's brother's apartment.

"This is terrific," Tom said, standing in the living room of the apartment. The ceiling and walls were white, there was a roll—top desk in front of two windows that looked down into the street, a stereo record player next to the desk, and on the floor, stacks of books. The remainder of the room was vacant away from the desk, except for a black rug, and a geometric pattern poster on the opposite wall.

"I usally stay here when I'm in the city," Baseheart said raising a hand. "Why not, my father pays for it."

Pam went back the door to the hallway. "Back in a flash," she said.

"Right," Base said, watching her go out.

Looking at the giant desk, Tom said, "This place looks and <u>feels</u> like a good place to do some writing."

Baseheart rolled up the desk shutter.

"This is his typewriter and stuff," he said.

"Wow," Tom said, "this is ideal. Every writer dreams of having a desk like this to work."

Looking down at the stacked books, Tom saw the titles of most the contemporary writers, and "Ulysses," "Memories of Things Past," several of Camu's books, most of the Russian classics, Shakespeare, Eugene O'neil, Thomas Mann and Kafka.

"My younger brother," Baseheart said, "is sort of an intellectual butterfly. Don't be impressed by all these books," he said pulling down the desk top. "I think he's going to be a student the rest of his life. This week, I found out, he's out on some anthropology trip digging with friends, upstate, for Indian relics."

"But he does want to be a writer?" Tom asked.

"That's what he says."

"Well, writer's need all kinds of experiences," Tom said. "Nothing is ever lost on a writer. He stores up information in his head, stuff he may use later in his writing."

Baseheart walked away, then said, "I'm going to turn on the air conditioner, This place is getting warm. There's a mamouth unit in the bedroom, I'm going to turn it on."

Pam came in from the hall, followed by a tall girl with blond hair, who slammed the door.

"Tom," Pam said, "this is Martha Harvey, my room mate. Then Pam held up a bottle of wine she was carrying, "I'm going to make sangria. I'll be in the kitchen."

"Hello, Martha," Tom said grinning. "I'd offer you a chair but the're arn't any."

"Ther's a chair at the typewriter," she said.

Pam and Art were laughing out in the kitchen; then Art shouted, "Somebody put some music on."

"Right," Tom shouted back, and going to the stacked records, turned to Martha, "Anything in particular you want to hear?"

"I like <u>all</u> kinds of music," she said.

"I'll just play what's stacked here then."

Martha was looking down at the books on the floor, checking the titles.

"Pam said you are some kind of writer," Martha said, still looking at the book titles, "I mean besides being in the army, that's what you do?"

"Yes, I plan to be a good writer."

"What do you write about?"

"Myself."

They both smiled.

Martha was wearing Bermuda shorts, and Tom could not stop looking at the roundness of her calves.

"At least you're candid about it," she said. "Most writer's are not."

"You know a lot of writers, Marty?"

"A lot of writers get angry when they can't get published," she said. "They just don't realize they are writing out of self—pity: their stuff is too personal to be real fiction. They try to pass it off as fiction, but editors can sense someone spilling—all on paper. Then, too, there is the writer reporting something that happened to him, all the details; that sticks out also. It's not hard to spot."

"You seem to know a lot about writing, Marty."

"Yes," she said, "last summer, I worked as a first reader at Harper. I read the slush — book submissions — that came in over—the—transom, unsolisited writings sent to the publishing house. It was ghastly. Never again."

She sat down on the chair at the desk, looking up.

"I guess you need an agent," Tom said. "I mean to get your writing a good reading; it takes connections."

"There are a lot of people writing, Tom," Martha said quietly. "Very few make a living at it."

"But it can lead to fame, and fortune," Tom said.

"Writing that sells big, well, you'd be free to do anything you wanted, live anywhere, go anywhere. You'd have money and — fame — to boot."

"I think, Tom, that's why most people write. They want fame — and — the money," she said without patronizing.

"I guess, so," Tom said.

He sat down on the floor, his back against the wall. From here he had a good view of her legs, so he tried not to let her catch him looking.

"I'm not talking about actual writing," she said. Quietly. I'm talking about how a publishing house works. The nuts and bolts of getting into print. Not writing itself."

"I know that, Marty."

"People say, things," she said, "like, 'I want to be a writer. I'm going off to a farm house I rented in Vermont to write a novel.' Then, two months later you see them in the Ceder Street Bar, talking about writing with other people who call themselves artists. You know the writing show was just a show."

Tom nodding, said slowly, "Writer's write because they have too, every day. It's a part of them. The publication part is important, but the writing itself is <u>more</u> important. They are the <u>real</u> writers."

Tom folded his arms around his knees.

"What do you write about, Tom?"

"Mostly about trying to understand some phase of life that needs understanding — like tragedy needs understanding, or their is no meaning, just bad luck," he said.

"Yes," Martha said, "That ought to give you — a theme. You've got to have some sort of theme."

"Not a conscious one," Tom said. I just keep writing. Eventually my writing will evolve — into something that you call a theme. Some kind of pattern or statement is bound to occur, and re—occur in my work."

"Tom, try to imitate Dickens or Mark Twain. Write emotionally; straight from the heart. Then everyone will read your books. Everyone, even intellectuals feel; have emotions."

He looked up at her, over her legs, wanting to put his hands on her.

"Yeah," Tom said, "you're right. I see what you mean."

Baseheart and Pam came into the room both carrying glasses with the sound of ice tinkling.

"Try this," Art said handing a glass down to Tom; when Tom reached up, Art rolled his eyes toward Martha, grinning.

"Thanks," Tom said, and winked.

Pam handed a glass to Martha and everyone took a long drink. She and Art continued standing above Tom, when she said, "We thought we'd go to the spaghetti place down the street and have dinner. Would you two like to join ..?"

A loud pinging noise came from the bedroom air conditioner.

"That's the second time that machine has done that," Baseheart said. "I better unplug it."

Pam followed him.

Tom sipped the sangria, then said to Martha, "What you said about writing for the heart, is true. I agree, but my problem now is jamming things I know, the events I've seen, and things that happened to me, into a story form.

"I don't want to write like a reporter, just tell what happened in the present tense .... I want to put things into the story in such a way the characters will make the reader feel what has happened."

Nodding, holding her glass in both hands, Martha said, "Exactly. That's what writing is. Writers have to get good at just what you said. When they do, they become artists."

Baseheart and Pam came back.

"I might be buying a new air conditioner," he said, and after sipping sangria, turned to Tom. "Now, would you two serious—looking people care to join us for spaghetti?"

"It's too warm," Martha said, before Tom could answer, "for a heavy pasta dinner."

Baseheart smiled at Tom, regarding Martha's answer, then took a long drink.

Tom nodded, grinning.

"I have the craves for spaghetti," Pam said. "With a salad...Antapasta... and. breadsticks, garlic breadsticks."

"I'm just plain hungry," Baseheart said. "Italian, Chinese or Mexican, I don't care."

Pam smiled at Art, Then, looking down at Tom, she said, "There's more sangria in the frige." Following Baseheart to the door, Pam added, "If you join us later, there's a dance club next to the restaurant. If you're interested."

She and Baseheart went out.

Martha made a blowing sound, and said as if relieved, "What some people have to put up with for half the rent."

Tom smiled, then asked quietly, "What is she studying?"

"Pam's not in school here at Columbia," Martha said. "She and I went to the same high school up in Ithaca. She's been modelling — wandering all over Europe in the process. She stayed with me a couple of times, then we agreed to split the rent — become room mates. She's not around much," Martha said. " It work's great. I have the time to study for my history classes."

The record player next to the desk made a click noise and the music stopped, the stack of records played.

Tom set his glass down and started to get up.

"Why don't we leave it off," Martha said. "Since the air conditioner isn't working, why don't we go down to my apartment. I have one that works. And I can make some tuna sandwiches."

"All right," Tom said as he got to his feet. "Do you want me to bring the sangria?"

"No. It's making me drowsy."

"Okay, we'll skip it then."

Later, when they had finished eating, and were still sitting at the small kitchen table, opposite one another, drinking iced tea in tall glasses, Martha said, "Yes, he is almost a religion." She moved the mint on the rim of her glass and took a drink. "Just look how the famous writer's life — almost every facet — of his personal and profession—al life has been documented and re—documented."

"People," Tom said, "demand that his life be documented. They want to know every scrap of information about him. And I think I know why; people want to get close to greatness like the famous writer has, like some sport figures have, people with talent and success, who have become winners. Someone who has won, against all odds, in the game of life. It gives people something to hold on to, simular to, like you say, a religion."

"But," Martha said, stirring her tea with a long spoon, "is it good? Healthy? Positive?"

"I'm not sure," Tom said, "but it helps people. Everyone has a hero. It might be or even an opera singer."

"What troubles me," Martha said setting the long spoon on the table, "is that the day—to—day life of the famous writer is becomming equally as popular as his writing. What is lost in the shuffle is that he is supposed to communicate with people through his craft — and only his craft."

Tom, shaking his head, said, "People find escape in his writing; they become him in his stories. But they need more, so they escape further by delving into his daily life they read about in the newspapers and magazines, which in the case of the famous writer, is as interesting as his fiction."

Tom was drinking from his glass, when Martha said,. "Yes, you're right. But it must be tiresome with people pressing to meet you all the time. That being a celebrity where ever you go."

Tom finished the tea in his glass, jiggling the ice.

"Do you want to go to the discoteque?" he asked.

"I guess I should go and talk with Art and Pam. I feel guilty; I haven't talked with them much."

"Okay," Martha said, standing and collecting the dishes from the table. "But I would like to get back before midnight. I've got a ton of research to do tomorrow in the library. My classes began this week, you know?"

"Maybe," Tom said taking the two glasses to the sink and dumping the ice, "I'll tag along tomorrow with you. We can strain aour eyes together."

Waiting the elevator in the hallway, Tom asked Martha quietly, "do you go with someone — steady?"

"I did," Martha said, "up until the beginning of this summer. He's on some field explori-tory trip for oil in west Africa — he's a geologist. I haven't heard any thing for over a month. Does — that — answer your question."

As they entered the vacant elevator, Martha turned around as Tom came through the nar-row door; they were face to face and Tom kissed her.

The next morning, they were laying in bed with a sheet over them, Tom, his eyes closed, facing toward Martha.

A car honked down in the street, the sound coming in the open window covered by a window shade. Tom woke up.

"No woman will ever hold you, Tom."

He looked at her in the sunlight slanting from around the shade, feeling the day's warm-ing beginning. The air conditioner was off.

"You don't have to say it," he said blinking. "Even if it is true."

"It's true, you know it."

"Do you have to start ..." he stopped, his defenses up, looking at her face. He caught himself feeling he had to refute her comment, and he did not want to. Suddenly, he thought of what the famous writer wrote in his most famous short story about a writer dying on a cot in Africa. The writer in the story says to himself that it is easier to get along with women if you tell them lies; tell them what they want to hear instead of the truth.

"Admit you know it's true," she said.

"I guess what you say could be true," Tom said looking at her face, getting aroused again. "But who can be sure."

"Tom, the plain truth is," she said pulling the sheet under her chin, "is that I know for sure and you don't know yet."

He almost smiled, but instead said, "You sound like a lawyer."

"You can't get out of it by being flip," she said.

"Listen, Martha," he tried to touch her face, but she pushed his hand down, "I don't want to argue — I don't see how either of us will benefit from arguing."

"I'm not arguing," she said calmly. "I'm simply saying no woman will ever hold you ... you don't want to be tied to one woman."

"I never thought about it in that sense," Tom said.

"You know," she said, "what I'm asking; what's going to happen to us from now on?"

"I honestly don't know, Martha. Not for sure. I'm going to finish school here at Fort Slocum and go to Germany." He raised up on one arm, looking at her. "I don't know what 'to say."

"And last night?" she said. "Can you say anything about what happened right here in bed?"

"It was wonderful," he said. "I'd be lying if I said otherwise." He bit his lower lip to keep from grinning. "We both enjoyed ..."

"You are like a thief, Tom. You make women fall for you, then you sneak away," she turned and looked at the ceiling.

"No, that's not true. I'm just a young man trying to be a writer." He was up on both elbows. "I have to go places and see things and meet people. It's part of the process."

She turned to face him, pulling the sheet.

"Then, what about love?" she said in a flat tone.

"Writers are supposed to know about love too."

"Yes," he said.

"Is that all you can say?"

He nodded.

She lay silent, looking at him.

There was only the sound of the traffic down in the street.

He lowered himself off his elbows, closed his eyes, and put his hand on her.

"I like you a lot," he said.

"You'll be here at New Rochelle six or seven weeks, Tom? Is that part true?

"Yes," he said opening his eyes.

"Good," she said.

Chapter 7

Tom was in Europe five months before he travelled to Paris. It was April, like the song, he thought, the best time. He took four color transparentcy photographs of the garden archways in the Tuileries, trying to sight down a line from the door of the Louvre to the Arc de Triomph; he had read in the Frommer Soldier's guidebook all the arches are in alingnment.

It was the first time he used the camera, borrowed from another soldier in the barracks back in Bamberg, Germany. He hoped he had the right settings on the complicated camera. He had photographed the Moulin Rouge and the Sacre Cour up in Monmartre near his hotel, and he hoped the films were good.

Now, from the Tuileries, Tom wanted to go to the Latin Quarter, over the Seine to the Left Bank. He took out the map of the city he bought to find his way around Paris. The famous writer and his wife lived over there in a cheap room when they first came to Paris in the Roaring Twenties. That was where the young famous writer began his career. The room was near a graveyard. Tom wanted

Chapter 7
(SECOND VERSION OF PAGE)

Tom was in Europe five months before he got to Paris. It was April, like the song, he thought, the best time. He took four color photographs of the garden archways in the Tuileries, trying to sight down a line from the door of the Louvre to the Arc de Triomph; he had read in the Frommer Soldier's guidebook all the arches are in line.

It was the first time he used the camera, borrowed from another soldier in the barracks back in Bamberg, Germany. He was trying hard to get good pictures. He already photographed the Moulin Rouge and the Sacre Cour up in Monmartre, near his hotel on rue de Chabrol.

From the Tuileries gardens he wanted now to head for the Left Bank, over across the Seine to the Latin Quarter; he studied the Paris city map bought for directions.

Over there in the Quarter was the cheap room, near a graveyard, that the famous writer and his wife lived, when he first came to Paris in the roaring twenties. That was where a young famous writer began his career. Tom wanted to see the famous writer's room, and the cafes, that he wrote about in his early stories. And he wanted to see the Shakespear and Company bookstore he had seen in photos.

It was exciting for Tom being in these well—know haunts of the famous writer; it gave him a feeling of accomplishment for trying to be a writer too. Tom had seen a news photo of Plimpton sitting in one of these cafes, editing his Paris Review. Plimpton, dressed like Tom in crew—neck sweater and raincoat, must have been bitten by the same bug.

Crossing the Seine on the Pon des Arts bridge for the Latin Quarter, Tom saw the sunlight on Notre Dame Cathedral, and stopped to photograph it, thinking how lucky he was to be here.

Walking, he thought it was best to travel alone. You can take your time and see the sights when you choose and for as long as you choose. Alone, there is no bickering with someone about where to go and what to see. Besides, not everyone is interested in the places the famous writer had lived and worked.

On the Latin Quarter side, Tom walked along the bookstalls, getting really excited, picturing himself as the young famous writer walking here, Notre Dame in the background.

Wa1king these same quais was like visiting a shrine. They were beginning to mean that only time seperated Tom from becoming a famous writer too.

At the Boulevard Saint Michel, the Boul' Mich' as Tom remembered reading it was called in the famous writer's first novel, he turned away from the Seine, walking all the way to Boulevard St. Germain. He was tired from walking, and looking up St. Germain, he saw the tables and chairs of the cafe Les Deux Magots. He smiled; luck has it. This was one of the places he wanted to visit.

Walking toward the cafe he wondered why he was getting tired so quickly, lately. He grinned, telling himself it must be all the army's field training excercises in Germany, wearing him out, or all those girls who he met at the Taverna Bar outside the cascerne gate in Bamberg.

He sat down in a chair in front of a small, round marble-top table. Smiling, he thought, here's Tom Cohill right smack in the Deux Magots, the cafe the famous writer and his "Lost Generation" made immortal. Who knows, he thought, he may even be sitting in one of the chairs the famous writer used.

When the waiter came, a middle—aged man with grey hair combed straight back, Tom ordered beer. He thought of showing off by ordering <u>absinth,</u> but changed his mind.

The sunlight was beginning to fade, shadows getting long, and Tom wanted a photograph of him sitting here at the Deux. He set the time exposure on the camera, then put it on the next table, hoping the picture included him with the empty inside bar behind. The old waiter stood in the doorway watching. There were only four patrons sitting at the tables; and Tom figured the old waiter did not want anyone leaving without paying.

There was an automatic click from the timer, and Tom reached for the camera hoping the photo was good.

Looking up, he watched two girls in raincoats walk off the sidewalk and sit at the table opposite him. They had to be Americans, the way they dressed; college girls.

"The book says he lived over a sawmill," Tom heard with short blond hair say. "And it's supposed to be near a cemetery ... so it has to be this Momartre Cemetery. It's the only one on the map."

The other girl, her long brown hair hanging forward, was looking at the map.

"I understood he lived on Rue Cardinal Lemoine," the long haired one said without looking up, "but there's no cemetery, that I can find."

Suddenly, the old waiter appeared, and stood between Tom and the girls, picking up Tom's empty beer bottle and said something in French. Tom nodded, supposing he was asking if he, Tom, wanted another. Then the waiter went to the girl's table, and Tom heard them both order citrons.

"I remember the sawmill thing," the blond said. "I remember that for sure. But it sticks in my mind from an article I read once, someplace, that his room overlooked a cemetery.

"I remember poignantly about the cemetery, because whoever wrote the article, said that the famous writer was fascinated by death ... had a death wish thing… and even liked living over a cemetery."

The girl with the map, looked up, "but the cemetery," she said, "doesn't fit in with what I've read about where the famous writer lived."

Tom had heared enough; he had to speak.

"The famous writer," he said to the two women, "lived at 113 Notre Dame des Champs above the sawmill." They both looked at him. "It's down there where the Boul' Mich' runs into Boulevard Montparnasse ... between the Luxembourg Gardens and the Montparnasse South Cemetery. You can see the cemetery from the sixth or eigth floor of his apartment building. He lived on a lower floor room, and wrote in an upper floor room."

"Thanks," the blond said just before the waiter returned, blocking Tom's view again, serving the girls first.

Tom watched the waiter set another bottle of beer on his table, then he said, "He also lived at 47 Cardinal Lemoine.

The waiter looked at Tom, and flipped, his hand towel.

"Ah—h," the waiter said, "you are speaking of the famous writer, No?"

Tom nodded.

"He came here quite often," the waiter said, slowly lifting Tom's beer bottle, then pouring the beer into his glass. "I remember him well, as if it were yesterday. He was a large tipper."

Tom watched as the waiter set the bottle next to his glass on the table, and at the same time, seeing the two girls listening, and watching, the waiter, he said, "What about the Cafe Select, and the Rotonde, and Bal Musette? Can you tell me how to find them too?

"No—no," the waiter said and waived his arm with the towell. "They are all gone now, those places. They have been gone for a long time."

Tom nodded, then took a drink of beer.

"That," the waiter said, "that will be all, Monsieur?"

"Yes," Tom said. "For now."

The two girls, drinking their lemon drinks using straws, had been listening to Tom and the waiter.

"Do you think he really knew — served — the famous writer here in this cáfe the blond hair girl asked.

"Could be," Tom said and set his beer glass down. "Where are you girls from in the States?"

"Virginia," the blond said, stirring her with the straw.

"Do you go to school — college — there?"

"No," the blond said, her eyes meeting the other girl's.

The long haired girl turned to face Tom.

"We're in school — the university — over here," the long haired girl said, pushing the hair from her face.

"Paris?" Tom asked.

"Geneva," the blond said.

"I'm from Michigan," Tom said. "I went to the university there, but only briefly."

"Are you here in Europe," the blond asked, rolling her eyes up to belittle Tom in front of the other girl, "taking some kind of tour?"

"I'm a soldier," Tom said.

Everyone smiled.

"I suppose we are all English majors?" Tom said.

Both the girls smiled, looking at one another.

"Can you tell us," the blond asked, "where the contemporary of the famous writer lived? We like him also. He was here in Paris when the famous writer was becoming famous."

"I think it was 14 rue Tilsitt," Tom said. "He and Zelda lived there, as far as I know."

The long haired girl wrote the address on the map.

"I like the contemporary's book that takes place on Long Island," Tom said. "It might be the All—American Novel: <u>the</u> modern classic. The plot is perfect, so's the characterization."

"Yes," the long haired girl said, folding the map. "And do you know anything about the lady doctor who helped the famous writer with his craft?"

Tom stood up.

"Mind if I join you?" he asked. "I'm tired of shouting over to your table."

"Sure," the long haired girl said, and made a quick look at the blond for approval; it was a furtive glance. "I mean, we don't mind you sitting here."

Tom set his glass of beer on their table and sat down.

"Gertrude and her friend lived over at 27 rue de Fleurus. Gert was a pediatrician. Her friend and companion, specialized in making cookies — with hashish," Tom said leaning forward in his chair. "I forget the companion's name," he said testing the girls.

"Alice," the blond said. "The same name as her's," she added, pointing at the long haired girl, who was putting the folded map in her coat pocket.

"I don't see how we are going to see <u>all</u> these places in just two days," Alice said to the blond.

"That's always the problem," Tom said. "I'm going back to Germany on a bus tomorrow afternoon. I'm on a tour with a group — I sneaked off on my own. The tour included a ticket to the <u>Follies Bergers</u>," he said and flashed an orange colored ticket from his sport jacket top pocket, grinning. "But these literary places, are a must."

"Where are you stationed in Germany?" Alice asked.

"Bamberg. It's a town about forty kilometers east of Nurnberg, over near the Checkoslovokian border."

"What do you do in the army?" the blond asked. "I mean do you drive a tank — or shoot cannons?"

"Oh, I more destructive than that. I write the regimental newspaper. I'm an editor."

"Well, that figures," Alice said, smiling, "I mean with you're — literary man's back-gound — and all."

"I've got an idea," Tom said, "Why don't we take a tour of the literary sights together? We can split the cost of cab fare and all that. We're àll interested in seeing the same places... we can look together, help each other."

"I guess it would make things easier," the blond said, looking at Alice, who was nodding.

"Good," Tom said. He waved to the waiter for the check, then finished drinking the beer in his glass.

"Think of what this cafe," Alice said, "must have been like back in the twenties jazz—age. Think of all the people, who are famous now, who had come here. It feels like we're intruding in history that we've read about. Don't you think so?"

Nodding, Tom said, "It's more like a hero—worship than intruding, I think. We liked and admired the way the famous lived, and where they lived, and did their art."

The waiter came with the check. "I'll take care of it," Tom said getting to his feet. "You can buy the next one." Both girls, stood up and walked out to the sidewalk, talking and smiling.

"Which number is the amount you pay?" Tom asked, holding the small slip of paper.

"This, Monsieur," the waiter said pointing to the upper corner of the stub. " This is the amount."

"That looks like the check number," Tom said.

"No, Monsieur, it is the amount for the cost of the service to the table."

"Oh, yeah," Tom said, "then what is this number with the two zeros in front of it? Right here," he said holding his thumbnail in front of the number for the waiter to see.

He did not like the waiter's comment about the famous writer being a big tipper. It made him suspicious; it made him think the waiter was out for all he could get. Tom knew the famous writer could not have been a big tipper because he was poor when he lived nearby during the twenties.

"That is the check number, Monsieur."

"What are you trying to pull?" Tom asked quickly.

"No, Monsieur. That is the total cost for the two beers and the two citrons."

"I'm no damn tourist you can just cheat ..."Tom started, but saw the girls looking. "Awh—h, here's your damn money," he said and set it on the table.

"Tip, Monsieur," the waiter said flatly, his hand out. Tom turned to the sidewalk, the waiter followed.

"Tip."

Tom turned. "You probably charged me double the price," he said. "That's your tip." People on the sidewalk were looking at Tom. "What do you want, blood?"

The long hair girl said under her breath, “That’s how they make their living. They don’t get a salary. All the waiters earn a living from tips.”

“I’m trapped like a rat,” Tom said. “I guess there’s no way out of this. I’m the bad guy.”

He handed the waiter ten francs.

“That ought to take care of things,” the blond girl said, as the waiter, nodded, then walked away. She turned to Tom, “I want to call you by name, but ...”

“Tom. Tom Cohill.”

“I’m Ann Lawrence. And this is Alice Durant.”

“We’ve decided to walk instead of taking a taxi,” Alice said. “Is it okay with you?”

“All right,” Tom said.

While they walked on Saint Germain to where it met the Boul’ Mich’, Tom noticed that the blond took long strides. They turned in the direction of the Sorbonne, and Tom said, “Hey, I know a student hangout near the Pantheon from one of the guys in the barracks. Jazz. Want to stop?”

“I don’t think so, really,” Ann said. “Time is short.”

No one spoke as they began walking, again.

Tom thought the silence was brought on by his dispute with the waiter, he offered, “Sorry I acted like a soldier with that old waiter. I’m just tired, I guess.”

“Paris needs time to get accustomed to,” Ann said, smiling at Tom.

Ann was better than the other one, Alice, Tom thought. He like partly for her blond hair, partly for her smile, and partly for her good legs that showed below her rain coat. And the way she walked, hands in the pockets, pulling the coat tight, reminded him of Harriet.

Looking at Ann, made Tom feel the way a young soldier should feel on a three—day pass in Paris, and he wanted to tell her,

Tom reached over and held Ann’s hand.

Alice stopped, as if shot with a bolt of lightening.

“It’s getting too dark to walk around,” she said. “we won’t be able to see anything now.”

Ann looked at Tom, then back to Alice, and let go his hand.

“Well, Alice, if you don’t want to try…”

“I’ve had enough touring for one day,” Alice snapped. “Even if we do find the apartment where the famous writer lived, we’ll probably find some young writer living there,” Alice said showing contempt, “probably thinking that by being in the same room, will make him rich and famous too. Or something silly like that.”

Tom shrugged when Ann looked at him,

“It would still be a kick,” he said, “to see the room, apartment, what ever, where the famous writer started out.”

"I'm beginning to get hungry," Alice said to Ann. "I think we should go to the hotel and change for dinner."

"All right," Ann said, "but I thought we decided to locate the sites of the writers we read about in our literature courses — you agreed it would be fun. Remember?"

"Maybe," Tom said, "you'd like to stop for a drink. There are a lot of student hangouts near the Pantheon."

"No," Alice said bluntly.

"It might be fun," Ann said, "to see how the students enjoy themselves here."

"Maybe tomorrow," Alice said and looked up the boulevard. "Let's call a taxie."

"What's the matter, Alice?" Tom asked softly. "Did I say something — wrong?

"It's nothing like that," she said. "It's just that I suddenly realized how stupid we are acting."

"In what way?" Ann asked her, then looked at Tom, then shrugged.

"Can't you see all this crap of looking at rooms of famous writers is neurotic?" Alice said. "It's sick," she said pulling her raincoat tight. "We can't re—live what the writers had, and did, in those cheap rooms."

"Yeah," Tom said, "I see what you're getting at."

"You mean," Ann said, "We're carrying this hero—worship thing too far. I thought of that too, sort of."

Alice waved her hands, "It's not important where the writer lived, or where the writer sat in a cafe. What's important is what the writer wrote."

"Wow," Tom said, grinning, "you're all right."

"She's a writer," Ann said to Tom. "She won the short story contest at school, three years in a row."

"I did realize you were a writer," Tom said to Alice. "I'm working on my second book. I guess that makes me a writer. It's a book about people I knew at the university; characters."

"I'm just learning to write," Alice said. "I haven't tried a novel ... just short stories."

Overhead, the stree lights came on.

"Are you girls really in a hurry to go to dinner?" Tom asked feeling comfortable asking. "Couldn't we ...?"

"No," Alice snapped.

"Can I call you girls tomorrow?" Tom asked looking at Ann.

Then he saw them look at one another.

"We're staying with Alice's relatives," Ann said to him slowly. "They have some plans for us tomorrow. We're at the George Sanc. We're meeting some movie people."

"I thought," Tom said, "we could get together tomorrow. Someone mentioned it earlier. We could take—in the sites, together."

He spoke, looking at Ann, who was shaking her head.

Alice stepped off the curb and raised her arm for a taxi, and one pulled up and stopped abruptly.

"I wish," Tom whispered to Ann, "you could somehow get away tonight. Come out for a while."

She smiled, looking down.

Alice opened the cab door, then climbed in. "Coming Ann," she said, holding the door. "Good—bye, Tom. Luck with your writing ... and the army."

"See you," Tom said to Ann, watching her get in the cab. Then to Alice, "Luck with your writing too."

"See you," Ann said, looking up at him.

As Ann was closing the door, Tom heard Alice say, "You bitch, you held his hand."

"I thought so," Tom said. "I thought they were like that. Well, one of them is, for sure." He shook his head.

The next morning, Tom felt too fatigued to get out and walk around Paris. It was not tired, but a fatigue, something he had not felt before. When the other soldier's on the tour of Paris where getting ready for going out, Tom told them he felt sick, and wanted to sleep. They laughed.

He slept most of the day in the musty hotel room, then about six o'clock, dressed, and went downstairs to the restaurant and had an omelette. While eating, he decided, that once back at the barracks, he would go to the dispensory for a medical check—up.

In Strasbourg, where the tour bus stopped the next morning, crossing into Germany from France, Tom was sick in the men's room. The other soldier's laughed; making a joke of what he caught in Paris.

Tom followed the group tour of Strasbourg, taking photographs of the delicate, one—spired cathedral like the rest of the crowd of soldiers. But the lone spire made him think of Paris, and the famous writer's apartments; he wished he would have gone to see the apartments.

Chapter 8

"The amazing thing about it," Tom said to Irmgard, "is that it doesn't hurt. There's no pain."

They were sitting in the dining room of a gasthaus named The Salamander; the ceiling of the room was glassed— in the same as a greenhouse.

"Oh—h, Tom," Irmgard said, shaking her head, upset.

"You think I would be coughing blood," he said.

"Only a romantic ... like you, Tom, believes he has Tuberculosis at nine o'clock Sunday morning," said Irmgard patronizingly, then took a sip from her small coffee cup.

"I've got it, for sure," Tom said, "I feel it. And when the army reads my x—ray at the dispensary tomorrow, they will know I have it too. I practically had to beg those jerks at the post dispensary to take the damn x—ray.

Irmgard, smiling, slowly set her cup down on the saucer.

"Oh—h, I hope you don't have it," she said. "You would enjoy having it ... too much, I think. You are so much a romantic.

Tom leaned back in his chair, hands behind his head, looking out the windows. It was an overcast spring morning, and cold. He could see across the valley to the Altomann castle on it's hill. Bamberg, down in the vally, was mostly covered with mist, but he could pick out the old part of town by the steep rooves of the Medieval houses.

"That's what I like about you, Irmer. Your'e so soft hearted and sympathetic," Tom said showing his teeth.

"You are such a complicated man," Irmgard said quietly. "Maybe that is why I like you so much. You are not like the others." when Tom leaned down on the table, looking her in the face, she patted his hand.

"And I thought," he said quietly so the other guests in the dining room could not hear, "there was more to it than that." He smiled. "Like what we did last night in room four."

"You—u," Irmgard smiled, slapped his hand, then put both her hands over his, covering them.

"See," Tom said, grinning, "I was right."

"Tom," she said softly, looking at his face, "can you get a leave from the army? I want to show you the Dalmation coast. It is so—o beautiful." She patted his hands. "I must go soon on a buying trip for jewelery to Split. We could spend the afternoons in the sun at the sea shore." She squeezed his hands. "Your health would be improved, I am sure."

"But that's Yugoslavia," Tom said. "Uncle Sam won't let his soldier's go to a Communist country — even to buy shell jewelry. I don't think Tito would like having me in his country, either. Wandering around taking pictures.

"We can go to Italy. They must have shell jewelry in Italy too. And, 'The sky in Italy is the bluest in the world,' Tom said, remembering the sky color statement from one of the famous writer's short stories.

"The sky and sun in Italy is <u>too</u> bright," Irmgard said disappointed. "On the Dalmation Coast — everything — is not so intense as Italy. You would like it there, I know, for sure."

Tom, looking at her thin face under the wide—brim hat, her dark blond hair, thought of the famous writer's girl friend, the nurse that the writer met as a young soldier, wounded, in Italy during the First World War. The nurse was older than the young writer, just like Irmgard, and wore a floppy—brim hat, just like Irmgard. Tom remembered the photograph of the nurse from a biography of the writer; the similarities came to Tom just now, and he did not know why.

Another thing suddenly came to mind for Tom, was about the famous writer's girl having a "von" in her last name, the same as Irmgard does. The way she explained it to Tom, Irmgard's family, some sort of aristocrats, raised prize horses on a "ranch" outside of Leipzig, now in the Russian Zone of Occupation. When the Russians broke into Germany at the end of the Second World War, Irmgard's family fled the "ranch" they had owned for centuries. To make a living, Irmgard, displaced, began selling jewelry made from sea—shells. She somehow got permission to sell jewerly to GI's in Bamberg at <u>Werner</u> <u>Cascern</u> beer hall, that was on the army post. That was where in 1956 met her.

Once, when they were drinking at a club in Bamberg, Irmgard showed Tom a ring, he remembered. The ring had a crest or shield, he rembered, that was divided in half; the top had the image of a unicorn, the bottom half a running horse. Irmgard said the unicorn represented the symbolic source her great—great grandfather was supposed to have gotten their original stock of horses.

Tom rembmered that around Germany in 1956, everybody had a fall—from—riches type story. He half believed her: cripe, she sold jewelry and could have got the ring anywhere. He had once asked her if she was ever married, and she said her husband, a sergeant with an anti—aircraft unit, was killed in an allied bombing raid. Tom half—believed a lowly sergeant could marry an aristocrat in Germany.

Looking at Irmgard now, thinking of the wounded famous writer falling in love with the-older woman, a nurse, Tom knew he was not in love with Irmgard. He liked being with her, ever since, seven months ago, payday night at the camp service club, and she was unpacking her jewelry on a table, and he talked with her and they went out later.

"I'd like to go to Split," Tom said. "It sounds great, the Dalmation sea coast and all, but I'm going on a one—way trip to a hospital in the States."

Tom was sorry after he said that; he saw Irmgard's eyes blink, as if she had been struck in the face.

"Are you sure you have the tuberculosis?" she asked and squeezed his hands.

Tom pulled his hands free.

"It's more than just a cold, or influenza, or bronchitis, or any of those diseases, I'm sure," he said quietly. "I've had it too long for it to be any of those."

"But — you do not — look like a person with the T.B., Tom."

"I don't get it either, Irmgard. So I looked in up in the post library. The night—sweats, poor appetite, and the constant fatigue. T. B. is the only thing I could have."

"Have the doctors at the camp looked — examined — you for this?" she ask slowly, her eyes on Tom's.

"That German quack at the post dispensary said I had a bad cold," Tom said. "It was only last week that I talked Herr Doktor into giving me an x—ray." Tom smiled. "I was coming to the dispensary so much, that he threatened to have me charged with malingering."

"Tom, that is terrible," Irmgard said, concerned.

"Well, anyhow, tomorrow we read the x—ray," he said, and to avoid Irmgard's eyes, put his elbows on the table, and holding his face, began looking out the windows.

"Can I do something, Tom. Anything."

"Believe it or not, Irmmer," he said looking out the window, "I'd — like to go over there to the castle — Schloss — and go through it. See what it's like inside."

"You talk as if — Tom, I am sure you are not that bad sick."

He turned, not speaking, and reached for a magazine from the stack that was piled on a bench under the windows. It was a German picture magazine; he could not read some of the writing, but he continued looking at the photos to avoid talking to Irmgard and slowly turned the pages.

Suddenly, he saw a recent photograph of the famous writer sitting in a crowd at a bull ring. The writer was dressed in a tweed jacket and hat, and wore steel frame glasses. His face was covered by a white full—face beard.

Looking down the page to a smaller photograph, the famous writer was shown standing with his second wife at the railing of an ocean liner. They were both young.

"What does this say here?" Tom said to Irmgard, sliding the magazine across to her. "It's in German."

"Ah," she said seeing the world famous writer's face in the photograph. "He has arrived in Spain, the setting of his first novel, and is planning to stay for the bull fight season this year — he is writing a bullfight story for a magazine. It also says —

"No more," Tom said. "Don't read any more. I can't stand any more." He was quiet for a moment. "You don' have to go on a buying trip to Spain, do you?"

She smiled at him.

"You would go there? "she asked. "You would go there to meet with him?"

Nodding, Tom said, “But there’s always something that holds me back. Something always blocks my path. Now I’m sick. Damn.”

“I was at Pamplona,” Irmgard said quietly. “Two years ago. Since the famous writer wrote that book about the thing San Fermin Festival, everything has been ruined there. Too many young people geting tipsy. The’re no hotels to stay, no train seats. It is no fun. Trash everywhere.”

“Still,” Tom said looking at the photos, “I would like to go there — meet the famous writer. I would go to Spain if it wasn’t for those damn x—rays tomorrow.”

“I know a writer in Munich,” Irmgard said. “He’s not a famous ...”

“Who?” Tom said, looking at her calmly.

“Gephardt Rausch,” Irmgard said, “he writes charming children’s books.”

Tom put his hand over his mouth so Irmgard would not him smiling.

“No,” he finally said. “I would rather go to Spain.”

“But Pamplona is in July, Tom.”

“I know. The famous writer is in Spain, now. I could go there and meet ...”

“Tom, I know two Yugoslavs. They make films in Munich near where I live. Maybe I could get you some writing work with their film company in Schwabing.”

“That’s okay,” Irmmer. Thanks but no thanks.”

“How can I help you, Tom? Tell me ... your wish.”

“For beginners,” he said sensing her concern, and wanting to blunt it, “I’d like to go to the Altemann Schloss and take a tour though it. I’ve seen it up on the hill since my first day in Bamberg. Will you come?”

“You must be serious, Tom. You are making a joke. You must decide plans for the future. We must ...”

“That’s just the point; I don’t what my future is going to involve until tomorrow at the dispensary. Until then ... I mean ... we just have to wait.”

Irmgard looked straight at Tom for a moment.

“All right,” she said pulling up her fur coat that she had let drop off her shoulders onto the seat.

“You mean ... ?” Tom asked.

“Yes, I understand tomorrow for the out come...” she said tilting the brim of her hat. “So now, we go to the Schloss. That is what you wish, no?”

“Dunka,” Tom said.

Irmgard telephoned for a taxi, and when it came, they rode down the long hill from the gasthaus into the town of Bamberg, passing the Cathedral, Zur Dom, then stopped on a narrow cobblestone road.

“What’s this?” Tom asked, huddling with Irmgard for warmth in the back of the taxi. “It looks like Shakespear’s Globe Theater.”

People dressed for Sunday services passed the taxi on the way to church. Some looked into the taxi at Tom and Irmgard.

"It is the Alte Hofhaltung, Irmgard said with pride, almost, to Tom's ears. "It was built in the fifteenth century as a residence for princes and bishops who came visiting to Bamberg." She opened the taxi door, and getting out, reached back with her hand for Tom's, and said, "Come."

Walking through the courtyard of the Tudor—style buildings, Tom turned up the collar of his sports coat. "I'm getting numb from this damp, Irmmer," he said folding his arms over his chest. "This is too much."

"Pope Clement the Second is buried over at the cathedral, there, she said pointing. "He was bishop of Bamberg here before he was pope."

"Wonderful," Tom said shivvering. "Can we go back to the taxi now?"

"Of course," he said. "I am sorry the cold is so bad today. Come."

Sitting in the back seat of the taxi again, Tom put his arm around Irmgard's shoulders.

"That building is a historic place," Irmgard said. "There are few in the world that old. Did you you enjoy it?"

"Yes, I did. Very much," Tom said grinning.

Irmgard pressed her face against Tom's.

"You ..." Irmgard whispered, "are a light in my life. You are good at so many things. That is why I am ... desperate ... for you."

"You make me 'desperate' too," Tom said, rolling his eyes up, deriding her.

She turned her face up, and he kissed her.

"You are my darling," she said. "We have fun together."

"Yes," Tom said, and dropped his hand from her shoulder on to her breast where her fur coat was open.

"We enjoy doing things, together," Irmgard said. "We enjoy just being together, don't we, Tom?"

"Yes we do," Tom said and cupped the roundness of the breast, then removed his hand. He could sense what she was leading up to with all the references to "together."

"We will fight this disease together, my dearest Tom. But, I hope very hard that you do not have it. But if you have it, we will not let it be ruiness."

The taxi was driving through a part of Bamberg that Tom had not seen before.

"I feel bad about having the disease," he said. "Now, for a while, I don't want to think about it."

"Maybe it is not the Tuberculosis, for sure," Irmgard said in a brighter tone. Maybe it is your — imaging — imagination — that says you have it."

She smiled up at him.

"Possibly," Tom said, looking out the taxi window, trying to spot something familiar that indicate where they were they were. Then, the taxi turned, and headed up a steep road.

"Yes, Tom, it is a possibility."

"Let's not talk about it for a while," he said.

"Let tomorrow come," Irmgard said. "We can do nothing to stop it. We will enjoy today and being together.

Tom rolled his eyes, gathering time to keep silent. He knew she wanted to go to the United States with him.

When the taxi drove into a clearing, suddenly the castle appeared, it's stone walls high up to the parapets that overlooked a deep moat. There was a narrow foot bridge across the moat that lead in the main gate.

"We came at a good time," Irmgard said. "It Is too early for the tourists."

Tom opened the taxi door and said, "Looks like we have the place to ourselves." The hard wind caught him when he stepped away from the car.

Irmgard spoke in German, rapidly, to the taxi driver, who nodded.

She stepped out of the car, and had to push hard to slam the door in the wind.

"I told the driver to wait until we come back," she said pulling her fur coat up to her face.

"That's expensive," Tom said folding his coat collar across his chest, trying to keep warm.

"No, no," Irmgard said as they walked to the bridge. "Rudi is an old friend. I asked for him when I telephoned from the gasthaus. He will have a sleep while we go."

Tom shrugged his shoulders, then followed as Irmgard lead the way over the moat on the narrow bridge. He had to hold his sport coat collar with both hands, the wind coming hard now. Irmgard was holding the brim of her hat with both hands.

When the wind gusts picked up, there came a deep even, moaning, sound from the open spaces of the castle walls.

"Now we are out of the wind, here," Irmgard said after they passed though a small door in the gate made of iron bars and entered a courtyard.

"This is better," Tom said looking up at the high walls on every side.

"They have a bear in a pit here," Irmgard said as they walked toward a door in the wall. "Poldi, they call him. Short for King Leopold."

"They don't let him roam around?" Tom asked, smiling.

"No, silly. He is at the bear—pit. He sleeps much."

"Show me where Irmmer. I'd like to see him."

She pointed at the door ahead of them.

"We must be quiet, otherwise we wake the custodian. He will make us leave. The bear only performs in the afternoon," she said straightening her big hat.

"I'll be quiet."

"This way," Irmgard said and opened a thick wood door.

The bear—pit was sunken and looked like a swimming pool without the water. In the middle of the pit was a heavy tree stump with thick limbs for the bear to climb.

"Where is the bear?" Tom said looking down. "I don't see him anywhere. Maybe they took him away."

"Just there," Irmgard pointed down to an opening of a room below where they were standing.

Tom leaned over to look down, and saw the foot with claws and the rear black—haired leg of the bear.

"He's sleeping," he whispered to Irmgard.

"We should have brought eggs," Irmgard whispered back. He eats eggs. They let the children throw him eggs. But no candy."

"He's a late sleeper," Tom whispered, looking over the edge again. "Or maybe he's worn out."

"He has a busy time," Irmgard said, "when all the tourists come. He performs for food, and the tourists keep him very busy."

Tom smiled as he straightened up and looked at Irmgard. "I wish we could wake him up," he said softly. "I'd like to see the rest of him. Is he big?"

"Quite big," she whispered. "As high as that tree down in the pit."

"Wow. Wish I could see him."

"Let him sleep, Tom. We go up in the tower now."

"Oh, all right, Irmmer. I guess you're right." He followed her across another courtyard with a slate floor to a small door at the base of the tower. "Looking up at the outside of the structure, he said, "you can see this thing from anywhere in Bamberg. Since the first day I saw it, I wanted to climb up and take in the wiew."

"Yes, Tom, you said this in the cafe. That is why we are here," Irmgard said as she lead the way up the narrow steps against the spiralling wall. At the top, climbing out of the semi—darkness through a trap door, they came out into the light and cold wind again.

"Wow," Tom said holding his coat collar to his neck, "that wind is something." When he stepped to the edge of the opening, he stood silent, looking. "You can see the whole valley," he said slowly. He turned around completely to look in all directions. "Wish I had a camera," he said and took hold of Irmgard's hand.

"Very impressive," she said, holding her hat with her other hand, and very cold. Oh—h, that wind..."

"I read some where that cold is good for TB patients, Tom said squeezing her hand. "I mean ... crazy people, I meant to say... crazy people." When he saw a shadow pass over her face, he added, "Hey, there's Werner <u>cascerne</u>, see it, Irmer. Right down there," he said pointing with his free hand. "I can even see the flag pole at the end of the parade field.

"And over there is the <u>bahnhof</u>, he said to distract her more away from the disease problem, "and there is your hotel, just across the street. A lot of good that does us."

Irmgard would not take Tom to her hotel room. She said there were too many business people, who knew her, coming and going at the train station that might see her going to the hotel with a soldier. It was not good for her business. And many of the people were from Munich, and that was not good for her reputation.

"Yes," she said, "I can see the hotel."

"Don't be so ... enthusiastic, Irmmer.

"You don't have to be cruel, Tom."

"Okay, no cruelty on such a morning ... filled with art works. He waved his arm. "Just look at the way the fields form a pattern ... like a quilt ... the light green, then the dark green. Isn't that terrific?"

"Yes. It is beautiful. A beautiful… picture, like a painting," she said.

"Okay, Irmgard, so you've seen it all before. If you're cold, go bak down."

"How will you get back down, Tom, if I go?"

I just follow the steps down," he said, then quickly crossed the platform and looked down into the courtyard. "There's a man, a woman, and a child coming in the gate, down there. What are they doing in my castle?"

"They are coming to the tower?" asked Irmgard.

"Looks like it," Tom said, stepping back, looking out at the valley again. "Guess they like the view… can't blame them."

"Come, Tom, we must shout on the way down the steps," Imrgard said and took his hand. "That way they know to wait until we come down. Come — come."

"Clever," Tom said. "Very clever."

"It is just politeness," Irmgard said to Tom. Then she shouted down the stairwell, "<u>Moment</u>! <u>Moment</u>!"

"I hope they hear you," Tom said following her down the narrow passage. "We'll soon find out. A traffic jam."

"Are you going to be cruel again?"

Tom did not answer. Then he heard a man's shout from down below. "<u>Bitte</u>. <u>Bitte</u>."

When they got to the last few steps, Tom saw the family looking up at them intensely.

"They must think we look like astronauts, or something," he whispered to Irmgard. "We're desending to earth."

"<u>Morgan</u>," Irmgard said to them and they all answered the same word in chorus. At the doorway out, she said, "It is uncommon for tourists to be in the tower so early. They were surprised." She reached up to hold her hat with both hands when they stepped out into the wind.

Walking across the courtyard, Tom said, "It would be very hard to describe what we saw from up there. Even with a thousand words. A couple thousand words. It would be better to just photograph it," he said holding his lapels closed with both hands.

"Yes, Tom, there are some things that cannot be — written."

"Well," he said, when they began walking across the bridge over the moat, "I wouldn't know what to do with a place of landscape like that in my writing. I really wouldn't have much use for it. Besides, writing is about people; landscapes are for painters."

They were walking to the taxi; the driver spotted them and began folding his newspaper. The motor was running.

"Your famous writer writes landscape, does he not? Irmgard said as Tom pulled open the taxi door.

"Yeah," he said as Irmgard climbed into the back seat, him following," and I think the way he does it — is one of the tricks — of becoming famous. Ah—h," he said opening his lapels, "finally we got some heat," and shook himself.

"You are in a cruel mood, Tom. You even attack your hero."

"I'm just using insight, Irmmer. You have to use a lot of insight when you want to become rich and famous."

"Tom, you are talking — complicated. I do not understand. You are too fast with your ideas."

"I realized it first in Paris, when I was in Paris."

"What are you talking about, now, Tom?"

"You can use places, Irmmer. You can describe places and use them for your own purposes. The famous writer did it — and became famous."

"I do not understand," Irmgard said as the taxi stopped at the bottom of the hill, then turned onto the road into town, heading back to the gasthaus. "I cannot — follow

— what you are talking about. You go to fast ... your ideas are too ... complicated."

"I first realized it, Irmmer when I was there in Paris last month."

"I cannot follow, Tom."

"You can use places, Irmmer. You can describe places in your stories, and when people go to the places, and you become famous, people say, hey, the famous guy was here and did this and that here. They see the places through the eyes of the famous. The famous writer did it and became famous."

"Tom, explain it so I can understand. Please."

"Very simple, Irmmer. You see the famous writer wrote about a place everybody can go to, like Paris, Madrid, and even Africa." Tom rubbed his hands together, feeling the warm inside the taxi reviving him. "Most people who go to these places are also readers, and what they read they remember the story about the place and who wrote it. After a while, the famous place itself does not seem as important as the famous writer who wrote a story about the place.

People don't even care what the story was even about after a while. It becomes the famous writer's place, Paris, Madrid, and Africa, they are no longer places known just for themselves."

"Tom, I am not sure," Irmgard said looking out the taxi window," but I think there is something in what you are saying. She turned to him, "We will have a cognac at the gast..."

"It first came to me," Tom said slowly, "when I was there in Paris; but in a negative way. I suddenly realized how stupid it was to go clomping around to visit all the places the famous writer had been in his youth. From that, I came up with the equation that famous places, plus a famous name, equals imortality. That's a bit on the rough side, but it's essentially the germ of my theory."

"You are too confusing, Tom. Stop for a while."

"Irmmer if you can get your name associated with a famous place, then you're practically assured of fame as long as the famous place does. Understand?"

"Yes," she said. "Here we are at the gasthaus. Maybe you should lay down for a while. For a rest, Tom. You must have a fever." She looked at his eyes. "My poor Tom."

Chapter 9

Two days after Tom was admitted to the Army Hospital at Nuremberg, Irmgard came to visit him. He was laying in the bed opposite the door, and when he saw her, he raised up on his left elbow.

"You 1ook provocative wearing that mask," he said as she walked toward his bed… "just the eyes showing, you look very sexy, Irmmer."

"Tom, how do you feel?" she asked sitting down on the chair at the end of the bed. "What have the doctors told you? I worry so much for you."

Earlier that day, Tom's Company Commander had sat in the same chair, his Executive Officer standing behind him. Tom thought the two officers, dressed in Class A uniform, with their medals and bars, looked ridiculous wearing cloth masks over their faces. Besides, he figured they came for chest x—rays for any sign of TB, not out of compassion for him.

"The doctors found two lesions — holes — on the x—ray of my left lung," Tom told Irmgard. "And there might be some on the right side too. They have to test me more. It's the damn Tuberculosis, Irmmer." Then he added, almost boastfully, "My instincts were right. Right on the money."

"To—om, that is terrible," Irmgard said and grabbed his foot at that end of the bed. "That disease is from the devil."

As if he was indifferent to her emotion, Tom said, "I've been trying to trace where I caught it. I've been in Europe a year and a half — living in a barracks — now I come down with this damn disease. Crap, what bad luck."

"I am sure, Tom, the doctors will cure you quickly. They have drugs now. They know much about this disease."

"Yeah, they have me taking some medicine called P—A—S," he said trying to act heroic. "Fifty pills three times a day. Tomorrow is a complete examination, and that means they tell you the whole story of what they're going to do. What they're going to do for a cure."

"Very good," Irmgard said. "Is there any pain?"

"No. There's no pain," Tom said and put his hand on the left side of his chest. "Except, there's kind of a — tightness here — like a pulled muscle. That's about all."

"I have a gift for you," Irmgard said, and opened her wide leather handbag. "These will calm your nerves."

She handed Tom a box of miniature chocolate bottles filled with cognac. Then she set her handbag and wide-brim hat on the vacant bed next to Tom's.

"Terrific, Irmmer. I can really use these," he said and slid the box under his pillow. "Thanks a lot."

There were eight beds in the ward, but only Tom and two other patients occupied the room. The other two, and old sergeant and a young negro, were in the beds at the end of the room near the windows. The doctor wanted Tom isolated from the other patients until his examination was completed.

"Tom, do you think you will stay here — in Europe— for your treatment?" Then she whispered, "There are fine sanitoriums in Switzerland — the best of clinics."

"Yeah," he said whispering back. "I'd be just like Thomas Mann up there on a mountain in the Alps..."

"Be serious, Tom. This is serious, your convalescense is very important — for you getting well."

"I know, Irmmer. No. No, I haven't heard anything — official — yet, and I appreciate your concern."

He did not tell her what the other patients told him about soldiers who contracted Tuberculosis, about how they were collected at the Frankfurt Army hospital and flown back to the United States for long—term care.

Tom watched as Irmgard's eyes above the mask were welling up with tears. He could not stop looking at the eyes as she leaned forward in her chair, her left hand on the bed.

"Tom, I want to be with you," she said in a low voice. Then, in a whisper he could hardly hear, she said, "I'm in love with you, Tom. So much."

"Irmgard ... I don't know what to say. This disease has me now and I have to think about my getting better ..."

He could not look at her eyes after he said that.

"If you go to the States, Tom," she whispered hoarsly, "take me with you. Please Tom."

The tenderness was gone from her eyes now, and when Tom saw this, he said, "I'm in the army, Irmgard. A private. I have to go where they send me. I can't ..."

Irmgard slid down her mask.

"Tom, we could be married, here, in this hospital." She leaned forward. "Then the army would ... ship me to the States ... I would be your wife.

"Oh—h, Tom, I <u>must</u> go to the States. Please, Tom, take me with you."

He squinted at her, still up on his left elbow in the bed.

"I suppose, Irmgard, you plan to make a lot of money and all that in the States?

"But, for sure, Tom," she said as if sensing a glimmer of hope of going to America. "You know I am a business woman."

"Like Lille Marlene, huh?" Tom said and smiled.

"Tom, I don't understand this about Lille Marlene."

"You're a business woman, Irmgard, and it looks like you've been giving me the business ... all along."

"What are you saying, Tom?" she said leaning back in the chair, pulling her mask back up. "Tell me your meaning."

"What the hell you think I mean?" Tom shouted.

At that outburst, Tom saw the old sergeant in the bed at the end of the room, turn, smile at Tom, then turn back to looking out the window.

"There is no need for shouting," Irmgard said.

"I always shout when I dissolve a business partnership," Tom said. "It's good for my lungs. For the liver and spleen too, not to mention the kidneys. But I'm not too sure what it does for the brain."

"This means you will not take me to the States, Tom?"

"That do you think, Irmgard?"

"I thought you would marry me sometime," she said. "I thought you loved me. In Munich, when we were together for so much time, I thought you were in love with me, Tom. You said it. You said you loved me in Munich last summer."

To Tom, now, she sounded like a lawyer.

But she was right. Tom remembered taking the three— day pass in Munich last summer. Irmgard's apartment was in the Schwabing section of town, the student and artist quarter near the university. Irmgard rented the room above her apartment for Tom, so they would have a place away from her two—year old daughter, the people who took care of baby Katerina, as well as Irmgard's business partner, who with his family, lived next door.

Tom never asked who was the father of Katerina.

That morning of the day Tom had to get back to post at Bamberg, he and Irmgard went for breakfast at an outdoor cafe. They had fresh strawberries and cream and sat watching people rushing to work along the sunny street. Later, they walked over to the City Hall, and from the tower, Tom saw where the Alps began in the south, off in the distance across flat plain.

It was at the Munich train station, that when Irmgard asked if he loved her, Tom lied and said he did, because he liked her a lot; she was something new.

"Things were different then," Tom said to her there at the end of the hospital bed. She was now an intruder. He moved to lay on his side in the bed for comfort, his hand and elbow supporting his head up.

He saw that Irmgard's eyes above the mask had grown narrow.

"You are hateful, Tom. A hateful person," she said in an even tone. "And you are deceptive."

A nurse came in the door and when she saw Irmgard, stopped. She was a stout woman with captain bars on her collar.

"Miss," she said standing behind Irmgard in fresh white uniform, "you will have to leave the ward, it is the patient's rest period. I must ask you to go presently."

"Yes," Irmgard said, "I was just going, now."

The nurse walked down to the end of the ward and pulled down the window shades.

"Good—bye, Tom," Irmgard said in a low voice. She picked up her large handbag and her hat off the next bed. "Good luck, too. You will need it, you devil."

"Good—bye, Irmgard, and stay well."

She turned quickly, then went out the door, the nurse following.

Tom laid back on the bed, then reached over to hide the cognac—chocolate miniatures in the drawer of the bedstand next to the bed. Then, he rolled out flat, laying with his hands behind his head.

"Well, that's over," he whispered, feeling relaxed.

"Gettin' your lumps, today?" the old sergeant said from his bed down the ward. Everyone called him, 'Pappy.' Earlier today, Tom talked to the sergeant and the colored kid, Clifford, about the letter he was writing home, telling why he was in the hospital. Tom found it hard to explain how he caught the disease of Tuberculosis to his parents.

"That's about it," Tom said back to the sergeant's referrence to the conversation with Irmgard there in the ward. "But it had to be done."

"Yep," the sergeant said. There was silence in the darkened ward for a while. "After chow," the sergeant said, "maybe the three of us can play some cards. When the day nurse takes off."

"Okay," Clifford said.

"Okay," Tom said.

Tom lay thinking of the famous writer's story about a young wounded soldier in Italy during World War One, who begs a nurse to marry him. She tells him she will follow him home and marry him, but she never does.

It was apparent to Tom that his, and the famous writer's life, were very much the opposite. It seems now, he thought, this was happening more and more. Take Irmgard, for instance, it was the young soldier, Tom, who had to break it off.

Tom smiled, thinking that all the time he was with Irmgard, she was working for a ticket to the United States.

"She was all business," he whispered, grinning.

Chapter 10

They had set the stretchers in a row on the runway at the airport in Romulus, Michigan, and Tom laid on his side to watch the army medical transport plane take off. The wind from the plane fluttered the identification tickets wired onto the stretcher handle behind Tom's head. It was a hot August afternoon and Tom was sweating under the wool blankets. Medical orderlies loading the stretchers into ambulances took off their white jackets and were working in t—shirts.

Tom was back in Michigan. The ambulance would take him to the Veteran Administration Hospital in Allen Park.

All the time Tom was being transported from one hospital, he had to lay on a stretcher. He felt uneasy about being carried because he was able to walk, but the Army said he must be carried. He had been on a stretcher in the ambulance from Nurnberg Hospital to the one in Frankfurt. Later, from Frankfurt he again laid on a stretcher on the medical flight across the Atlantic Ocean, carried off again at the Azores Islands, where they had to land due to bad weather, then carried back on the plane again the next morning. From the Azores the plane flew to Bermuda, stopping only for gas, no one getting off. From Bermuda they flew to an airfield near Philadelphia, and from there were taken on ambulance busses to Valley Forge Army Hospital near Phoenixville, Pennsylvania.

Tom had been treated with chemo—therapy for eight months at Valley Forge before the Chief Medical Officer, a Colonel, told him he needed surgery on his left lung. Because of the operation, the officer said, the Army must know if Tom was planning to stay in the Army, or be discharged when his enlistment time was ended. The officer said the Army did not operate on those who were taking their discharges. Tom said he was not staying in the Army, and he was discharged and put in the care of the Vereran's Administration Hospital at Allen Park. It was here the operation on the left lung would be done, followed by the post—operative treatment.

Even lying on the stretcher, Tom felt good being on home ground again. It was good to have the Army behind too; being a civilian again. When the orderlies came to pick up his stretcher, he even thought of getting off. No, he was not ready for that yet, he told himself. Not yet.

Riding in the ambulance, Tom thought of the famous writer, who as a young man, wounded in the First War, came home and was asked to speak at his old high school, and who held up the pants he wore when wounded; the pants were full of shrapnel holes.

Tom wished his own "wound" was more honorable than just tuber bacillis holes in the left lung. He wished he had a wound he could be proud of. Something he could show around like holes in his shirt, or something. But Tom knew he would be denied all that; nobody could see the holes in his lung. If the young famous writer had caught Tuberculosis, he would have found a way of showing people he had it, Tom was sure of it.

But Tom began thinking now about telephoning home tonight, and talking to his mother and father, and breaking the news about his upcoming lung operation. His parents came to visit him at the Valley Forge Hospital once, but he asked them not to come again, saying the drive from Michigan to Pennsylvania was too hard on them. In reality, it was too hard on him, Tom had to admit. It was going to be difficult telling about the operation. And being near home now, his parents would be coming to visit more to the hospital. That was going to be difficult also. They made him feel — guilty — of something.

It was not until the second week of September that the chest surgeon called Tom for a conference on his operation

"What we want to do," the doctor, whose nametag read, "Trojanowski," said, "is take out this part of the infected lung."

Using his fingers, the doctor formed a triangle over an x—ray showing Tom's left lung. There were other x—rays of Tom's lungs on the rack, lighted from behind, that cover ed the wall of the office.

"We will seperate the ribs here — push them apart," the doctor said, looking at Tom in the face for an instant, "then go in here and cut out a wedge—shape piece of the lung."

"The medication," Tom asked, "that I have been taking to calcify the germs in that infected area, won't that hold? I mean, doctor, back in the Army hospital, they said the Tuber 'bug' can be encased in calcium by taking that PAS and INH medication."

"In some of the mild cases, it might hold, the doctor said thoughtfully. He wore a t—shirt; his arms were heavy, like a day—laborer. Nurses and hospital people had said the doctor was an outstanding specialist, too good for the pay he was making here at the VA. Someone said that the doctor had been a TB patient himself, and had initiated this chest surgery method of dealing with the disease. "But in the case of the size of you lesions, calcification would not hold," the doctor said slowly. "The lesions are too wide to be held by calcification. You could take a chance. But it looks to me likely the lesions would break down very easily and the disease could become active again."

Tom looked at the doctor's face in the pale light glowing from the x—ray rack.

"Why doctor," he said, "didn't you just operate in the first place? Why did I have to lay around the hospital for nearly nine months?"

"We had to make sure the disease was inactive," the doctor said calmly. "We had to make sure the lesions were encased in calcium. Otherwise, when we operate, the disease will leak — spread into the good tissue of the lung — while we'er operating."

Tom leaned forward to look close at the x—rays on the light rack.

"Then the operation is the only sure way — to be sure — I won't get the disease again?" he asked.

"There is no real gaurantee," the doctor said. "But operating is the most effective way we know about today to lessen the chances of the disease reoccuring."

"It's quite a complicated operation, isn't it?" Tom asked, looking at the doctor's face for a reaction.

"Yes. Yes it is. It is what is called 'major surgery.' We will be working directly over your heart in this case."

Tom, shaking his head, backed up and sat on the edge of the doctor's desk.

"When do you have to have my decision, doctor?" Tom asked, folding his arms over his chest.

"In a day or so," the doctor said, piling the x—rays in a stack, then sliding them into a large envelope. "We have to schedule the operating room ... and before that we have to make several tests. It could probably be schedualed for late next week."

Tom nodded. "I'll wait until tomorrow to give my answer. Okay?" he said.

"Surely," the doctor said. "Another thing is that you, or your family representative, will be required to sign a release to allow us to administer an anesthetic to you. You have told your family about the operation?" Without waiting for an answer, the doctor added. "If there is anything your family ... or you ... would like to know about further, I'll be glad to explain."

"Okay," Tom said. "But I think I've explained the operating procedure to them pretty thoroughly, doctor. We've talked it over quite a bit."

"Yes," the doctor said looking at Tom, smiling,

"I think you were the one who requested a transfer to our VA Hospital in Ann Arbor — but changed his mind."

"It was my father's idea," Tom said flushing red in the face and lowering his head so the doctor could not see. "He pulled some strings to get me there. I backed out."

"You don't have to worry," the doctor said smiling widely. "The quality of care in Ann Arbor — with their renown medical center — is the same as here at this hospital. The same operating team which operates on TB patients here, is the same team that operates in Ann arbor."

"I know that," Tom said nodding, his head low, "but I didn't know it before."

"Is there anything," the doctor said putting the envelope of x—rays in a cabinet and closing the door, "that I can do for you now?"

"No, I think we covered everything," Tom said.

The doctor turned on the bright overhead lights, and went over to his desk.

"You talk to your family, "he said from behind his desk, and sat down. "Let me know when you are ready."

"Right," Tom said, and before going out the door, turned, and said, "Thank you doctor."

Walking in the hallway, wearing the paper mask that was required at all times outside the isolation ward, Tom remembered in the famous writer's book about First World War Italy, where the main character, a wounded American, is having his wounds treated in an Italian hospital by a major—doctor.

Tom thought of how, in the story, the major—doctor said he would operate the next day after examining the wounded American. The major—doctor then took a drink of brandy — and was entirely unaffected and good at his job despite the brandy. The famous writer had contrasted the major, and his easy manner, with three incompetent and hesitant captain—doctors, who had wanted the wounded American to lay in bed for six—months in order to "encyst" the shrapnel in his legs before operating.

Tom felt now his lung—doctor was like the major— doctor — competent — even though he did not drink brandy. Tom was going to say yes about the operation. He did not need any further consoltations. He had known it all along.

Another thing that bothered Tom, was that the famous writer drew a lot story material from his wounds. Tom hoped he could use this operation on his lung as story material on his way to becomming famous also, but somehow he felt a lung operation is just not the same as shrapnel in the legs.

Tom thought about it a moment. It was the war in the background that made the famous writer's stories work. That was it, Tom thought. It had to be the war.

After the dinner hour at the hospital, the same day Tom had discussed the operation with the doctor, he decided to telephone his former girlfriend, Harriet. He called her from the pay telephone in the hall of the hospital ward.

"When are you coming to see me?" Tom asked her in a tone of mock disappointment. "I haven't heard from you — since I called last week. I thought you'd come by for a visit by now, or something."

"I —I know, Tom," she said, quickly. "I feel bad about not coming to see you. But I'm so busy. There is no way I can come see you right now."

"What could tie you up that much, Hare?"

There was a pause from Harriet's end of the line.

"Didn't you get my letter?" she asked slowly. "The one I sent to you in the hospital in Frankfurt."

"Yes. And I still have it, Hare."

"Then ... you know about me being engaged to somebody?"

"Sure, babe. But what's that go to do with coming to visit a sick friend?"

"Well, he's very ... jealous. He knows we went together for a long time, Tom. And, he asked me not to go see you in the hospital."

"That creep," Tom said in a low voice. "You're not going to let that stop you, are you, babe?"

"I know how you feel, Tom. But you have to look at it from his point of view; after all we are to be married next month.

"I know how you feel — right now, Tom — but in a while, none of this will mean anything to you."

"Hare, I just want to talk." After he spoke, he caught himself begging; that was what it sounded like, to him. So he added a soft sentence, "I just want to talk about what has happened to the both of us, and all that."

"I'm sorry, Tom," Harriet said in a tone that was growing distant. "Things have changed since you went away to the army. There is no going back to that time we had. And it would be upsetting for me to see you in that hospital. Very up setting."

"You should be in my shoes, babe," Tom said, defiantly. "It's a hell of a lot more than upsetting."

"Stop it, Tom. I know you're working on my sympathy to break me down. I sorry, but I just can't come to see you. Please — understand."

"You know I always loved you," he said.

"Stop it, Tom. You don't mean it — you just want to say it for the effect."

"You know I still love you, Hare?"

"Stop it, Tom. Stop it."

"I've always loved you."

There was a pause on the line from Harriet's end.

"Now ... Now, Tom, you see why I can't come there to the hospital. I knew you say things like that. You say things that can break people's heart."

"You know it's always been you, Hare."

"No, Tom — no more. You are just saying that now, because you are back, and you want a girl. You really never loved anybody. I know you never really loved me."

"Don't talk like that, Hare," Tom said trying to be defiant again. "I always loved you."

"No—o you don't, Tom. No more and not again. The only real love you have is — for yourself. Even your writing is for yourself, to make yourself famous, so you can satisfy your giant—size ego."

"Harriet, you're going way overboard."

"I have to say it Tom."

"Why? And don't tell me you're going to save me from myself, and all that."

"Tom, you know I once loved you. And you know I have the right to say it is over with you and me. But you won't let go."

A Negro patient came up and stood near the telephone, his back to Tom, jingling handful of coins, and looking at his watch from time to time.

Tom turned, and cupping his hand around the telephone mouthpiece, said, "Harriet, I'm going to have a serious operation in about a week. Maybe ... I won't come out of it. Some people don't. All I'm asking is you come see me, before I go under the knife."

Tom had heard other patients using the phrase, "Go under the knife," and he thought it was descriptive, in a general way, and now he found a chance to use the phrase as his own, so he did.

"Tom, there you go again, playing on my sympathy. But it won't work. No, no. No more."

"I know, Harriet, that the whole thing sounds a little melodramatic about the operation, but it just happens to be true ... this time."

"I'm sorry, Tom. I can't come there. Really.

"Hare, I have to go right now, a guy wants to use the phone. Can I call you back, Hare?"

"Sorry, Tom, but I'm going out.

"Well, I'll call tomorrow."

"No, I don't think you should, Tom.

Tom's face turned red; he slammed the phone when he hung it up.

The Negro man picked up the phone when Tom turned away.

"Hope you have better luck than I did," Tom said walking down the hallway.

Chapter 12

At nine—thirty the next Thursday morning, Tom lay covered by a sheet on the cart—table, a gurney, and was silently pushed down a sunlit hall to the operating room waiting for him. He was drowsy from the shot of demerol the head nurse had given him in the arm earlier; she twisted his right ear and smiled after giving the shot, but said nothing. Tom smiled back.

Rolling along, Tom thought that are some things in life a person must do alone, go alone, no one can go for you. He was thinking that this operation was for himself, alone, and he, alone, had to go through it, alone. No one could do it for you.

He suddenly had the premonition that he would come through this operation without any problems. While still feeling the elation of the premonition, he told himself it was brought on because he wanted to be a writer, but somehow, he realized, the telling himself he wanted to be a writer was coming from himself. He wished he could tell himself he was going to be a writer and feel it the way the knowledge of how the operation would go successfully did. But it did not.

The next day, his mother and father visiting him was upsetting. They saw the mercury—pump on the floor next to the bed, keeping the blood from flooding his lung where it had been severed by the surgery. Their faces showed the strain. He was almost glad when they left; his guilt left too.

On the television set in the room, the news was all the Russian "Sputnik" that was orbiting the earth. Tom looked at the picture of the electronic device that appeared nothing more than a ball with several aerials sticking out, and wondered what all the fuss was about. The news report on the television program said the "Sputnik" was launched into space yesterday morning, indicating the Russians were ahead of America in a technology sense,

Tom smiled. The launch was the same time he was going into the operating room. "Unbelievable," he wispered.

During the six—months post operation convalesence, Tom read and studied books of fiction to see how they were made. He found a book also, on how to write fiction, and studied it diligently. Then he scrapped the two—hundred and fourteen pages of a book he had written

about the wild people he had known at the university, and turned to writing two pages each day about the past in his own life. He was plotting this new book with a girl and Tuberculosis. All the people in the new book were disguised making it a work of fiction.

During this time, he also wrote two short stories about girls he had known in Europe. But he could not sell the two stories. In order to sell these stories, he would have to twist the plots, make a trick ending, but he resisted doing that. He thought it phoney. He knew most writers did it; a surprise ending was the way to make the story sell to a magazine. But he was above that stuff. He told himself he did not need the money, now, so he would not write that way. He was determined to be an artist, not a commercial hack.

At Christmas time, the doctors at the hospital let Tom go home for a week. When the holidays were over, he decided not to return. The hospital sent a letter saying he should return for at least two more months of therapy. He stayed home in Grosse Pointe. The hospital sent a letter he had left "against medical advice," and he was solely responsible for any medical mishaps which might occur.

He had time now to write fiction, and he wanted to get his degree at the university in the city; take the few remaining classes required. And the food was better.

Tom lived at home until spring, then decided to move to an apartment near Wayne State University in Detroit. He was not fully recovered physically and never would be the same. He tired easily when walking, and sometime had to stop and lean against a tree to catch his breath. Going up the stairs to classes was the most difficult, but some of the newer buildings on campus had elevators.

He mentioned to his parents that an apartment would give him freedom to write and all hours. There had been several incidents at night, late, when he woke them with his typing.

Having an apartment, he would have a place to take a girl, but he never mentioned this to his parents, who probably new this already. They did not oppose his moving out.

The money Tom received from the Veteran administration for disability was enough to pay rent and buy some food and other necessities. Rent was not too costly near the college, which was located in the older section of the city, called the Cultural Center; The Detroit Museum of Arts and the Main Library were just across a wide lawn from the university.

At the corner of Palmer Street, where Tom lived, facing the campus green was the Karl Rolfson Bookstore. It was not the paperback kind of bookstore. Rolfson, in addition to teaching a class on the history of writing, a class he designed and prepared and presented, was an expert on rare books and first editions. His store had many fine prints on the walls in frames, also, and frequently instructors and professors from the university could be seen browsing in the store along with wealthy book collectors from the suburbs.

Tom did not like the sophistication of the store, its black door and the front window framed in black and the gold and black block letters on the glass. The outside could pass for a bank or funeral parlor. Tom did not like the rows of old books on the shelves that covered the walls, nor the steps of bare wood that lead up to a loft where there was a walkway with more shelves. The unpainted wood of the shelves and steps gave the place the look that it belonged back in Charles Dickens' time.

But worst of all, Tom disliked the way the rare books were displayed, open, on a black velvet cloth in the window, a tinted plastic sheet blocking the sunlight. To Tom, the bookstore seemed to cater to people interested in printing and bookbinding rather than to someone interested in the ideas and information written in the volumes.

Tom not only did not like the upscale bookstore, but he did not like Rolfson himself, specifically the way Rolfson dressed. Several times walking past the store, Tom had seen Rolfson standing near the window in a pressed suit with a vest. A gold chain dropped from his lapel to the breast pocket, where there must be a watch. He wore his gray hair clipped short, military style, but it was the clipped mustache that that Tom's dislike centered on. With that mustache, Rolfson looked like Thomas Mann, whose picture was on the jacket of the book Tom was reading for his English Literature class. Tom did not like Thomas Mann's mountain book about Tuberculosis; he thought it clever but far—fetched. As for Rolfson, he looked like he belonged at Harvard, not at a city, working—class, university.

The third week of summer classes at the university, Tom, passing the window of the bookstore, saw the red— haired girl from his English Lit class, browsing at a shelf. Tom had been talking to her since the first day of class, but he had never gotten to talk with her outside class; she was always rushing to someplace. Although, once she offered she was graduating in January, had two papers to reasearch, and study for her German language test. Tom blurted out she should have taken care of the requirement long ago, and he hit a nerve. She did not like the comment. She avoided him this past week.

Tom knew the foreign language requirement trick, where a student took the class several times, taking incompletes each term, until the student was sure to make at least a B grade on the test, then taking it and not lowering your overall grade average. Language courses like German had a lot of students doing repeat courses.

Tom walked into the bookstore to talk to her, tease a little.

"Well, if it isn't Virginia Handley," he said, smiling. "You looking for some cowboy literature?"

"Tom," she said turning around. She wore a western jacket with fringes that swayed when she moved. "I didn't know you were a book collecter."

Tom stood smiling; "I live in the neighborhood."

Rolfson came out of his office, "Hello," he said to Tom. "Can I help you with anything?"

Tom saw the handkerchief in his suit breast pocket was a Peasley print.

"I'm still looking for a book of western prints, Karl," Virginia said. "A gift for dad... but there's so much..."

"This whole section," Rolfson said. "Back to the wall. Take your time."

The telephone back in his office rang, and Rolfson darted back to his office.

"There are a number of good volumes ... on western art," he said without looking back... "just to your right."

"He's very nice," Virginia whispered to Tom. "Women can't leave him alone. He's so charming."

Smiling, Tom said, "I think I saw a wedding ring."

"Yes, of course he's married."

"You sound as if you know him," Tom said, looking at the row of books in front of him.

"Yes," Virginia said, and began looking at the books again, leaning to read the titles.

"Hey," Tom said, "you're a Psychology major, right?"

"Right," she said, and as she did her red hair fell forward as she leaned over. And the fringes on her jacket were hanging on the books.

"I meant to ask you before," Tom said, trying not to watch her too closely, the grace in her movements, "then what are you doing in an advance English Lit course?"

"I like to read," she said looking up at him, smiling. "No," she said straightening up. "My minor is English Lit." She stood looking at Tom, twisting one of the fringes on the arm of the jacket, thoughtfully. "It comes easy for me, literature. I read a lot anyway, so it was just natural, I thought, that I should major in it."

"I'm a Journalism major," Tom said watching her face. He thought if she was going to be forthright, he would be too. "I don't really like it, but I've gone this far, so I might as well finish it up for the degree." When she turned back to the books, he wanted to impress her, so he blurted, "I'm a fiction writer," he said watching her face for a reaction, hoping to see her impressed. "That's what I want to do ... for a living ... write fiction stories. That, and travel all over the world."

Virginia smiled up at him, "Like Ernest, the famous writer."

"Yeah, like the famous writer."

"Man, who doesn't want to live that way, Tom. Free to travel all the time, wow. Big game hunting. Deep—sea fishing. The whole bit."

As she was talking she was moving along the shelves now, looking at book titles.

"Like the man says," Tom offered, feeling now she was not bowled—over with him spilling his dreams out for her. "You only live once."

They stopped moving along the shelves when they came to the large glass windows that looked into Rolfson's office. In front of the windows, there was a worn leather couch. Turning around, Tom realized that a view of the couch from the front of the store was blocked by a chest—high line of book shelves. He smiled, thinking what the couch could be used for.

"You're right, Tom. You know ... that's how I feel about life too ... you're only going around once ... so, you should do what you want ... go your own way."

Tom saw Rolfson through the windows, talking on the telephone, intently. It was hard to determine, Tom thought, if it was business, or a woman, Rolfson was talking to in such au involved manner.

"It's got to be because you only get one chance to prove what you can do," Tom said to Virginia. "There doesn't seem much left in life if you don't think that way. Working, you just get old."

Virginia was looking at the books in a glass cabinet that stood at the far end of the leather couch.

"Tom, all these books were written in the Depression Era. It supposed to be one of the most complete ... one of the best collections ... of that nineteen—thirties period. Karl collected all these books when he lived in New York city. Malcolm Crowley, or whatever his name," she waved her arm making the fringes on her jacket sway," asked Karl to lecture at Harvard. They would have a double—barreled course: Crowlèy teaching the twenties, and Karl teaching the thirties. Karl is supposed to know everything that happened in the thirties era."

As Tom stood listening to Virginia, Karl hung up the telephone and came out of his office.

When Virginia saw him, she said, "Isn't this a collection of all the novels published in America during the Depression?"

Rich And Famous Page 137

"Yes," he said lighting a cigaret with a Zippo lighter, and snapping it shut, "as far as I know. And they are all first editions. It has taken me over twenty years to collect all of these — to find all the titles listed."

Tom looked closely at the books in the glass case: some were coming apart, crumbling, due to the poor quality of the materials used. It must have been real hard times, economically, during the depression, he thought, it even showed in the books from that time. Many of the book titles were faded, hard to read, or not legible at all.

"What I'm extremely proud of is my Mississippi collection," Rolfson said to Tom and pointing to another glass door cabinet in his office. "I've collected Faulkner's works since his first book 'Marble Fox.' That was back when I was working in New York City, just beginning to learn the book business at Brentanos. Faulkner was a talent."

"I see," Tom said; when he looked at Virginia, she was smiling, knowing he was impressed by Rolfson. "Is there any famous writer in the nineteen—thirties collection? I couldn't see ..."

"Of course," Rolfson said, "look at the top shelf, right side. There is a first edition of 'Have Not,' and 'Death In the Afternoon,' and 'Green Hills,'"

Tom followed Virginia to the cabinet again, and looking where she was pointing, smelling the shampoo fragrance in her red hair, said, "And these are first editions?"

"They are worth quite a bit, arn't they Karl?" Virginia said.

"Yes, dear," Rolfson said, crushing out his cigaret in a ashtray on a narrow table at the end of the couch. "That is why I keep them — both cabinets — near my office. And I won't sell them, unless I absolutely must. Then, I will only sell them as a collection, not seperately. A foundation, or library would be a likely customer."

An elderly man and woman, both wearing poplin tan raincoats came into the store. Rolfson turned to watch them.

When the old man lifted a framed lithograph picture of Fort Detroit from the wall, and both the old people began looking at it with magnifying glasses.

"I think you have a customer," Tom said.

"Yes," Rolfson said, and turned quickly to Tom and Virginia. "Please. Will you step away from this office alcove. It is not thet I mistrust you ... but, if anything is damaged, I would hav e to hold you responsible. I would not want to do that. You understand, I sure."

Following Rolfson out of the alcove, Virginia whispered to Tom, "Those books are ... fragile, Tom." Then when Rolfsonson was out of earshot, and talking with the old couple, she added, "He borrows money with those books as collateral. Frequently."

Where they were standing, outside the alcove, on the wall just above them was a picture frame with medals moun— on black velvet.

"What are those for?" Tom said pointing up. "Karl's father was an Olympic Marksman, or some thing," Virgina said. "He was an officer in the Danish army, I think, if I remember right."

"You've known Rolfson for some time, right, Virginia?"

"He's a friend of our family," she said. "My father knows him from fishing up in Canada, some fishing lodge up there. And, whenever my father's law firm needs an estate appraisal on a private library, or print collection sometimes, they call on Karl."

"Do you come here to the store a lot?"

"Not really," she said. "Sometimes when I get tired of the library, and studying, I drop in to talk with Karl. You should hear him tell stories ... and he knows a lot of things ... to talk about. Like an uncle."

Out in the store, they saw Karl lift the framed map out the elderly man's hands and hang it back on the wall, smiling all the while he did it.

"Looks like no sale," Tom said.

"He's very expensive."

"He's got to be," Tom said, "to cover the high cost of his clothes."

"He told me once that no matter what the price, if people really want something, they will always pay it."

"That's what he's figuring on with that old couple," Tom said, grinning. "If they give p eating for two weeks, they might be able to buy it. He's giving them time to go home and discuss it. They face the compulsion of owning that print."

"Okay, wise guy," Virginia said. "You're not being funny... just sarcastic."

Karl, after holding open the front door for the old couple, talking and smiling, came back across the store.

"Would you two like some coffee?" he asked.

"Sounds good," Virginia said looking at Tom, who was nodding.

"Think those old people will come back for that print?" Tom asked, following Virginia and Karl into the back room.

"No," Rolfson said. "I told them it was too expensive for them. It's an original. I told them in about a month, I would have several reprints of that map, at half the cost."

Virginia was smiling, turning a fringe on the front of her cowboy jacket, when Tom looked at her. She was saying in body language that he was wrong again, so he smiled back.

The narrow back storeroom was almost filled by a heavy walnut table and three chairs; the kind of furniture used in a library. On the table was a jar of spoons, four coffee mugs, and a jar of instant coffee. There were books stored in open cardboard boxes under the table, stacked along the wall, even under the sink.

When Rolfson filled a steel pot with water, he set it on a glowing hot plate sitting on top of a metal cabinet.

"Virginia says you fish up in Canada," Tom said as he sat down on the chair at the end of the table. "I've always wanted to go up there."

"I try to get away to my cabin every summer, now, with my boys," Rolfson said, spooning the instant coffee into each cup. I've been going up there for about twenty years. Before I built my own cabin, I went to fishing camps… I met Ginny's father one summer at a camp. We've been friends ever since."

"Where is your cabin in Canada?" Tom asked.

"Georgian Bay, Rolfson said. "It's the eastern part of Lake Huron. The cabin is actually on Key River, about fifty miles south of Sudbury." He looked at the water in the pot, then said, "I'll show you on a map."

When he stepped out of the store room, Virginia said, "He likes talking about that cabin." She sat back in the chair near Tom, smiling.

"I can see that, 'Ginny;" he said, smiling back, his head to one side.

Rolfson came back with a large Road Atlas and a small match box used safety matches.

"Will you pour the water, Ginny," he said opening the pages of the Atlas flat on the table. "The cabin is here on this narrow blue line, which is the Key River. I'm about half—way between the highway, the Trans—Canada, here," he showed pointing with a pencil, "and the Georgian Bay over here."

"You're not too far from Manitoulin Island," Tom said, looking at the map, leaning forward.

"Well," Rolfson said, "Key Harbour is here at the mouth of the river on the Bay, it might be fifty or so odd miles from Manitoulin."

"It's really primitive up there," Virginia said as she was pouring hot water into each cup. "No electricity. No running water, or outside plumbing," she said setting the pot in the sink. "My father took color slides, I've seen them."

"Yes," Rolfson said, taking one of the cups, stirring, then sipping the coffee, "it's quite wild up there.

I've seen moose and bears, foxes, beaver and skunks and porcupine." Then he opened the safety matchbox and dumped out three sets of rattles from snakes; one set quite large. "And a lot of rattle snakes."

When Rolfson shook the largest of the rattles, Tom set his coffee cup down, slowly, on the table, listening to the dry sound, intently. He was fascinated.

"With those things outside," Virginia said, "I'd be afrain to go out of the cabin. I can't stand snakes."

"The boys don't mind," Rolfson said. "The dog doesn't either. These are Mississagua rattlers ... they warn you when you're too close. They rattle a warning. They are fair."

"You seem to fit right in up there," Tom said to Rolfson. "That kind of life isn't for everybody."

"I can't wait to get up there in the summer," he said. "The boys and I take all our stuff on the train. We go to Windsor, buy supplies, and a little whiskey, and ride the CP train up."

The front door of the store opened, then closed.

"I have a customer," Rolfson said getting up from his chair. "I'll show you a photograph of the cabin."

He walked out quickly.

"How may boys does he have?" Tom asked Virginia and drank a sip of the hot coffee.

"Two, and there's a girl in between," she said. He's been married twice," she whispered. "And he's naughty… I heard father tell my mother that Karl had to leave New York because of trouble with women. They can't seem to leave him alone, and visa versa. I don't know how many children he has from the first marriage. But he's married now to a woman that was a fashion model. Young, when he married her. She drinks now. A lot. She's a real problem."

"Karl's quite a boy, Tom said, smiling, shaking his head, then taking a drink of coffee. He set the cup down. "Maybe you should be ... careful…"

"He knows better to start anything with me, it would ruin his business," Virginia said after sipping coffee; she held the cup with both hands. "I think he's afraid of father." She set the cup on the table. "Like you, he wanted to be a writer, so said my dad once to my mom. He tried until he was about thirty years old, then finished work for a Master's Degree to earn a living. But it was during the Depression Era, the degree didn't mean anything. There were no teaching jobs, so he took a job in a bookstore in New York. He was married to his first wife then."

"What kind of stuff did he write," Tom asked, "do you know?" He drank what was left of his coffee, tilting his head back.

"Short stories, I guess," Virginia said, pushing her cup forward. "How can you drink this stuff? This isn't coffee. Yikes."

When Rolfson did not return from the store, Tom and Virginia washed out their cups and set them on the sink. Passing the office, they saw Rolfson through the glass window talking seriously to a man wearing an expensive dark suit. They did not wave.

Tom could not help but start thinking about Karl's cabin up on Georgian Bay and how it might be a good place to write stories, and might even lead to writing a story like the famous writer's "Up In Michigan."

Stepping out the door of the bookstore behind Virginia, Tom said, "Up In Canada."

"What about Canada?" Virginia asked; she was looking at the books displayed in Karl's front window.

"I'd like to go there, that's all," Tom said, quietly, standing next to her. "It might be good for my writing," he said looking at the book on the velvet—covered stand.

"Not to mention it would be a good place for a vacation for you, eh, Tom."

When they turned away from the window, walking, Tom said, "There is no vacation for a convalescent."

She looked up at him, quickly, as if to study his face. Then, when they came to the corner, she said, "Walk me to my car. It's late, I should be getting home."

Chapter 13

Tom and Virginia were sitting on the grass in front of the university library. It was a sunny May afternoon, the campus grass green, the trees full of buds in every direction on the campus mall.

"Can't you get out of it?" he asked and stretched out full length on the grass next to her.

"Not really," she said quietly. Her hair looked orange with the sunlight behind it. "It's a family thing and all the relatives will be there. And I'll be back next week." he picked a blade of grass and threw it away.

"Wish you didn't have to go, Gin."

They had been seeing each other every day now, since meeting at the bookstore. last month.

"Honey," she said, dropping her hand on his arm, "you can work on your book with no distractions. You can really work on that chapter that's giving you so much trouble."

"Maybe so," Tom said, and raised up on his elbows to look at her, "but with you gone, I'll get another kind of distraction; loneliness. Gin, with you gone, every day is going to have a big hole in it." As he was talking, he looked across the lawn where two boy students and a girl were playing catch with a frisbie. He watched until the girl missed a catch. "But you're right about I would have time to work on that damn chapter, get the book story moving again... I have to come to a place in the book where I'v just run out of gas."

"Tom, maybe it's just a case of plane old writer's block," Virginia said, and picked another blade of grass and flicked it away. "It's nothing serious. It happens to all writers."

"Writer's block is <u>very</u> serious, Gin. Some people never recover from it ... their careers go right down the drain. Some shoot themselves."

"Tom, nenver, never talk about shooting yourself. Don't even let it cross your mind." She put her hand on his forehead. "It's not healthy to think of shooting yourself."

"Sorry. I don't want to upset you, but I was just saying what other ... some other ... writer's do in the extreme."

"Tom, I just don't want to hear about people shooting themselves. Okay?"

"Okay, Gin. But I have to talk about war ... in relation to writer's block." He sat up, crossing his legs, Indian style.

"Is this more about shooting?"

"No. No, Gin."

"What about war, then?"

"Well, I discovered the famous writer had a good thing going for himself ... by writing about war. You know, Gin, he had at lot of his stories with war in the background." He looked at her face. "Or his stories had stuff about war itself."

"Is that it?"

"Let me explain, Gin."

"I'm waiting."

"You see, Gin," Tom said picking up a blade of grass, "by using a war, you have a ready—made framework for your fiction characters to perform in. They are always coming or going to the war in your story. That way, you can do all kinds of situations and problems with your characters. You never run out of gas. You never have writer's block, because if you run out of stuff to write about your charaters, you just swith back to writing about the war, or… visa versa.

"That's pretty good, Tom. A good analogy. But if you can do it with a war background, why can't you do it with some other subject?"

"Yeah," Tom said smelling the blade of grass, "you can use other subjects, like the old west, the Yukon and outdoor stuff ... but its got to be adventureous, romantic, action—packed."

"Tom, some everyday things are adventurous. Why can't a writer write about everyday stuff?"

"I don't see going to work in an office as adventureous, Gin."

"What about love, then?" she said.

"Love is a good subject, but it's better to write about love and war together, or love and some kind of other adventure together. It makes a better story ... plane love is just not enough. Even the famous writer knew that. That was why he used the two together so much."

"Tom, I'm not so sure it's as simple as you make it out to be."

"There are variations, babe."

"Let me hear them. This is interesting, Tom."

"Well, for want of a better label, I call it the war background—background type. The famous writer used it in the direct method in the story he wrote about a young wounded soldier home from the war who sits on the front porch looking at battle maps in a book."

"Tom, I read that one. He says he likes the girls' bobbed hair and their dickie—collars, but he just doesn't want to get involved with a girl. Imagine that."

"Okay, it's something like that, Gin. You're right about his liking the girls part, but he's tired of going through the prerequsites you have to go through with them to make love. During the war he took short cuts with women and went straight to the love making. He wasn't ready now at home to go through all the prerequsites again."

"Well, whatever his problem was," Virginia said thoughtfully, "if he was normal about girls, he would have to get over it in a hurry or else he would find out he was creating more problems for himself. War or no war."

"We won't go into that," Tom said laying over on his side, still looking at Virginia. "What I started out to explain is that in this story about the young soldier, we are told in the story that the young guy has been to war. So it's a fact..."

Virginia picked at the grass. "And that's an example of your direct—method," she said not looking at Tom.

"That's right," he said. "Now, the in—direct method is more complicated.

"Let's hear it, Tom."

"The famous writer was a little older. The war experience is fading back in his memory. He is living in Paris with his wife and their baby son and trying to make a living writing stories. Maybe all that had something to do with it…"

"I should think it would, Tom," Virginia said smiling, then moving to lay out on the grass next to Tom, supporting her head with her hand and arm like him.

"I call it the 'indirect method' of war background because the war is never mentioned in the story," he said to her face to face.

"You sure of no mention of war at all, Tom?"

"Nope."

"Then how does the reader know about the war?"

"Simple, the reader knows the famous writer's life so well, that they know that war is looming in the background and has something to do with the story."

"Tom, this is getting complicated," Virginia said sliding her hand under her jaw.

"I'll explain it with another fiction piece, Gin. The famous writer as a young man in the story, gets off a train in the Upper Peninsula in Michigan. It's all wilderness, and alone he hikes across burned — out woods, and eats canned apricots, that he says taste better than fresh ones, puts up a little tent, then goes trout fishing, and when he baits a hook with a grasshopper, he watches the hopper spit at the hook ..."

"That's not a story, Tom. And where did he get the apricots?"

"Okay, it's not a story but a vignette, Gin, and don't act silly about the apricots — you know he carried the can in his knapsack."

"Don't call me silly, Tom. I know the story too."

"Okay, smartie, you tell me then, what I was leading…what point ... I was trying to explain."

"All right, Tom, hear it is. The sad part of that non—story is that the main character throws a log on the fire that night. There are ants living in the log, and they come out, run around the log, and eventually fall in the fire. The main character feels bad for the ants and states he will never hurt another living thing again."

"Does that go for grasshoppers too?" Tom asked.

"Silly, Tom, you know it does," she said sitting up,

"Well, you see then, Gin, the ants were kind of a symbol of maybe all the people the main character killed in the war. He was not going to do that again. But what I'm getting at, is there is no war mentioned, outright. Ergo, we have the in—direct method of the war background. You see what I mean?

He sat up next to her, resting his arms on his knees.

"Tom, this grass is beginning to feel wet. I just noticed it."

"That's about all I've got to say, Gin, about the famous writer's use of war in the background of a story. By the way, he wrote that 'Big Two Hearted River" story in a Paris cafe ... it was sort of an excercise in description. Back in nineteen twenty—two."

"Fascinating," Virginia said smiling, and standing up, brushing her rump. "Am I wet back there?"

"No wet, I can see, babe," Tom said getting to his feet, brushing her Bermuda shorts slowly, and smiling. "Big Hearted is a very good peice of writing ... if you look at it as just an excercise."

"For guys who like trout fishing, Tom," she said quickly.

"No, Gin. Cripes. It's a lot more than that. It makes you feel everything that is described in the story. The reader is made to feel the inside the tent, tastes the apricots, and smell the dry weeds, or whatever, just as the main character does."

"Okay, Tom. It's a great description and if that isn't enough, it has a war background too. How's that?"

"You know Gin, this young man in the story is the famous writer as a young man. He's going off on a hike alone. The war background comes on strong because you know he's on the hike expressedly to forget the war."

"Tom, I think you are mixing the famous writer's life into his story subjects ... just leave it as a good story ... about trout fishing."

"I can leave it as a good trout story, Gin, it's everbody else that can't."

"Let's go someplace for a coffee, Tom. Someplace I can sit on a chair instead of the ground."

"Let's go over to my apartment. It's just across the campus. I'll get some beer."

"I don't know," Virginia said. "I have to go ..."

"I want to tell you about my short story, the one I wrote for McGregor's writing class. I got it back yesterday; McGregor critiqued it, read it in class, and they all stomped on it. It's about a soldier, home from Germany recently, who caught TB, and the girl in the story tells him she can't see him anymore. Her mother doesn't like the soldier—protagonist."

"Really," Virginia said looking at Tom earnestly. "Tell me what did McGregor say in his critique? What did he say about your story?"

"Well, he said the story was all right. But Gin, he was just being polite . He said I should look around for my own themes."

"Is that all McGregor said?

"Naw, then he said ... something that makes me want to puke..."

"What was that? Tell me, Tom. I want to know."

"He said, 'you know, the famous writer's stories carry much more impact — because of his war background.'"

"Tom, is that what upset you so much?" She stood looking at his face, her hands on her hips.

"I could have punched McGregor right then and there," Tom said looking down. "You know how McGregor got his job teaching at the university? One slim volume; a book about the life of his sea—captain grandfather — and that is his qualification to teach creative writing at a university. Cripes, Gin, I can't do anything about this whole war back ground thing. How can I go to war?"

"Tom, you're getting into this whole problem too deep, if you ask me. We've only known one another a short time, but this writing thing is becomming obsessive with you — that a sick — you've got to let it go."

"Gin, cripes, it's not the writing; it's that damn war—experience thing that's driving me bonkers. How can I get around the war—experience? Tell me?"

"Write about some other subject, Tom. There are plenty. Let the war thing go, and write about something you know."

"Yeah, Gin, I guess that's what I have to do," Tom said running his hand over his hair, then down to cover his eyes. "You know what the lady in front of me in writing class said after my story was read?"

"Can't let it bother you, Tom. People react differently."

"American girls arn't like that;" Tom said making a pinched face at Virginia. "This middle—age old crow said that. She turned around in her chair and said it to my face."

"Maybe we should talk about something else, Tom. Let the subject of writing— rest for a while. She waved her arm. "We can go someplace, and ..."

"I want to go to my apartment, Gin. Maybe drink a beer." Tom grinned. "It may be a dump at the bottom of an air shaft. But It's as good a hideout as any."

"Okay, Tom. But just for a little while, I've got to get home and pack ..."

They walked holding hands across the new grass in the direction of his apartment house.

"I'm sure having a hell of a time, Gin, getting a toehold in this writing racket. Wonder how the famous writer did it."

"Stop thinking about it, Tom. Ple — ase, Tom."

"Okay, Gin."

They were sitting on the couch in the front room of Tom's apartment.

"Um—m," Virginia moaned.

Tom kissed her there again.

"You—u," she said.

"Move this way," Tom whispered. "Let me kiss the other one."

When she moved, the couch made a groaning sound.

"Tom. Tom."

She was holding his neck, pulling him against her.

"Beautiful," Tom said in a low voice. "So soft and beautiful."

She pulled him close, their faces touching; she kissed his face, searching for his mouth.

"Gin, I'm going to — explode. I want ... want..."

They were sitting on the couch that was opposite the two windows where the blinds were drawn. Sunlight shone at the edges of the blinds. There was a desk next to the couch stacked with books and papers. A small television set was on a chair in the corner.

Tom pulled Virginia slow, moving her full down on the couch, as he knelt on the floor.

"Oh, Tom. I want ... you ... I ... do."

His face was against her red hair as he pulled himself up on the couch next to her, pulling at he Bermuda shorts.

"Let, me," he whispered. "Oh, ple—ase ... let me."

He put his hand on her.

"Tom. Tom, I want to ... but I can't. I can't do it, honey."

"Gin ... I'm going ... crazy. Oh, Gin," he said pulling off his clothes. "I want you ... so bad—ly."

"Tom, I want you ... too," she, and held her body rigid. "I can't. It's not right ... now. We just met."

Tom eased his hold from her back and ran his hands down her thighs.

"No honey," Virginia whispered softly. "No."

"Gin .., I'm going out of my ... mind."

"So am I, Tom—honey." She pulled him by the neck and kissed him.

He tried to force his leg between Virgina to open her thighs.

"No more, Tom. I can't ... you ... stop."

"This ... is unbelievable," he said to himself.

"I'm sorry, honey. I'm sorry ... really."

"I could ... force you ..."

"I know, Tom."

He held her hard against himself. “You’re so beautiful. That orange patch down there drives me crazy, Gin.”

“Tom, you’re beautiful too. Every part of you, honest.

“Ginny, I think you own me. That kind of scares me to say. And I can’t stand how much I care for you. I sort of knew it from the start. I ache ... I ache, I need you so much, babe.”

“Tom, I want to be with you too, you can’t believe how much,” she said and put her face against his, then kissed him.

“We’ve — got to settle this, Gin.”

“Not now, honey,” she said softly. “When I come back — next week — we can talk.”

“Gin, there really isn’t anything to talk about; the whole thing has been decided, already, for us.”

“Maybe — but I think we should wait before we — do anything serious, Tom. Besides, you’ve had a bad day with your story and you are tired, too tired, to discuss anything.”

“Yeah,” Tom said quietly, “to say I’ve been under a strain today is — putting it mildly. And those people jumping all over my short story in writing class, yesterday, well, that really shook my self—confidence. Those lumps wouldn’t know a good story if they fell over it.”

“See,” Virginia said looking into Tom’s face, “when you get low — you start insulting everybody.”

“All right, Gin. All right, we’ll have our talk when you get back next week. We’ll settle our problems; until next week, everything is on hold.”

“Thank you, Tom,” she said and kissed him.

They lay on the couch for a few moments without speaking, looking at each other.

“I....should get some sleep,” Tom said. “I feel like an elephant sat on me.”

“And I’ve got to run, honey. I’m really late. I’m going to be late for dinner at home. I’ve got to go.”

“How can I sleep, Gin, when you have to go — for a whole week yet. With you gone, I might as well be dead.

“Tom, don’t make going away harder than it already is. Ple—ease.”

“Gin, I’m trying to be pleasant. But it’s hard. It goes against the way I feel.”

“I know.” She smiled. “I guess for some people being plesant takes an awful lot of energy. Some people just have to work hard to be plesant.”

“I should save my energy for my writing,” Tom mumbled. “But right now, I’m stuck on what to write next in my book, so energy, or no energy, I don’t know what I should do.”

“It will come to you, Tom, what to do.”

“Most books,” he said quietly, “are written — plotted — so the main character and his girl are together most of the story. But — my book isn’t like that — my main character wanders to all kinds of places. The girl is not with him. Not, at least, until the final half of the story.”

“She must miss him, Tom.”

"Be serious, Gin."

"Okay, Tom."

"My main character does not meet his girl until late in the story — the book — I should say.

"Well then, Tom, begin the story there. Shouldn't you begin where they meet? I mean, that's what's important, isn't it, honey?"

"No. This isn't a love story, Gin, this is serious stuff. This is about a guy who travels a lot and catches Tuberculosis. It tragic and beautiful because he wants to be a writer."

"Well, Tom, I think you should write a love story."

"And I just knew you were going to say that, Gin."

"Books with love stories sell a lot quicker than the other kind. Tom, everybody likes a love story."

"What I started to tell you about, Gin," Tom said moving his arms up, behind his head; the couch moaned when Virginia moved to make room for his arms, "is that my story is coming out in a straight line. It should be more of a circle — with all the parts connected."

"Wow, Tom, you lost me now. I don't understand all those technical problems about writing a story. "You'll have to explain all that to me, honey."

"Okay, Gin, here it is, babe, short and sweet; there's no conflict in my book." Tom rolled up on his side to face Virginia. "You know how the famous writer always has conflict ... his characters are always struggling to solve monumental problems, blowing up a bridge, or bringing home some giant fish. Me, my stories don't have that kind of conflict."

"Tom, maybe you're just a different kind of writer. You write about a different kind of struggle."

"What you are saying is that I write psychological books, as opposed to the physical sort of book."

"Yes," Virginia said, "that's about it. I don't know if a book is written in a line, or a circle, but I know that all writers can't be the same." When Tom laid back down, Virginia, leaned up on her elbow, her breasts touching his chest. "What do you mean exactly when you say your book is coming out in a straight line."

He reached to touch her, but she took hold of his hand.

"It's as if my book," he said smiling at her face, "is just a string of episodes, incidents, whatever you want to call them. They don't move the story along toward a solution of a problem. And there isn't supposed to be anything in a book — like an incident or episode — that doesn't have something to do with moving the plot along to solving the problem the main character is fighting."

"This is where you are now, right Tom?" She stroked his forehead. "This is your' writer's block' thing?"

"The only thing the incidents have in common is that the main character is in all of them," Tom said slowly, enjoying her interest in his problem and effort to help.

"Is your book interesting to read, honey?"

"Sure, Gin. At least I think it is."

"Then what does it matter, Tom, if the incidents are in a string or not. The main thing is that the book is interesting."

"That makes me feel better, Gin; what you just said. In fact I just remembered something I read once, that no classic book ever resembled any other classic book that came before it."

"That statement seems appropriate, Tom, in kind of a general way. But, it seems to fit."

"Thanks, Gin, for your... help," he said and put his arms around her and kissed her, the couch groaning when he moved.

Then she pushed him away.

"I've got to go home, now," she said in an even voice. "I've got to run. I'm late already."

She slid off the couch and began dressing.

"What am I going to do with you gone, Gin?"

"You have a week to work on your book, Tom. Use it wisely ... get some work done."

"I will, I will," he said and stood up. "I'll walk you to your car."

"No. I'll never get away if you come out. Stay here, Tom. Ple—ase."

He sat down.

She bent down, kissed him, and went out the door, quickly.

Sitting on the couch alone, Tom said out loud, "Damn, I knew I should have bought some beer before."

Later, taking a shower, he decided to go home for the week. He could write at home, and he would be away from the apartment that reminded him of Virginia, now.

When leaving for home, he put his book draft in his briefcase while standing over the desk, and when he saw the typed sheets of the short story he had writter for Professor McGregor's class and put them too in his brief case.

"What can McGregor do?" he said going to the door, turning the lights out in the apartment. "He can't help me with my writing. No one can," he said pulling the door closed.

Chapter 14

It was raining hard the next morning, Saturday, when Tom woke up in his bed at home. Only ten minutes to eight; he knew his parents would not be up for an hour at least. Turning from looking at the clock, he tried to sleep.

Lying with his face agains the pillow, he reached for the other pillow as if it were Virginia.

"Man, he said in a low voice, "I'll go crazy if I don't quit thinking about her.

He pushed the pillow away and turned to look at the rain hitting the window.

"I think today I'm going to send that short story to a magazine. Screw the class and Professor McGregor, I think it's a good story — even if it doesn't have a 'war background,'" he said quietly to himself, grinning.

Getting up out of bed, he put on khaki pants, a blue t—shirt, and his worn tennis shoes with a Jack Purcells' label. He went downstairs quietly so not to wake his parents.

Downstairs in the kitchen he filled the coffee maker with water, added coffee, amd plugged it in. Then he went out to the den where he left his briefcase last night on his father's desk. Sitting down, he turned on the desk lamp and began reading the pages of the short story.

Finishing the reading, he seperated the first and last pages from the stack.

"Some magazine will snap this story up," he said. "I think it's as good as some I've read. I'll just re—type these two dog—eared pages, and send it out." He smiled.

As he slowly pulled open the desk drawer, he smelled the coffee brewing in the kitchen. He took two large, manuscript size, envelopes from the drawer and laid them on the desk. In another drawer, he found a labelling pen.

When he heard his mother coming down the stairs, he stood up, then turned out the light.

Back in the kitchen, he poured a cup of coffee and sat down at the long table, scraping the chair on the floor.

"Terrible morning," his mother said to Tom, her back to him, looking out the yard window. "I wanted to work on my flowers today, but it's raining. Oh, well, the rain will do them good."

"It won't rain <u>all</u> day, mom. Just wait a little."

She poured a cup of coffee and sat down at the table across from Tom. She wore a pink, quilted, bathrobe.

"What are you up to today, son?"

"Well, first, I have to do a little typing. Then I want to go to the post office."

"Is this typing for that book of yours?"

"No, mom. This is a short story I want send out to a magazine… that they might buy."

"Which magazine?" she asked and took a drink of the coffee.

"Esquire."

"Is that one of those sex—crazy magazines?"

She took another drink of coffee.

"No. Not really."

"Tom, I don't know where you got this writing habit you have. We've never had any writers in my family; your father's as well. I just don't understand it, son."

"I know, mama," Tom said smiling. "I chose it. I like writing, and I'm trying to make a living doing it."

"You made your father very happy by going back to the university — finishing, ah — working for your degree, even though you're sidestepping law school."

"I'll keep working at the degree," Tom said. "It won't be long ... I'll get it; one of these days."

"What will the degree lead to, Tom? Work on a newspaper?

Tom nodded, and said, "Yes, I think so." He was lying to her. "Until I start selling fiction stories, and books."

"I see," his mother said smiling. "Is that what your famous writer did? Is that what he did when he was first getting started?"

"Yes it is, mother," Tom said smiling, knowing he could not hoodwink her.

"Well, I hope, son, it all works out for you. You get what you want. Soon. For your sake, and us at home here."

"It will, mom," Tom said, getting up ,and lifting the coffee pot. "You want more coffee, mother?"

"Please, dear," she said holding out the cup to him. "Who is this Handley girl I heard you telling your father about last night?"

"Dad just wanted to know if I was seeing any girl on a steady basis, that's all."

"Is she the Handley from Birmingham?"

"I'm not sure," Tom said filling his mother's cup and handing it back to her, "but I think she is from out there in the Birmingham area. She mentioned it once."

"Her father is Calvin Handley," Tom's mother said business —like. "His law firm represents the company that supplies abrasives to auto companies — all three of the big auto firms."

"Mother, I never asked her what her father does."

"The last I heard of her, Tom, was that she was attending school out east. I can't help but wonder what she is doing in that city university back here in Detroit."

"Her father had a heart attack recently — in the spring," she told me mother. "She came home, and just stayed. "She's finishing her last term here. She just wants a degree."

"I see," Tom's mother said in a calculated tone. She took a sip of coffee and said, "I think it's very fortunate for you, Tom, to meet a girl like that — in that working—class type of a city university."

Tom nodded, grinning.

"Doesn't she feel bad about not graduating with her class back east?"

"I guess not, mother. She said she just wants to graduate."

"Doesn't she like it back east?"

"It's not that, mother. She mentioned once she wants to go to Columbia University for post—grad work. She's in a hurry, I guess. But I don't think she is sure about it, yet. I mean, she hasn't mentioned it a second time."

"Does she have a lot of boyfriends?"

Tom smiled, "I'm not sure, but she's only been home from back east a couple of months."

"She sounds like a nice girl, and seems very intelligent. I would like to meet ... Tom, you know what I mean."

"Yes, I do mother."

"I hope you two are getting serious, Tom."

"Yes and no."

"That sounds like a yes, son."

"What about career problems, mother?"

"That should not interfere. You can work that sort of thing out easily..." She took a long drink of coffee, thinking. "I remember you had' prob1ems' with Harriet Mallory — 'career problems' — that writing like that drunken famous writer of yours. Now, Harriet is married to someone else."

Tom, grinning, shook his head as if trying to dislodge from his brain what he was hearing.

"Take it easy, mother."

"Well, I'm your mother, and I'm saying it's time for you to find a nice girl and settle down, son."

"Mother, it's not as easy as that."

"Tom, everybody goes through it. You must too." She drank coffee, then said, "Better soon than later."

Tom stood up and said, "You're right, mother."

"Before it's too late, Tom."

"I'll remember that, mother," Tom said, setting his cup on the sink. "I've got a little typing to do. Do you think it would bother dad if I type in the den?"

"Not at all. He's snoring like he's cutting logs... Tom, he works so hard on those patent—infringement cases. He's so conscientious about his law work; it's taking a toll on him too. I'm worried...bout his health"

"I've got to get this typing done, mother," Tom said quietly. "Then I'm going to the Post Office before it closes."

After Tom was done typing the two pages, he addressed one of the brown envelopes to Esquire magazine, printing the letters with the marking pen. Then he paperclipped the story pages together and slid them into the envelope. Addressing the second envelope to himself, he folded it and slipped it into the first envelope; this was the return envelope, if the magazine chose to return the story. He would have the envelopes and story pages weighed at the Post Office for the postage cost, and buy the stamps, to send the whole package.

Tom always wondered what the editors did with the return postage when they bought a story, when he sent out a envelope with the return postage inside.

Going out to the kitchen, Tom saw his father, alone, having coffee at the table.

"Hi, dad."

"Good morning, Tom. What have you got there?"

"A story I wrote," Tom said and held up the envelope. "I'm sending it out to a magazine."

"Good luck with it," his father said, sounding tired. The loose bathrobe he wore made his shoulders look slumped. He drank coffee slowly, and set the cup down as if it were heavy. "If it sells, son, I'd be able to crow that my son, the writer, has an article printed in such—and—such magazine."

Tom smiled, "Yeah, dad, getting published would settle a lot of problems."

For some reason, lately, Tom felt responsible for his father's careworn appearence and he could not explain why.

"Have you had breakfast?" his father asked holding up his cup. "I had coffe with mother. She went up to get dressed. She said the rain stopped and she wants to work on our roses some more."

"No time for breakfast, dad," Tom said trying not to act abrupt. "The post office closes early on saturday — so I've got to run."

His father nodded, then took a drink of coffee.

When Tom walked to the back door, he saw the worn corduroy sports jacket his father used for garden work hanging on the doorknob.

"Can I borrow your jacket, dad? In case it rains again, I don't want the envelopes to get wet."

"Just bring it back."

At the post office, Tom bought stamps from the confused girl clerk, who did not understand why the envelopes needed to be weighed twice, and who watched him put half the stamps in the envelope, then lick and stick the other half on the outside of the open envelope. Tom saw her watching, and quickly licked and sealed the flap and handed her the envelope.

"Thanks for your help," he said, and stepped away from the counter, grinning. He was not grinning about the clerk being confused, but moreso from the feeling of optimism — hope — that comes when a story is mailed out for publication, and the possibility of it being accepted, brings the writer's mind to a high pitch of anticipation.

"Walking across the Post Office parking lot, Tom saw Harriet Mallory getting out of a Volvo station wagon with a ski—rack on the roof.

When she turned, he saw she was pregnant under her raincoat.

"Oh geez," he said to himself. Then, raising his voice, "Harriet. Hey, Harriet, over here," he said waving an arm.

Her face was drawn, Tom saw when she looked over at him, and with her hair pulled back in a knot, she looked like a school teacher who would tolerate no nonsense.

"Tom? Tom Cohill," she said and made a thin smile, as she watched him walk closer. "Well."

"Well, yourself," he said pointing at her abdomen. "I see you've been busy."

"That's not funny, Tom," she said grinning. "And how are you doing — feeling — after all that lung business?"

"Well, so far, so good," Tom said trying not to sound flip. "I still go once a month for a check up."

"You look okay," she said, "considering what you went through."

"You look good, too, Harriet. When's the big day?

"The doctor says the end of the month," she said, and flapped both hands, which were in her pockets, making the front of her raincoat jump, "but it could co me any time now." She shrugged, then said, "What are you doing with yourself these days? You still trying to be a famous writer?"

"Of course. What else? " Tom said smiling. "An—nd, I finishing school for my degree — here in the city."

"Oh, your degree — after all," she said. "Is that for insurance? Something to fall back on for a job, if your plans to make it big in literature don't work out."

"Still subtle as ever, eh, Harriet?"

"Still a dreamer, arn't you, Tom?"

"It hasn't hurt anyone," he said quietly.

"Hasn't it?"

"We can go on like this all day," he said, grinning.

"Well, Tom, you're right on target for making your life match the famous writer's; home from Europe, wounded, restless, and all that. What next? Florida, fishing for giant marlin?"

"Sure," Tom snapped. "Why not."

"Have you sold any of your stories?" Harriet asked, tilting her head to one side, looking at the worn jacket.

"Yeah," he said, knowing she was unsure, so he lied. "I'm just mailing another one out now ... to Esquire magazine."

"You sold before?" she asked doubtfully, but she could not hide a trace of being impressed.

"I'm working a novel now. A bigger work."

"What's it about?"

"Ah, sort of a life story — before I got sick."

"Did you put me in your story?"

"You'd be disguised, of course."

"Of course, Tom. And I bet you make me out a character that everyone will hate."

"Ah-h, you peeked at the manuscript."

"You haven't changed at all," Harriet said, pushing down on her hands in the pockets of the raincoat. "I've got to run, Tom; get in there," she nodded at the Post Office, "and get back home."

"How do you like married life?" Tom asked. "No regrets?"

"It's okay," she said nodding. "I want lots of kids."

"Well, you have a good start. Where do you and whats— his—name live?

She smiled, looking at the ground.

"We have a temporary place, a rental, near City Hall, in Grosse Pointe Park," she said smiling, "and now I really have to go — before what's—his—name starts to worry."

"Possessive is he?"

"Wouldn't you be?"

Each looked the other in the eyes.

"I don't know," Tom said slowly.

"You should have known, Tom."

Nodding, he said, "You better get going before we get serious, here."

"The only thing you're serious about, Tom, is writing. You save everything for that writing. Right?"

"Well," he said pointing at the ski rack on top her station wagon, "I think it's more contructive then ski—ing downhill the rest of my life."

"I guess, I asked for that, Tom, "Harriet said smiling. "Are you — seeing — anyone? Would I know her?"

"Now, I have to go," Tom said.

"No, I'll go first, " Harriet said smiling then walking away.

"Harriet will always be Harriet," Tom said watching her go, hands in her raincoat pockets. "That's why it's got to be this way."

In the car, Tom sat thinking what it would be like to be married to Harriet. What could have been. But the same answer was always there; they would never get along. It was odd, he thought, to know the answer and still like her.

He turned the key and the car engine started.

Driving, Tom thought of writing a story about a young writer who meets his former girl friend, who is married and pregnant. But, he caught hiseif remembering that F. Scott had done a super job on the same subject. Scott's story involved revolving doors in a New York hotel lobby and ended with the main character sneaking out of the house where he had been invited by the girl, and her husband, to spend the night.

Everything seems to be in favor of the girl, Tom thought, both with Harriet, and the F. Scott story. Maybe that is because writers never really seek contentment; they always seem to pass up good things, while looking for some thing else — and they're always on the move.

When turning onto the street to his parent's house, Tom thought it was too bad Harriet did not see life the same as he; she would not buy his tomorrow—I'll—be—famous talk. She was practical. She was no nonsense about tomarrow.

"She should have known — I'm the sum total of all my tomorrows," he said, out loud. "They are all I have." Smiling, he added, "I think she's given me something to write about," then he turned up the driveway.

Chapter 14

"Why wouldn't you come out to the house?" Virginia asked Tom.

They were sitting at a small marble—top table in the cafe at the Detroit Art Museum. Above them stretched a wall—to—wall skylight, a cloth underneath to block the sunlight, so the light came through filtered, soft.

"I don't know, Gin. Maybe it's from writing so much — I'm just nervous — or call it tense."

"I know what it is, Tom."

"All right, let's hear it," he said, picking up his empty tea cup, looking in it, then setting it down with a rattling noise on the saucer.

"We have been away from each other for over a week and you want to have ou± first day together on neutral ground — the museum.

He smiled at her as she drank her tea.

"Are — are you finished?" he asked, his voice cracking.

"With what? Guessing why you're nervous, or with the tea?"

"Let's walk up to the second floor," he said taking hold of her arm. "We can look at the Brueghel painting of the wedding feast — sixteenth century style. I think it must be the most valid work they have in the whole museum."

"All right," Virginia said looking at him closely, as if trying find the source of why he was so adjutated.

When they started up the dark—red marble steps to the next floor, Tom took her hand.

Then, when they were walking through a gallery of Renaissance paintings, he said, "I met a girl I used to go with at the Post Office. Ah, last week."

"What? You're hanging around the Post Office now?

"No, wise—guy, I just met her in the parking lot — by coincidence."

"Oh, I see," Virginia said slowly. "And why are you telling me this? Are you trying to make me jealous?"

"No—no, Gin. Nothing like that," he lifted her hand and squeezed.

Virginia stopped walking, pulling her hand free.

"What happened then?" she said. "Tell me, please."

"What I was leading up to ... well, seeing her again gave me the idea ... for a new short story."

"That's all?" Virginia said putting her hands on her hips. "That's it?"

"Yeah, that's all," Tom said slowly. "Why?"

"Oh—h, Tom. I was scared to death…"

"How come?"

"I ... didn't know ... what you were leading too telling me about this other girl, you, went with and all that. I thought you were going to tell me, well, you were going start seeing her again. You were acting strange."

"Naw, that's over for good," he said and took Virginia's hand. "Hey, you're shaking," he said, "I can feel it." He wrapped his arms around her. "Jeez, I'm sorry, Gin. I was just thinking out loud. I'm sorry if I upset you. Honest."

"Tom," she said leaning back, "what did you expect me to think? Meeting me down here in the museum, then telling me about you meeting an old flame. I thought you were telling me it is over, or something."

Tom grinned, "What do you mean — 'acting strange' — he asked, holding her in front of him with both arms.

"Nothing really," she said, "and stop grinning. You look like a simpleton, Tom, grinning like that."

She took his left hand, pulling him along in the gallery, he following. His left rubber tennis shoe made a long screech, and she stopped pulling.

"Gin, what do you mean by 'acting strange'?"

"Nothing," she said. "I meant to say ... odd or maybe ... unusual. Okay?

"Tom, your hands are cold.   What are you so nervous about, honey?"

"C'mon, Ginny," he said taking her arm, "let's go look at the Brueghel wedding painting.

When they were standing in front of the painting showing a large group of Flemish peasants, dancing and drinking, some watching, and some talking in groups, all in an outdoor setting, Tom slid his arm around Virginia's waist.

"Which one is the bride?" Virginia asked.

"No one knows for sure, but they think this is her right here," he pointed, "in the foreground, in the white hat with flaps that look like bat wings."

"This has to be the groom here," Virginia said pointing to a contented—looking man on the right side of the painting, standing near a large tree trunk.

"That guy is the one most people agree seems to be the groom." Pointing with his free arm, Tom said, "See how three groups of people form three triangles in the picture ... each large triangle outlined by the white of the women's aprons and winged—caps."

"Yes, I can see that," Virginia said, "now that you told me, the three groups, wow." Kiddingly, she squeezed a handful of Tom's side, saying, "You know an awful lot you."

"Right," Tom said, "and I owe it all to an Art Appretiation class, I took one semester. When Virginia let go of the handful of skin below his ribs, he smiled and said, "See the codpieces? The things covering the men's privates?"

"Yes—s, Virginia said. "Why do they call them 'cod—pieces?'" She smiled looking up at Tom. "They certainly don't leave much to the imagination — sticking out like that. It's — obscene."

"Well," Tom said, "that was the fashion in the sixteenth century Flanders. But, you are right, some people found it offensive — that protuberance— and when lithographs of the painting were made, that part was retouched, painted out."

"So we're seeing the original, uncut version, eh Tom?

He nodded.

"But why," she asked, "did they call them 'codpieces?'"

"I guess," Tom said smiling, "the shape of' the thing, in general, resembles a filet of codfish, a codfish split open for drying and laid flat."

"They didn't cover that subject, 'codpieces' in Art Appretiation class, eh, Tom?"

"Not at all," he said, "among other things."

"Is Brueghel and codpieces why you got me down here today, Tom?"

"No, Gin. I wanted to ask you to marry me. I love you. I go crazy when you go away."

"Oh—h, Tom," Virginia said looking up, her mouth open.

"Say yes, Gin, and make the whole day perfect. The whole thing perfect for the rest of our lives."

"We have to ... talk, first, honey. It was so sweet, Tom, the way you did this whole thing about asking me. It is very ... clever, and I love you for it."

"Talk? Ginny, we don't have to talk. We love one another. There is nothing more to say, except a yes, on your part."

"Tom, there are ... complications ... and you know it."

"What sort of 'complications,' babe?"

Two girls, followed by a woman carrying their coats, came into the gallery.

"Let's go where we can talk privately," Virginia said. "Better yet, let's go outside."

"I'm dying here, Gin. Tell me what the 'complications' are before I collapse."

They were going back down the red marble steps.

"It's this obsession of yours with Hemingway and the whole thing you have about writing, Tom."

The came to a large landing between the floors, but did not stop walking.

"Hey, Gin, what about my writing? And Hemingway? You want me to chose between you and Hemingway, or what?"

"Nothing <u>that</u> drastic, Tom. Besides, I know you could not do it, anyhow. Realistically. Not right away, that's for certain…"

Virginia's voice was drowned-out by clattering dishes as they walked past the kitchen for the museum's cafe on the main floor.

"Well, how 'drastic' a 'complication' are we dealing with, Gin?" The were walking side—by—side, passing a uniformed guard wearing white cotton gloves. "Christ, give me a hint, at least. Be human."

"Just a second, Tom. Outside," Virginia said and pushed the heavy brass revolving door, Tom following, shaking his head, watching her through the thick glass.

Outside, busy Woodward Avenue glistened with sunlight shining on the cars going in both directions. Across Woodward Avenue, the Detroit Main Library, surrounded by wide green lawn, shone like a white marble wedding cake.

Virginia sat down on the steps near a fountain, and Tom dropped down next to her.

"Gin, before I go out of my skull, tell me what makes my writing such a problem for us?"

"It's not a problem," she said, turning her head to face the sun, squinting. "I just said we should <u>talk</u> about it."

(PAGE 184 SECOND VERSION)

"Hey, Gin, what is this about my writing? You want me to choose between you, and my writing fiction stories?"

"Nothing <u>that</u> drastic, Tom, Besides, realistically, I know you couldn't do it anyhow. That's for certain."

Virginia's voice was interrupted by the sound of clattering dishes; they were passing the kitchen for the museum's cafe on the main floor.

"Well, tell me, Gin, just how 'drastic' a problem are we up against?" Tom asked as they walked past the Diego Rivera murals covering the walls here in the main gallery of the museum. "Give me a hint, be human."

"In a second, Tom. Outside," she said pushing the heavy brass revolving door, Tom following, shaking his head, and watching her through the thick glass. A woman. security guard, wearing white gloves, stood near the door watching them.

Outside, they came into the bright sunlight. Cars on busy Woodward Avenue in front of them, sparkled in the sun, as they passed in both directions. The Main Library, surrounded on all sides by grass, across the street, shone in the sun like a white—marble wedding cake.

Virginia skipped down the steps to the bottom where there was a fountain splashing, and sat down. Tom, following, dropped on the step above her.

"Well, Gin, if this is private enough for you...

"Tom, we have to talk about your plan to write stories," she said looking up, squinting against the sun overhead.

"Go ahead, babe, talk," Tom said touching her hair, then holding strands up to the sun to see the orange—color. "I'm all ears...damn, every part of you is terrific."

"Tom, how long do you expect to keep writing stories?" she asked, looking at him, then turing away. "How long do you plan to keep it up ... writing stories?"

"How long?" he said, dropping his hands away from her, but looking at the side of her face. "What kind of question is that?"

"Tom, it's a <u>fair</u> question."

"Oh—h, I get it," he said. "I know what you're driving at. You want to know how much money we will have to live on — until I start selling my stories. Right ?"

"Yes, Tom, that's part of it."

"Well, I have the money the Veterans Administration gives me every month for disability. That will be cut in half in about ten months."

"Then what, Tom?"

"If I'm not selling stories on a regular basis by then, I guess I could go back to writing for a newspaper. Or ... possibly get a job with an advertising agency. The pay is much better writing copy for an ad agency."

"Could you do that, Tom?" Virginia asked, squinting again, looking up at him, the sun in her eyes. "Could you quit your story writing and take some other writing job?"

"If I had to, yes."

"Oh, Tom, you really and earnestly do love me. If you had to quit writing your fiction stories, you would take a job doing other writing ... be responsible. That <u>proves</u> your love."

He smiled, nodding.

"That's what I've been telling you all along, Gin. He put his arm on her shoulders. "Now, Miss Handley, will you marry me?"

"Yes, Tom, I will marry you."

"I can't give you a ring ... an engagement ring, Gin. I don't have that kind of money."

"I don't <u>need</u> a ring. I've got you, dearest."

"Every girl wants a ring; it matters a lot."

"Nothing matters, Tom. We have each other. Forever, now."

He started stroking the back of her neck with his fingers.

"Well, anyhow, Gin, I'll get you a ring ... <u>sometime.</u> Some day you'll have it all. I promise. You'll see."

She rose up and kissed the side of his face. "Tom, I want you so much ..."

Her lips burned the cheek at the spot of the kiss.

"Let's go to my apartment," he whispered.

"You are very fortunate, Tom," Karl Rolfson said. Sitting on the worn leather couch, Tom leaned forward, elbows on his knees, looking up. "Virginia is a fine woman from a very good family. You are marrying into what most people can only dream about."

Rolfson was standing in the doorway of his office.

"Yes, I'm aware of that stuff, Karl, but the hitch now is that getting married is going to — well — put a limit on my writing."

"What kind of limit is that?" Karl asked and looked out into the store, lighting a cigaret with his Zippo lighter, then leaning back against the door jam, clicking the top of the lighter open and closed.

"Well, it looks like when they cut down my disability pay to half — in about ten months — my writing time will be cut with it. Ginny and I agreed, before we set the date."

"You mean, you'll have to go to work?" Rolfson said, turning the square lighter in his fingers. "Sounds very practical. You will have to earn money to live."

"But ... being a writer is not practical, Karl. Unless you sell your stories."

"It's the age old problem of all artists," Karl said, exhaling cigaret smoke. "Artists have one foot in the art world, and the other foot in the practical world. The artist must learn to hop on one foot, or the other, from time to time ... in order to survive."

"I'm beginning to understand what the famous writer was up against," Tom said slowly. "I mean when he was getting started. It's rough ... emotionally ... when you want to write every day and you have to worry about money. The famous writer and his wife were really broke over there in Paris when he was beginning his writing career."

"Tom, that's sort of a myth about the famous writer being poor and starving in Paris," Rolfson said and took a quick look out to the store and the front door. "He always had money. He had wealthy acquaintences who gave him funds so he could keep working, especially after he abandoned newspaper writing."

"I didn't know about the rich friends," Tom said, "only the part I read about him being broke in Paris in his early writing days."

"Well, he could have been broke," Rolfson said, "but I'm sure it was only for a short time." He looked out at the front of the store again. "He didn't have much money, but he was never destitute as he would like you to believe. His second wife was heiress to a cosmetic empire and he did not have any money worries after marrying her."

"It all boils down to this, Karl, I'm not going to stop writing my book. I've got over two—hundred pages of the first draft done. But the pressure now, well, it's slowing me down. This time deadline keeps popping into my thinking."

"Tom, this is just the beginning of pressure that you will have to contend with," Rolfson said. "There are all kinds of pressures that you are going to have to face." He took a long draw on his cigaret, then exhaling the smoke, glanced out into the store. “But, if you are really determined, you will stick to your guns. Not give up.

“That’s what worrys me, Karl. When the time comes to give up writing stories, if I will be able to do it. I mean, I promised Ginny— but what if I can’t let writing go? What if I can’t quit?”

“I’m confident you will work out a solution — you and Virginia. You are both level—headed.” Rolfson said, and while crushing out his cigaret in an ashtray, took a furtive look out to the front of the store. “When the time comes for you to make a decision, Tom, you will do what is right.”

“Are you waiting for sombody, Karl? You look a little…anxious…as if it were important.”

“Yes, I have an important customer coming today.” Then as if he never changed thinking about Tom’s problem, he added, “If a writer gives up his writing, he’s lost, and his life ... becomes meaningless.”

“Wow, Karl, I guess then for a writer, there isn’t much of a choice.”

“There is not much of a choice for anyone in life, my boy. Some are lucky, but most are not. People must do what they have to for survival, they have little choice of a job, they take what they can get. If it were an easy choice to be a writer, well, we would be swimming in writers. Writing is part of the proplem, selling stories steadily, and making a living is the other part.”

“Yeah, Karl,” Tom said leaning forward, his elbows resting on his knees, “but how does a writer ... know when he is a real artist?”

“Tom, how does anyone know anything about themselves?” Rolfson said evenly. “I’m not trying to be fascetious, but I am asking you — how do people learn for themselves?”

“I thought I was asking you that question?” Tom said, grinning.

“Don’t you have any thoughts of how a person knows he’s an artist, Tom?”

“Well, I know that once you have any thought of becomming an artist, do what artists do, well, Karl, it’s…very hard to stop. I mean you can’t get it out of your head. It’s like a virus ... or something.”

“Do you think that what sets you apart from other people?” Karl asked, slowly glancing out to the front door of the store, then back to looking at Tom. “Do you consider yourself different from other people?”

“Well,” Tom said wringing his hands, thinking, “to be honest, I ... have noticed ... that people treat me different, when they find out I’m a writer. I think, they think, I’m different,”

“In my writing days,” Karl said, “I thought I was different ... to the point of thinking myself superior.”

“Yeah,” Tom said, “I kind of figured you — for the writing type.”

“Ginny probably said to you that I was a writer,” Karl said, “but I won’t ask you if she did.”

Tom sat back on the couch, “Okay, Karl.”

"As a writer," Karl began again, "I thought I was above the problems of everyday life that everybody has. I thought I was superior, that once my talent was recognized, all the problems would be taken care of because of my success."

"Well, Karl, you were right in a way, success does solve a lot of problems."

"But not having sucess, and thinking myself superior, made it doubly hard for me to give up writing. It was a long coming down. And I hit bottom at the height of the Great Depression. I had to find a job and make a living at a time when you couldn't buy a job. There were no jobs, and I had a pregnant wife."

"Well, Karl," Tom said looking at the floor, "you had good reason to stop writing."

"Yeah, that sounds like a realistic soultion, but the writer who gives up, Tom, is the writer who suffers the most."

"He didn't have much choice, Karl."

"True, but remorse sets in anyhow," Rolfson said slowly, turning again to look at the front door. "What could have been gnaws at him the rest of his life."

Tom smiled, looking up at Karl, "You are trying to tell me something — two things, actually— and I can't follow you."

"It is not that complicated, Tom."

"Well," Tom said smiling, "you seem to be saying to keep writing, if you quit —— ever — you'll be sorry, all the rest of your life. You will always wonder about success."

"Exactly, Tom," Karl said, looking out at the front of the store. "That is about as far as one man can advise another ... and still be honest."

"You're a big help," Tom said smiling, "Arid, now, I'm being facetious, Karl."

"I envy you, Tom. You can't imagine how much. You have all the good things — ahead of you. Do your best and I'm sure it will all work out as you want them to."

"Well, Karl, while you are in a good mood, there is one more thing I've got to ask you."

"What is it?"

"Do you allow honeymoon couples to use — rent — your cabin up in the Canadian wilds?"

"Not usually," Rolfson said smiling. After taking a quick glance at the front door, he added, "But in your case, I could make an exception."

Tom smiled, watching Rolfson glancing toward the front door.

"It isn't too rugged up there?" Tom asked. "No bathroom?"

"It's too beautiful to be called rugged. And it's the perfect place for a honeymoon, I think, but you would just say I was prejudiced."

"How much do you charge for the use of your Shangri— La, Karl?"

"I'll make you a wedding present of the front door key, and a map on how to get there. But, you'll have to find your own good fishing spots."

"What do I need be the usual groceries."

"Nothing," Rolfson said, taking another quick look at the door. "Everything you'll need ... except a girl like Virginia ... is already there."

"Great, Karl," Tom said standing up from the couch. Don't say any more about the cabin, I'm really getting excited about going up there. But for now, I've got to trundle home."

"Are you going home now?" Karl asked.

"Yeah, our family is going out to the Handley's for dinner ... and a discussion over the wedding plans."

Walking with Tom to the front door, Rolfson said, "The Handley's are nice people. I've known them for over a dozen years. You couldn't meet a nicer family."

"Well Karl, I'm really interested in only one member of the family; Ginny." Then Tom added, looking out the store window, grinning, "Not very busy today."

"Business is always slow toward summer ... people go away. That's when I go up to the cabin, usually."

"How come... you're not ...?"

"Tom, I'm expecting an important client any moment."

"Sure, Karl, I'll be running along. Bye."

"Bye, Tom. Stop by any time."

Walking outside to the corner of the street, Tom hesitated, looking back, just as a silver Lincoln pulled up in front of the bookstore. Thin stepped around the corner of the brick building, then looked back again, and saw a middle—age woman, wearing a white pleated skirt and a wide— brim hat, step out of the car, and vigorously slam the door.

"Some client," Tom whispered, smiling, watching the woman enter the bookstore.

Chapter 15

Tom and Virginia were tired when they pulled the boat up on the narrow sand beach at Rolfson's cabin. It was the evening of their wedding day. Inside the cabin, Virginia unpacked the box of supplies in the small kitchen, while Tom took off the window shutters, then put up the screens on the front porch. Just inside the front door he found two folded canvas chairs, and as he was opening them, Virginia came out to the porch with a bottle of Champange.

"Congratulations, Mrs. Thomas Cohill, and welcome to paradise. Nay it go on forever," Tom said, holding up his glass of Champagne. Then leaning back in his chair, he held out his free hand, as if offering the view through the pine trees, where the fading light shimmered on the river up to where it turned, going, between the steep rock cliffs to the bay.

"The view is fantastic, Tom. How could you not love this place?" She put her hand of his arm, "Smell that cedar smell, just heavenly. Everything here but that eagle in the front room, is just wonderful. That thing scares me •"

Tom had seen the stuffed white Snow Owl the instant he opened the cabin front door. It startled him; the wings spread, eyes wide for a kill, mounted on a branch between too tall bookshelves in the main room of the cabin. A small brass plate he saw on the branch, read: TO KARL FOR AN UNFORGETTABLE STAY AT KEY RIVER CABIN. BOESEN FAMILY.

"It's just an owl, Gin, but maybe I can turn it around, or something, while we're here."

"Those eyes," Virginia said, "they're so big, they're scarey."

"Maybe you have a guilty conscience, Gin," Tom said grinning, lifting his glass for a sip.

"Yes, yes," she said, smiling, "I have so much guilt— for being so-o happy."

She reached over and took Tom's hand.

"I love you, Ginny," Tom said quietly. "I'm so lucky for having you — and this — eden." He was quiet for a moment. "I — I must of done something good to deserve all this. But — the only thing I do is write stories."

He leaned over and kissed Virginia, holding the glass of champagne out at arm's length. Then, she stood up and moved over to sit on his knees.

"Tell me," she said, "that we'll always be this happy, my darling writer, that you will make it go on forever."

“We will, Gin. We will. And this is only the beginning. Why, I have plans ...“

Lowering her head, she kissed him, first soft, then hard, holding the back of his head.

“Are you hungry, Tom?” she whispered at the side of his face. “I don’t want to fall down on the job of being a good wife ... and not feed my husband.”

“I couldn’t be fuller,” he said in a low voice, then rising up, he carried her into the cabin and set her on the bed. The Champagne glasses were left on the floor next to the chairs.

It was after eleven o’clock at night when they got up, and Tom lighted a kerosene lamp.

“I’m starved,” he said, looking at the black windows; there was no light outside in any direction. “You too, hon?”

“Me too,” Virginia said pulling on her Bermuda shorts. “I brought pork chops in the cooler. There’s potatoes too.”

Tom put the lamp on a high shelf in the kitchen, lighting the whole room evenly. He was lighting a second lamp on the front table, but stopped when Virginia came near on the way to the kitchen; he kissed her mouth, then her forehead, and she smiled, before entering the kitchen.

“They don’t call it a honeymoon for nothing,” he said, lighting the second lamp and replacing the glass chimmney.

“And just think,” Virginia said, “my mother suggested we go to the Bahamas,” and dropped the pork chops into the frying pan, then adjusting the height of the flames of the kerosene stove.

“We have each other,” Tom said , “that’s what counts. Admittedly, the surroundings are a bit primitive, Mrs. Hemingway, but, I’m sure, your honeymoon will be a memorable one. Tomorrow, we’ll take a tour out on Georgian Bay in the boat, and have a shore lunch with the fish we catch.”

“Tom,” she said to him standing in the doorway, watching her, “you think I should open the applesauce?”

“Sure, let’s splurge,” he said.

“Okay, and how about coffee? You want coffee?”

“Let’s finish the Chapagne, Gin,” he said stepping close to her and putting his hands on her shoulders. “Hey, have I told you lately that I love you?”

“I can’t recall the last time,” she said and kissed him, slowly.

He looked at her, when she let him go, shaking his head, smiling. “What a cook,” he said, then turned the lid on the applesauce jar and set… it down. “I just can’t get enough of you. I want to <u>devour</u> you.”

“That’s impossible, but you can do me a favor.”

“Just name it Mrs. Cohill. I’ll do anything you ask.”

"Set the table for dinner, please, Mr. Cohill."

"Where are the utinsels, Mrs. Cohill?"

"There, on the tray next to the stove."

"Your wish is my command madame." When Tom collected the knives and forks, he lifted one plate off a back shelf. Wow, these are big," he said, "and they weigh a ton."

"Let's use the paper ones," Virginia said. "We won't have to wash them."

"Where are they?"

"In the food box we brought, Mister Hemingway,"

Setting the table with a plastic tablecloth and paper napkins, out in the main room of the cabin, Tom thought of that 'Mr. Hemingway' remark Virginia just made as an attack on the <u>whole subject</u> of his writing. As if writing stories was child-like, naive, and like a child, if his bad habit of writing, did not pan out, did not show a profit, he would have to give it up. She even made him promise, that after a while, he would go to work for wages if he was not selling. Work was practically a prerequesite for her saying yes to marrying.

"I don't know," Tom muttered, "what exactly I've let myself in for."

When he said 'Missus Hemingway' earlier, he had been referring to the famous writer and his wife on their honeymoon in 1922 up at the Hemingway family cabin on Walloon Lake, near Petosky, Michigan. Hemingway and his new wife were not flush with money, and the summer cabin, even though primative by city standards, was a Godsend for the newly marrieds.

It was his remark to Virginia, Tom calling her 'Mrs. Hemingway,' earlier, was meant to say, yeah, sure, it is primative living here in Karl's cabin, but the young Hemingway's did it, went through the same thing, and could have been a factor in his writing success later.

But now, Tom reasoned, Virginia had boxed him in with this time period of ten-months. If he does not sell in that time, his plans to be a fiction story writer are over.

Moving the kerosene lamp to one end of the table, Tom set down the paper plates, and then the silverware, on opposite sides of the table. He found the Champagne bottle and glasses on the porch and brought them in and set them on the table.

Sipping Champagne, Tom thought Virginia's calling him "Mister Hemingway" was a baldface mocking of his writing — throwing it in his face he had only the few months to prove himself.

"Tom," Virginia shouted from the kitchen, "did we bring catsup, honey?"

"I saw it next to where the paper plates were — in the box, Gin."

"Found it," she shouted. "Everything's about done, is the table set?"

"All set," Tom said. "When you're done in there, I'll bring that lamp out here on the table."

"Coming, but don't bump me. Let me come through the door, Tom, or our dinner might wind up on the floor."

"Okay, Gin, I'm waiting," Tom said looking at the two bookshelves, the owl, and the rows of books.

Tom mumbled, "I'll just have to fight to keep doing my writing," looking at the rows of books again. "No matter what it costs. "

He and Virginia sat opposite one another at the pic-nic-style table, eating their pork chops with their fingers, then licking their fingers, to pick up the fork to eat the fried potatoes, dip-ping them in the pad of catsup on their plates first. Tom had poured out applesause on both plates, and they used their spoons to scoop it up.

The only noise was the two lamps hissing at each end of the

"How come you're so quiet, Tom?" Virginia asked, pic-up her glass of Champagne. "You seem a million miles away."

"I'm just tired, I guess," he said wiping his fingers on a paper napkin.

"Tom, honey, don't be so distant. It scares me… I've never seen you like this before. Please talk to me."

Tom looked at her while drinking his Champagne.

Outside, on the dark river, an outboard motor boat went by, headed up to the bay. The sound, a whine, grew weaker as the boat moved away, then faded out in the distance, completely.

"Today has been long," he said setting down his glass. "We left St. Hugo of the Hills and drove all day to get here — the excitement — I guess everything is piling up on me. The wedding ceremony. I'm just pooped."

"Tom, why don't you lay down, honey. I'll clear this stuff off the table, and I'll come join you."

Tom stood up.

"There's a little wine left," he said.

"Here, take it, Tom," Virginia said pouring it into his glass. "It'll make you sleepy."

He kissed her, then went over to the bed and sat down and drank the last of the Champagne.

"You shouldn't do that to yourself," Virginia said from the kitchen. "You shouldn't get overtired like that."

Swinging his legs up on the bed, he said, "Well, it isn't every day you get married."

The next morning, the cabin was cold inside from the damp night air. Tom crossed the big room of the cabin, out to the screened-in porch in his bare feet. Outside, next to a tree, he relieved himself, standing under the dew-wet branches.

"Hey, Tom, I've got to go to," Virginia said from the front porch.

"Put your shoes on, Gin. I'll walk you back to the outhouse."

"I think it's warmer out here," Tom.

"Yeah," he said walking to the porch, "the cabin retains the cold and damp from the night."

"Tom, look right. Look at that river in the sun. It's like a painting by that guy that went west, a German."

"Bierstadt," Tom said.

"And look at the size of the grey rock formations," she said swinging her arms open, "the're all around. That's that Laurentian Shield you showed me in that book. Wow, it's so — so —"

"Primative," Tom said coming up the steps to the porch. "It's the cooled magma from a volcano. The oldest rock in the world. I learned that in my Geology 101."

"No wonder Karl loves this place so," she said before Tom kissed her.

Later, after a breakfast of oatmeal with raisins, they straightened up the cabin, and went out to sit on the porch, barefooted, to drink a second coffee.

They began talking about last night, then Virginia asked, "What was it, honey? What was it, really, that made you feel so down?"

"It was nothing, Gin."

"I love you, Tom, and I have to know ... if I did something wrong ... I'm going crazy trying to ..."

"It's not you, Gin," he said quietly. "And it's not <u>your</u> fault," he said with the coffee cup to his mouth.

"God, Tom, please let me help. Tell me what I can do."

"I can't," he said looking straight ahead.

Virginia, leaning forward to see his face, took his hand.

"Tom, I'm your wife. We face things together, now. You don't know what you are doing to me. All kinds of things are running through my mind. Please, please, tell me, what is the matter."

"It's nothing with you personally, Gin."

"What is is, honey?" she asked, setting her coffee down.

She sat on his knees, her arm around his neck, her eyes moist, looking at his face.

"It's my writing, Gin. That promise I made to you… and some of the cracks you make about my writing stories."

She leaned back at arms-length, looking at him.

"Oh-h, Tom," she said in a disappointed tone, "is <u>that</u> what you let come between us?"

"See?" he said sheepishly. "I told you it was nothing."

"How could you?" she said.

"How could I what?"

"I thought you were bothered by something dark and devious from your past ... a murder… or something."

"'From my past?'" he asked grinning.

"I thought it might be a life or death problem… a disease, or maybe a bad heart, you hadn't told me about, you monster."

"To me, my writing is 'a life or death problem,' Gin."

"Okay, honey, but nothing like I thought it was that made you so troubled last night. I didn't think of your writing as the problem."

"It's a damn dilemma," he said. "If I choose to write after the damn time-limit, I lose you, Ginny. And if I choose to honor the time—limit, I lose my writing. What you clamped on me ... it's destroying me."

"But, Tom, you agreed, she said getting up off his lap, picking up her coffee cup, sitting down in her own chair.

"Gin, you just can't hold me to it. You can't."

"Yes I can, Tom. I'm your wife now, and your best interest is mine now also. And we must have an income to have a life."

"No, Gin, it's just not fair ... not fair to let me run out with a rope around my neck, then jerk it back."

"I'm not doing that," she said after sipping coffee, looking over the rim of the cup she was holding in 'both hands. "Im not doing anything — remotely — resembling what you said about the rope."

"You are, Gin. You don't realize it, but you are. Tom stretched his feet across to the window sill of the screen windows. "And not only that, this time limit is— is spiking my work now. Every day I feel the axe above my head, and every day I know I'm one day shorter to it falling and chopping off my writing time. I can't live like this. I'm preoccupied — distracted — well, my work is suffering. And I need to do my best work on my new novel."

"You have to finish that book, Tom."

"I can't, Gin," he said, scratching the screen window with his toenails. "Not with this psychological millstone of a time-limit in my head. It's spooking me."

"But you promised ten-months, Tom."

He scratched at the screen with his toes again.

"Gin, for some reason, I can't write with this thing over my head. I don't know why," he said and drank his coffee.

"Well, Tom," Virginia said putting her feet up against the screen, "we'll just have to wait out your time. Then we will discuss, at that time, where we go from there."

"I can't waste a year just waiting, Gin."

"Then write," she said softly, "and use the time, the ten-months."

"I guess I can try."

"Now," Virginia said, lowering her feet to the floor, "that we hashed that out ... tell me some of the things I say that get under your skin. What wise cracks I make, that bug you so badly."

Tom looked at her, and squinted.

"I'd rather not," he said, lowering his head. "I'm sorry, I said that."

"Tell me, honey... so I don't repeat them. I want to be a good wife."

"It'll just make you mad."

"Tell me anyhow," she said, sliding her hand over his. "Make me angry."

"You're not some kind, of ... masochist?" He grinned.

"No, just a new wife trying to find out what displeases her husband. I have to know."

"Well," Tom said taking a quick look at the river shimmering in the sun, "it's just that you make me feel like a child ... whenever you talk to me about my writing."

"I do no such thing."

"Yes you do."

"How?"

"Well, you say things, like 'don't say that' when I'm ... just ... kidding you."

"How does that make you feel like a child?"

"When you made me promise to give up writing in ten months, hell, that made me feel real sheepish.

"Don't start that stuff — that was last night."

"Well, it's a big part of it. I lost control of my plans, I felt. I'm being led by the nose ... someone else is calling the shots."

"Poor baby Tommy," Virginia said pursing her lips. "Hims liddle feelings is hurt, poor baby."

"You-u," he said blushing. Then trying to make a stern face, said, "I'll do more than hurt your feelings… I'll paddle your rump ... so ... It'll match your hair on the other end … you ..."

He tried catching her arm, but she jump away out of the chair.

"No-o-o, Tom," she shouted, smiling,"don't you dare," and twisted free when he reached for her arm, holding it close to her body. "Tom-m don't ... you ..."

He reached for her over the canvas chair, then fell forward on the floor, tripping over the chair.

When she got to the doorway into the cabin, he caught her by the foot while he lay on the floor, and began pulling her down.

"D-o-on't," Virginia said smiling, then when Tom pulled her to the floor, let out a screech.

They both lay on the floor laughing.

"God," he said, his face next to hers, "I love you so much, I think I'm going burst out of my skin."

Both their faces were flushed from the playful chase, and they were winded, breathing heavy.

"Tom," Virginia whispered, "I'm crazy for you, honey. Absolutely and completely."

He picked her up slowly and set her on the bed.

The next morning the sun had been up for two hours and Tom and Virginia lay with their faces on the same pillow.

"'Guess we'll skip breakfast," he said, grinning.

"Who needs breakfast?" she said quietly. "D-on't take your hand away."

"Who wants pancakes, anyway."

"How can you talk about food, Tom?"

"I have to have food to keep my strength up, you red-haired sorceress: my beautiful red witch."

"Do that ... again, honey," she said. "Put your hand there again."

"You are sorley lacking in propriety, red witch of the east," Tom whispered.

"Especially when I'm with you," she whispered. "None what-so-ever."

"Gin, I can't restrain ... I'm on fire about you. You're consuming me ... so beautiful."

"I love ... love," she said, "you ... so much... I don't know what else to say ... the way I feel. Words don't ... work."

"Gin, I'm lost ... there is no me."

"And I am you, Tom. For ... ever."

"O—oh, Gin."

"Do that, Tom. There."

"Yes.

Later, in the afternoon a steady rain began falling, and the temperature fell. Tom started a fire in the cast iron stove in the big room of the cabin using dry wood from the porch wood box.

"Let's roast hot dogs," Virginia said, lifting the stove lid by the handle. Flames shot up. "We can put them on a little grill right over here."

"Yeah," Tom said smiling, "but don't burn them black."

"I brought two cans of chili in the food box," she said putting the stove lid back down.

"I think, one can of chili, babe, is enough."

"I know that," Virginia said opening the celephene wrapper for the hot dog buns. "I'm going to set the buns on the stove top to warm. Will you open the chili can for me, Tom?"

A heavy gust of wind made the cabin wall creek.

"Wow," Tom said as he was lifting the chili can from the food box. "It's really blowing out there. " Picking up the can opener, he went to the table and looked out the window behind it. "It's really dark off to the south. A real squall."

An outboard motor boat went by down on the river, headed up to the bay. It was running full speed.

"How is our boat, Tom? Is it all right down there?"

"Yeah, I was just looking ... the ropes are okay, but there'll be water in it. But I brought the cushions up when we came."

He opened the can of chili on the table using the opener, looking outside; Virginia came close, kissed him, and took the can into the kitchen.

"You're a good cabin wife," Tom said looking out.

When she came back from the kitchen, the chili in a pan, she set it on the stove.

"Honey," she said, "I hate to sound like a real cabin wife," and putting her arms around his neck, added, "the kerosene lamps need filling."

"Okay, babe," Tom said and kissed her. "The kerosene is in the outhouse. Are you sure you want the lamps?"

"I thought you might like to write some tonight, Tom. And I could read for a while..."

Tom dropped his arms to his sides, and tilted his head, looking at her face. He did not know how express the indignation that welled up in him.

"When I want to write," he said holding back the anger, "I'll write. Okay?"

"I just thought, Tom, maybe ... you want to."

"I'm ... too excited to write, Gin. Besides, I resent ... I don't need anyone telling me when to write. Ever. Understand?"

"Well, if you don't want to then don't," Virginia said and turned to stir the pot of chili on the stove.

"And I don't need anyone to tell me not to write either. Okay? My writing is off limits to suggestions, limits, advice, prompting and any urging. Okay?"

"Wow," Virginia said looking at him, "I guess I hit a nerve."

"All right," he said, and walked slowly to the window and stood watching the rain, blowing with the wind, move like a curtain across the water.

Then he walked over to the front door, and taking the rain poncho off the hook on the sideboard, said as pulled it over his head, "The kerosene ... I'll get it."

Virginia stood stirring the pot, smiling, watching him go out; then she blew him a kiss.

The rain made the narrow path back to the outhouse slippery, and once when Tom lurched, he had to grab a low, dripping, pine branch to steady himself. At the outhouse, he opened the door, and stood inside, back at the cabin. The waterproof poncho that covered his head, made the water run down his forehead and nose.

Over at the cabin was a small light from the kitchen window, and grey smoke rose from the metal stove pipe.

"There are just some things, like writing, that belong to a person. That he don't share," Tom said against the blowing wind. "If you take that writing away from a person, he is nothing, no matter how much you love him," he said, wiping away the water on his face.

Moving a life vest for the boat, and a pair of oars, out of the way, he pulled the five-gallon kerosene can off a shelf in the outhouse. He had seen it there when he walked Virginia out to use the latrine that morning.

"How am I going to explain to Ginny to just leave the writing part of our life to me, exclusive?" he said out loud, closing the outhouse door.

Ducking through the line of rain dripping off the cabin porch roof, Tom saw Virginia through the window, sitting on the end of the table-bench, rolling the hot dogs on a grate with a fork. She had not heard him comming back, so he stamped his feet while pulling off the poncho over his head on the porch. He left the can on the porch when he went in.

"Ah-h, it's really bad out there, honey," she said looking up at him. "I didn't mean for you to go out <u>now</u>."

"I had to cool off, Gin," he said putting his hand on the back of her neck. "Hey, babe, I'm sorry I snapped at you ... there, before I went out."

She reached up, putting her hand on his, "You were right, Tom. I shouldn't interfere with you're writing."

"I'm sorry I acted like a prima donna, Gin."

"But you're the writer, honey, and you should make all your own work decisions. I can see how important it is, now."

He put both hands on her shoulders.

"You're perfect, Gin. Oh, God, you're perfect. I'm very lucky to have found you, babe." He kissed the top of her head. "Thank you for saying that about the decisions. I could almost cry."

Virginia stood up and kissed Tom quickly, her arms around his neck, still holding the fork.

"I'm so happy," she whispered.

When she let go him, and turned back to the hot dogs on the stove, Tom inhaled, then exhaled, and said, "Wow, I'm starving."

"The hot dogs are close to being done," she said, and the other stuff is ready."

He sat down at the table, looking at the plates and the silverware from the cabin she had set out neatly.

"We'll have to drink the white wine," Tom said. "It's all we have left in the beverage department of the food box," he said getting up, going to the kitchen.

"That's okay," she said without looking up. "There are some nice wine glasses in there... on the shelf."

"Okay, okay, I see them," Tom said.

"Wipe them off."

"Yeah, " he said. "We got any onions? I don't see any onions in the food box, babe."

"No-o," Virginia said, then added under her breath, "who eats onions on a honeymoon."

"We'll put onions on the list of what we need; for when we go to the store, Gin."

"That's my job," she said stirring the chili. "Let me take care of that."

Tom smiled, sitting down at the table, watching her stirring the chili.

The rain stopped while they were eating, and after cleaning the dishes, they walked down to the shore to check the boat. The storm had moved off and the low sun, an orange ball, was setting to the west.

"Gin, I'll bail out the water in the boat, will you go up and. bring that fishing pole from the cabin ... near the kitchen door?"

"It's getting dark, honey."

"Go quick, then."

Pushing out from shore, they drifted in the boat, Tom casting along the still reeds, Virginia sitting next to him.

"This must be heaven,Gin," Tom whispered, not wanting to disturb the silence. "I can't tell if we're floating on water; that reflection of the sky. It' like a mirror up."

"Tom," she said softly, "I've never known this kind of happiness before."

Tom thought that maybe he could use this honeymoon in his writing.

Chapter 16

"I knew you and Virginia would enjoy the cabin," Karl Rolfson said. "It's perfect up there for a honeymoon."

"Everything just went great," Tom said from where he sat on the chair, across from Rolfson at the desk in the bookstore office,

Rolfson, wearing a tan summer suit, sat addressing envelopes from a list of names that covered a stack of typed pages at his left elbow. Using a Cross gold pen, he wrote out the names on the envelopes; he was sending out a new catalouge of his stock of rare books.

"I could of stayed for the whole summer," Tom said.

"Ginny's got the outdoor bug ... dispite the ... inconviences. I hear you're going up. When you going?"

"A week from Wednesday or Thursday," Karl said writing another address. "I got some business to clear up," he said taking another envelope. "The boys are all packed, they have their luggage in the hallway at home. And the dog had her shots."

"I sure envy you — for going up to the cabin," Tom said. He took a ring of keys from his pocket, and jingled them. "Here's the keys to the kingdom, I'm returning them," he set them on the desk. "The boat is chained-up at the last dock behind the store at the high way. I sure envy you; Ginny and I thank you."

"Did you drive up to Sudbury?" Karl asked, smiling.

"No," Tom said. "On the sunny days we were up on the bay fishing, taking photographs on the rock islands."

"And skinny dipping," Karl said taking another envelope, smiling.

"Man is that water up there cold," Tom said smiling.

"Invigorating," Karl said writing on an envelope.

"Okay, and stimulating, also."

"Where," Karl asked stacking his addressed envelopes, "are you and Virginia living now?"

"Out in Rochester. Ginny's parents rented it for us. They own part of the apartment complex or something. It's out in a woods. The actual name is Rochester Hills."

"You're very fortunate, Tom ... to marry into that family," Rolfson said quietly while reaching for another envelope.

"It's just temporary," Tom said as if had not heard Karl's remark. "When I make some money writing, Gin and I plan to buy a house. We were thin of buying propertyover on Harsen's Island ... we would be out on the wind and water. Her parents said they want to help us locate out there."

"Have you sold any stories yet?" Rolfson asked, his head down, writing.

"No. The one I sent to Esquire came back," Tom said quietly, "so I sent it to Cosmopolitan.

Rolfson, smiling, was reaching for another envelope, when he said, "How are you doing on that novel of yours? Have you fisished it?"

"Almost," Tom said. "Ginny said she'd help with the typing, when I start on the re-vision. She's great."

"Who you going to send it to; what publishing house?" Karl asked putting a rubber band around a stack of the addressed envelopes.

"Scribner's, because I like their stable of authors. And I've seen their building. I saw it when I was in New York with the Army," Tom said. "The famous writer was published by them."

"Scribners is an excellent choice, Tom."

"You know the famous writer was in Sudbury, Karl?"

"Yes, I think I read that somewhere."

"It was back in nineteen-twenty-three, and the Toronto Star sent the young reporter up there to cover a mining story. He stayed at the Nickle Range Hotel for three days, I think it was. I told Ginny about it, but we never got to Sudbury."

"I'm glad Ginny enjoyed the cabin," Rolfson said as he counted the edges of a stack of envelopes with two fingers. "Where is she today?" he asked, putting a second rubber band around the stack of envelopes.

"She's with her mother at the hair dresser's," Tom said, then smiling, added, "and I think they're going to do some shopping."

Rolfson nodded, counting a second stack of envelopes, "Did you take a lot of photos up at the cabin?"

"Oh yeah," Tom said. "I'll bring them in when they're developed." He leaned forward in the chair, elbows on knees. "I came down today to get the rest of my stuff from my apartment. They let me store it in the basement of that dump I used to live in."

"How was the fishing around the Bay?" Karl asked, leaning back in his chair, lighting a cigaret, clicking his Zippo shut. "Arn't those rock islands in Georgian Bay something?"

"It was unbelievable, Karl. We caught every kind of fish you can name ... including a 'ling.' We mostly ate pickerel for a shore lunch." Tom took one of Karl's cigarets from the pack on the desk, and reached for the Zippo.

"And that map you have on the wall in the cabin was a big help. I found the Shirttail Islands," Tom said while lighting cigaret, then snapping the Zippo shut. 'We found Fox Bay, Docus Island, and we wanted to go to Bad River, but it was too far; the Bustard Islands were out of our range too."

"You did really good," Rolfson said looking at Tom and smiling, then reaching for another envelope. "You're a natural for the outdoors ...

"Some pun, Karl."

They both smiled.

"And Karl, I found a whole bay where wild rice was growing. I think it was Genesee Bay. It would be a super place to go duck hunting in the fall."

Writing again, Rolfson said, "I have never been duck hunting. I don't like shooting game ... the blood sports."

"Well, the famous writer and I are," Tom said, "alike in that aspect ... if you will. I like to shoot ducks, pheasants, partridges, rabbits ... whatever. I'm no big game hunter, I just like wing shooting, and fishing. All kinds of fishing."

"A writer," Rolfson said, "should be involved in all kinds of activities, do all kinds of things. Hunting and fishing are wonderful for getting you outdoors." Then he added smiling, "And you never can tell, it might actually help you write better."

"Karl, I don't do it so much for my writing as I do because I <u>like</u> to do it." Tom leaned forward, elbows on knees, "I suppose, if I ever become known as a writer, everybody will say I hunt and fish to be like the famous writer."

"Well, there are all kinds of injustices in the world, Tom, and I'm confident you can handle that one."

"To tell the truth, Karl, I'd like to be world famous like the famous writer — live the life he does. In fact, that's exactly what I want. Writing, selling, a good life."

"You're not alone, Tom," Rolfson said reaching for another envelope.

"Yeah, I guess everybody would like to live like he does. You can't blame them," Tom said smiling.

Rolfson looked up, nodding, "No you can't blame them."

But Karl, they haven't got the guts to go after it. They settle for a wife, house, a bunch of kids and sports on television."

"Sounds quite normal," Rolfson said writing.

"I guess what I'm trying to say, Karl, is that people get — sidetracked — in life, and they wind up just dreaming about doing things."

Rolfson said, "Uh-huh," but kept writing.

"Well, I think it's wrong to get sidetracked if you have any kind of talent. And talent is a gift, and it's a sin, sort of, not to use the talent if you have it."

"Yes, Tom, but <u>everyone</u> cannot be an artist."

"People can sure talk about being an artist, Karl, or to be correct, people talk about wanting to be an artist. Especilly at parties. As soon as they hear I'm a writer, they launch into a spiel about how they are going 'to do some writing someday' just as soon as 'they can find the time.'"

"At parties," Karl said, "people drink and they are prone to lose their inhabitions." He finished one envelope, took another and began writing. "You have to be understanding. Everyone wants to express his or hers ideas."

"I can't understand it, Karl. If they want to do it so much — why don't they make it a priority — and set out to do it? Maybe they have their priorities mixed with something else, like making big money, quick. Either that, or they don't really mean what they say at a party. They just want to make themselves feel important, or in some way superior."

"Tom, that's a very good observation on your part."

Tom smiled, moving his hands as if washing them.

"I can just imagine," he said looking at his fingers splayed out, "what the famous writer goes through out in public; I mean about listening to every idiot who can hold a pencil, saying he wants to become a writer."

"Yes," Karl said reaching for another envelope, "that would get to you after a while,"

Tom sat beck in his chair.

"You know, Karl, when I say I'd like to live like the famous writer, that doesn't necessarily mean I want write the way he does."

"That's good thinking, Tom," Rolfson said writing.

"I think a lot of writers make that mistake ... don't you think so, Karl? They combine the two; the way the famous writer writes and the way he lives."

"Yes, I do, Tom." He stopped writing, still holding the pen. "In fact a whole generation has done it, but it is easy to spot the worse offenders. Some of those writers who wrote books after World War Two, attempted to write like him also, duplicate his style, but they were easy to spot also."

"They liked his way of writing uncomplicated prose, I guess," Tom said. "The famous writer's prose is sort of close to newspaper writing."

"Yes," Karl said, "his writing style is decievingly simple, in fact it is a compelling style, it's a milestone in literature. He created prose using everyday words with an economy that appears to be simplicity. But, Mark Twain did it first, writing simple prose ... the words people use in everyday talking ... Twain made the first American literature, writing that way."

"I think the famous writer's prose takes the reader, Karl, right there,as the action is happening, as it's taking place. Karl, his prose makes you feel every thing that goes on. It's like a movie, only better because there are three more dimensions than just seeing and hearing. You get touch in his writing, and smell, and you get the character's reaction in the story, how he feels."

"You're quite a competent observer, Tom. That's very good."

Rolfson set his pen on the desk, lifted his eyeglasses, and began rubbing his eyes.

"Yeah, Karl, observing is the simple part, writing is the hard part. It's hard as hell to write it down."

Rolfson picked up his pen, and looking at Tom, said, "I would like to read your book. When you get it typed, I would like to see the carbon copy."

"Why, Karl? You want to see if I'm just a talker: if I can write as well as I talk about writing?

"I guess you could say that," Rolfson, smiling, said while reaching for an envelope.

"You should read it, Karl, more for the overall impact — what the whole book says — then just pick at the techniques of the prose."

"You are very fortunate, Tom," Rolfson said writing, not looking up, " because you have both the inclination to write, and, the time to do it. I envy you for having the opportunity to develope your writing skill."

"Well, Karl, don't envy me too much because in ten months if I don't make a sale of my writing, I'll be in a hell of a fix. I may be writing for a newspaper to earn a paycheck."

"If possible," Karl said, " that should be avoided."

"I agree," Tom said scratching the back of his head. "I'm trying not to worry about it — I'll just wait until that bridge comes up, I keep telling myself, then I cross it."

"Maybe you will sell a story by then, Tom."

"It would settle <u>all</u> my problems, personal and financial, Karl."

The front door of the bookstore. opened and Rolfson stood up to see who came in.

Tom turned to look, and saw two girls standing in the aisle by the door. Both wore bell-bottom pants.

"Yes, girls," Rolfson said stepping to the office door, "can I help you with something?"

"Do you buy used textbooks?" the tallest girl, with black hair cut like Cher Bono, asked. The shorter girl carried a wide suede handbag.

"No, dear," Rolfson said, you have to go to the university bookstore over on Woodward at Warren avenue for that."

"Thanks," the tall girl said, and they went out the door.

"The shorter one wasn't bad, eh Karl? Tom had been standing, looking through the glass of the office window.

"I'm going to miss campus life."

"That's a fine thing for a newly-married man to say," Karl said. "Besides, they didn't look much like students."

"What? I just said, Karl, that I was going to miss campus life. That's all." Tom grinned, holding out his hands.

"I know what you said," Karl said, grinning back.

"If one of them wore a white pleated skirt, every thing would have been okay, huh, Karl?

Karl stopped grinning. "I'm not sure what you're referring…"

"I bet you don't."

"No. That was ... not what you're thinking."

"You should write fiction," Tom said, making a writing motion with his hand, the fingers together as if holding a pen, grinning.

"That was just a customer — you saw."

"Okay, Karl."

Rolfson walked back behind his desk, then looked out into the store.

"You won't say anything? ... To Ginny?"

"Don't worry."

Rolfson sat down in his desk chair and leaned back.

"Ny wife drinks ... heavily," he said quietly. "She isn't much ... company."

Tom shrugged. "You don't have to explain anything to me, Karl ," Tom said and sat down. "Before I go, I want ask your opinion about ... ah ... about travel." Tom was silent for a moment. "Hey, you said you 'envy' me because I have time 'to develope my writing skills.' Isn't that what you said a minute ago? "

"Yes," Rolfson said writing. "Something similar."

"I knew I heard that before, Karl. It just came to me. It was F. Scott's last letter to the famous writer back in nineteen-forty when "Bell Tolls" came out. After the letter congratulated the famous writer on the book, it said, something like you said: "I envy you'" and went on to say something like, "'because it will give you the time to do what you want,'" Tom said smiling. F. Scott died a month or so later after writing that. I read it in his biography, or someplace."

"Very good," Rolfson said, "you are a very good student of biography."

"It just rang a bell, Karl."

"No puns, Tom. You're wasting time with puns." As he reached for another envelope, Rolfson said, "Do not play with words. Now, what were you asking about ... travel?"

"I was thinking of Ginny and I going to Florida for a while ... living there for a time, not just a visit. There are a lot of things going on ... for a writer to learn about… and do ... down there."

"I have never been to Florida, Tom."

" I have, a couple of times, and I worked in Key West back before I went into the Army. I was the mate on a party boat for reef fishing — the kind of boat that takes tourists by the dozen and lets them drop a line."

"Your hero, the famous writer, lived in Key West for a while, right, Tom?"

"I almost met him."

"Yes, Ginny mentioned something to me about that."

"I never quite got the money together to ride the train ferry boat over to Havana. Then wham, he won the Nobel Prize and the crowd showed up."

"Tom," Rolfson said while flipping the address list page of book customers, "maybe it's better you never met him ... personally."

"What do you mean, Karl?"

"You might have been disappointed. Tom, I emphasize the might.

"We would have done a lot of talking about writing," Tom said slowly. "I have tons of questions to ask him."

"Well, he could be crude at times," Karl said. "He has no finesse ... he can be real tough. Actually, he is a simple man with a great talent, and I saw him and O'Hara at Costello's bar once in New York. They were trying to break a shillelagh by putting it on their heads and pulling both ends. They had been drinking all day."

"Who cares about all that," Tom said waving his hand. "He's a good writer. I like the way he writes and I like the way he lives. It all seems bigger than life, sorta."

Rolfson, sliding a blank envelope from the stack, smiled.

"Men are not gods," he said.

"I know, but so what if he gets crude sometimes; he's just letting off some steam after a long bout of concentrating on writing. You're overlooking the good his writing provides."

"You certainly admire him."

"Sure, why not," Tom said, lifting his heels off the floor and then, dropping them. "I have someone to look up to, someone who has given me a goal — something to shoot for. Kids do it with sports all the time. They have their heros."

"Well, just don let it get out of control, Tom. This hero worship of yours can get to be dangerous if you let it go to far."

"I know what you mean, Karl. But people like me use this imitation only until we reach success, and then we outgrow the hero's influence. We don't need it after we reach success, we go our own way."

Rolfson nodded, then reached for an envelope.

"Okay, I'm still interested in what you think of me and Ginny packing up and going to Florida."

Without looking up, Rolfson said, "You might meet your famous writer if you go down there again."

"I might get to show him my new book ... see what he thinks about it."

"You don't pull any punches."

"I haven't got time, Karl." Tom rubbed the side of his face. "I ... I've got to get rich quick."

"Everyone wants that, Tom.

"No patronizing, okay •"

"Give me mor credit than that," Rolfson said as he was writing. "Getting rich quick is the American dream."

"I think a trip to Florida for a while might just be the action I need. And there's Cuba down there too ..."

"Well," Rolfson said stacking the addressed envelopes, "I don't see how a trip to Florida would hurt."

Tom was silently looking at the floor, thinking.

"Maybe ... maybe we shouldn't say anything about Florida to Ginny," he said continuing to look at the floor, "until my publish or perish time runs out."

"All right, Tom."

"Going to Florida came into my head when we were up at the cabin," Tom said slowly, still looking at the floor.

"Yes, somehow the cabin makes us more aware of the world surrounding us," Rolfson said writing, "like a refuge."

Chapter 17

"Everybody on the boat is putting a dollar in the pool," Fred Terrel shouted to Tom over the engine noise. First one to catch a fish, and the one who catches the biggest fish today, split the pot."

Tom, holding the iron ladder going up to the pilot house deck of the seventy-foot party boat, turned his back to the waves, trying to avoid the spray. The grey water was rolling hard with the wind.

Fred had been in the Military Police in Stuttgart at the same time Tom had been in Bamberg. He was tall and boney, and still talked as if he was in the Military Police.

"Who ... do I give the dollar?" Tom shouted, then turned his face away quick to avoid a new spray.

"That guy there ... in the red windbreaker," Fred shouted, pointing.

Tom nodded, looking at the man in the red jacket who was holding a woman being seasick over the side of the boat.

Tom made a long face when he saw the woman being sick.

"Give me your dollar," Fred shouted. "I'll do it."

Tom watched him walk back toward the red jacket man, holding onto the backs of the fishing benches to steady himself on the heaving deck, then shook his head.

Tom did not like it there were twenty-two people on the boat. He thought that was too many to really enjoy the day fishing. Too many lines to get tangled.

Looking back, across the waves off the stern, Tom could see the sandy shore, and behind it, the rows of palm trees, and to the right, the thin black tower of the light house. But he could not see the inlet opening where they came out in the boat from the Intercostal Waterway to the ocean. Then he tried estimating where his house was located, the mile or so, south, from the lighthouse, and smiled.

In the four months Tom and Virginia had been in Florida, they had moved three times, and he thought that was funny. They moved from Fort Lauderdale to another apartment in Lauderdale-by-the-Sea, then to the house they rented in Pompano Beach. Tom liked this old stucco house; the ocean was just across the street, and the charter boats were close, up at the inlet. And, the house had a fireplace, and the windows had wooden jalousie shutters for the hurricane season.

The first week Tom came to Florida, he found a job as City Hall reporter with the Fort Lauderdale News He went to the newspaper to fill out an application, did so, and next day the editor phoned him for an interview; the reporter who formerly had the job at city hall was stricken with a heart attack and partially paralyzed. The paper was a man short on the writing staff. Tom was offered the job, and took it.

He did not like working on the News because it left him no time to write his fiction stories. His first novel had been returned by three publishing houses. He wanted to begin a draft of a second novel, but after work in the evening, he was too tired to write. He told Virginia this, and she said he should take a sabbatical from fiction; try something else, get his mind off fiction for a while.

When he said he did not want to take his mind off fiction writing, they came up with a compromise in their discussion. Tom would go fishing to relax.

Fred Terrel mentioned fishing to Tom when they were writing the Unsolved Gold Coast Murder Series for the Sunday edition of the News. Fred was the police beat reporter and had files on most of the recent murders, and some, on the older, but more spectatular ones. He thought he was a Sherlock Holmes, and even offered the police his services in searching for the Boston Strangler up there, but was turned down. Each week the Sunday paper offered a recent murder that was unsolved for the area running north up the seacost from Miami. The crime itself was dramatized by Tom, and the details of the investigation; suspects, and technical data, were explained by Fred in the following paragraphs of the news feature. The two reporters were popular for these stories, and it was said at some police stations, the detective bureau kept them on file because of the details.

Virginia, this Saturday, went shopping with Terrel's wife, Marge, to Jordan Marsh in Fort Lauderdale while the men were fishing.

On the party boat, Fred shouted, "We're both in the betting pool," when he came back to where Tom was gripping the ladder. "Some of the people want to ask the captain to go back in. They think it's too rough out here."

"He won't ... do it, will he?" Tom shouted, shaking his head.

"Naw, " Fred shouted, turning his face from the spray of water off the bow. "He don't want to give the money back."

Grinning, Tom shouted, "It's not ... that bad. Maybe it will calm down ...'

Suddenly Tom saw people pointing at the water up at the bow. Other people were moving to look over the starboard side.

"Somone fall overboard?" Tom shouted, pointing.

"Let's look," Fred shouted.

The crossed the swaying deck to the railing on the starboard side of the boat.

"Hammerhead," Fred shouted. "Hammerhead shark."

Tom could see the long dark outline swimming near the surface of the water, staying with the speed of the boat. Then, when the shark turned away from the boat, Tom could see the head was distinctly shaped like a mallet.

"Monster," Tom shouted to Fred.

"Twelve, fourteen feet," Fred shouted.

"Can we catch it?" Tom asked, shouting back.

"The fishing tackel — the poles and reels are too light — for a fish that size," Fred shouted, just as a wave broke over the bow and sprayed them.

"Damn," Tom shouted , "wish I had a rifle."

"Like the famous writer," Fred said, grinning and turning to Tom. "He uses a Thompson machine gun on sharks, I hear, down there in Cuba," he shouted.

"I don't blame him," Tom shouted, watching the shark swim away in the rolling waves.

When the boat came up to a black floating bouy, the captain cut the engines. Most of the people on board still wanted to fish and were taking the four-ought reel and fiberglass pole rigs the mates were handing out. Tom took a pole, and stood for a moment watching the bouy rise up on wave, and for an instant, loom higher than the boat.

"Down in Key West," Tom said turning to look at Fred, we used an ordinary chalk line." He did not have to shout now with the boat engines off.

"Yeah," Fred said unwrapping the monofiliment line from around his pole. "That's okay for reef fishing to use chalk line, in case you get a two-hundred pound Grouper, or some other of them heavy, slow, fish. But, we're fishing the ocean for Sailfish, Wahoo, kingfish, or maybe a bullhead dolphin. The're all fighters and speedsters; you'll see they ain't the kind you horse in."

"I never used a fishing pole this size," Tom said.

"Just use it like a regular fishing rod," Fred said holding up his, "except you see this thing that looks like a star, here behing the handle? This is the drag. If you want to slow a fast line going out, just tighten the star this way. When you want to ease the drag , turn it this way. And don't leave the drag all the way on, when your just sitting and fishing. A strike by the fish will snap the line. Leave the drag about medium."

"There's a wire leader at the end of this line," Tom said holding it up.

"Teeth," Fred said, "everything we're fishing has sharp teeth. King, Cuda, and the Sailfish has a small bill — eh, sword."

"I get a fish like those," Tom said, "hell, I'll win <u>both</u> the betting pools today. It would even pay for the trip out here."

"You ain't going to win, Tom, because I Am."

"Fat chance," Tom said smiling. When the ship's mate came and wired a small fish to Tom's hook, so it laid flat against the hook, he asked Fred, "what they using for bait?"

"Ballyhoo," Fred said as he was letting out line.

Tom started releasing line, he suddenly realized how fast the boat was drifting from the bouy.

"What happens when we can't see the bouy?" Tom asked.

"They always start the drift at the bouy because big fish hang around the anchor chain," Fred said. "Specially Sailfish. And when they hang a Sailfish back at the dock it makes the boat look good to the tourists — new customers. It looks like a lucky boat." Fred was lighting a cigaret from the pack in his shirt pocket, where Tom could still see the camel through the light material, when he said, Ginny told Marge you wrote a book about Germany and the Army and when you caught TB."

Tom sat, one arm on the boat railing, holding the pole out over the water. He adjusted his sunglasses, "Yeah, but I haven't had any luck in selling it," he said quietly.

"I've got a sister," Fred said, "Up in Wisconsin, who's been writing confession stories for years. She thinks she's a girl Hemingway, but she works for a dentist, because she never sells any stories to magazines. Everybody in the family tells her to quit, but she just keeps writing and sending stuff out. She's older than me. I can't understand why she don't give it up."

"Sometimes," Tom said, pulling up on his fishing rod, slowly, " I think the only qualification a writer needs is an unlimited capacity for disappointment."

"That's just the weight of the line," Fred said. "Sometimes it pulls like a fish."

"My line is a long way out there," Tom said, looking at the reel. "I bet there's not twenty feet left."

"All the lines are way out there, " Fred said. "Must be fifteen or sixteen — out in every direction from the boat. The fun begins when it's time to go in, and everybody starts reeling in. There'll be snags everywhere, some times three and four together."

A woman shouted from near the back of the boat; she had a strike.

Tom saw her line cutting the water like a blade.

The woman was smiling grimly as she held the rod trying to reel in the line against the pull of the fish. An old man was leaning out from the boat, guiding his line away from hers to avoid getting tangled.

When the woman brought the fish alongside the boat, the mate quickly gaffed it and swung it aboard.

Everyone cheered.

Tom saw the mate was untangling two other lines from around the woman's.

"Looks like she had some help," Tom said to Fred, who was lighting a cigaret.

"This is fishing for the working class," Fred said putting the match pack in his pants pocket. "It's kind of crowded, but at least it's ocean fishing."

"I think fishing should ... " Tom started, but watched Fred jump and pull back on his pole.

Out in the distance a fish broke the water in a splash.

"Geronimo," Fred shouted.

"Kingfish?" Tom asked.

"Yeah," Fred said pumping the rod and reeling in line," and I hope it's bigger than that other one — for half the pot."

Two other people, Kingfish on their lines, were shouting and laughing.

"Fred, you got two more competitors for pot."

The mate quickly gaffed Fred's fish, cut two notches in the tail for identification, and dropped it in the fish box, then went to help another fisherman.

"That one didn't look to hefty," Fred said, "but this time I'll do better."

An old man wearing a sweatshirt with Hawaii printed on the chest, pulled in a Yellowtail. It was not big.

"That ain't no competition," Fred said watching the mate take it off the hook, letting his line with a new bait, drift out. He put a cigaret in his mouth, and was reaching for matches, when he shouted, "H-ha," and the cigaret fell, as he pulled up on the rod with a second strike.

When he brought it in to the boat, and the mate gaffed it, this King was not as big as the other.

"You can't win them all," Fred said, lighting a new cigaret. "At least... we know who the better fisher man is of us two," he said grinning at Tom, exhaling smoke.

"Maybe, I need fresh bait," Tom said. "I'll reel in and get a fresh bait."

"You do that, Mister Hemingway junior," Fred said. "If you write books like you fish, you're going to starve."

"Once a cop," Tom said, "always a cop."

"You bet," Fred said exhaling smoke.

After fishing, Tom and Fred drove down the shore to the house Tom was renting. Virginia and Marge sat in lawn chairs near the porch, drinking from a bottle of J&B scotch they bought earlier while shopping. When Tom turned into the driveway, both women waved to the car.

"How did you do fishing, honey?" Virginia asked Tom as he was walking up from the car.

"Not to good," he said smiling, shaking his head. "I got two Kingfish," Fred said, proudly to Marge. "Young Hemingway here," he said pointing at Tom, "got skunked."

"You're the one who smells," Marge said. "That fish-smell is terrible."

"Scotch on tap," Virginia said, holding up her glass to Tom.

"Okay, scotch," Tom said, sounds good. "I'll get the drink of the day. You too Fred?"

"Is that all they had on sale?" Fred said. "Scotch is okay," he said to Tom after getting a hard-eye stare from Marge. "Fishing always makes me thristy," he said watching Tom go into the house, then he sat down in a lawn chair and crossed his legs.

"What did you do with the fish you caught? Marge asked him. "I can smell them on you."

"They're in the car," he said, grinning. "I brought them for our cats. I filleted them."

Tom came back with two glasses of scotch and handed Fred one before he sat down in the chair next to Virginia. She had brushed his leg when he crossed in front of her.

"Are you getting hungry, Fred?" Tom asked then sipped his scotch. "We can put those Kingfish on the bar-b-que if you like."

"We bought ground round, honey," Virginia said, not understanding Tom's joke with Fred. "Sweet corn and Idahoes and., some beer."

"Kingfish isn't much good to eat," Fred said, setting his drink on the grass. He took out a cigaret and while lighting it, said, "Some people smoke it and eat it, but I don't like the taste."

"We got Budwiser, Fred," Tom said knowing Fred did not care for the scotch. "I saw it in the frige."

"That Hemingway," Fred said lifting his glass from the ground, "I read somewhere, his father made him eat what ever he shot or caught on a line… when he was a kid at the cottage in Michigan." He took a long drink of scotch.

"That was just," Tom said taking his glass down from his face, "to keep the kid Hemingway from going around killing things for sport. Then just let it lye."

Virginia put her hand on Tom's arm.

"You-shoot-um, eh Tom, you-eatum," Fred said. "Only you got skunked today, Mister Hemingway junior," he said, holding up his glass.

"Fre-ed," Marge said, "what's the matter with you tonight?"

Virginia stood up, to interrupt a possible confrontation between the two, and said to Tom, "Honey, why don't you start the charcoal burning out in the backyard grill."

"Right," Tom said smiling at her. "Is there any of that starting fluid left?"

"Under the sink," she said. "Come, I'll show you."

Tom followed her into the house a back to the kitchen. It was getting dark and she snapped on the light.

"I think there's enough," Tom said shaking the can he took from the shelf under the sink.

"Honey," Virginia said, "I know it's difficult listening to Fred's wisecracks, but please, don't start a row."

"It's been going on all day," Tom said opening the lid of the can of charcoal fluid, "but the cracks about fishing are just kidding, it's the jabs about the writing that .. "

"Were you guys drinking before you came home?" Virginia asked opening the refrigerator. "Your stomachs are empty, you know?" She took a stack of raw hamburger patties off the shelf in the refrigerator and set it on the sink.

"We had two or three beers at the Yardarm Bar at the inlet when we got off the boat, that's all," Tom said pushing open the back screen door. "He might be showing off for Marge, or something."

He snapped on the backyard light, and went down three steps to where the grill stood on a cement slab.

"I'm sorry, honey," Virginia said in a loud whisper through the screen door. "I spoke too freely with Marge about you book writing plans."

Dumping charcoal from a bag into the grill, Tom turned to her, "It was bound to come sooner or later, here or at the office."

"I love you to pieces, Tom, for saying that," she said in a hoarse whisper through the screen door and turned into the kitchen.

"You're a hell of a woman," Tom said. "I never know what pleases you." He turned to look at the door, but she was gone.

Tom stood looking at the high flames burning on the charcoal. The yard was dark all around now, except for the yard light. He heard Virginia talking in the kitchen, then he heard Marge's voice, but he could not make out what they were saying.

Then the kitchen door opened, and Tom saw Fred come out. He had a can of beer.

"They're calling our baby sitter," Fred said, "to see if she can stay an hour or so longer." He drank from the can, and said, "'Need any help with the fire? I was a Boy Scout, you know?" He laughed. "We stayed out on the boat longer than was expected."

"It's catching pretty good," Tom said looking into the flames.

"I helped myself to a beer," Fred said holding up the can, jiggling it. "I'll get you one ..."

"Not right now," Tom said as he stirred the coals with a small stick. "I'll have one with my burger.'

"Tom, I apologize for what I said ... the Hemingway crack ...

"How you want your burger? " Tom asked. "Rare, or what?"

"Rare," Fred said, then took a swallow of beer. "Hey, you better let those flames burn down some."

Tom nodded, "Yeah, they are a little too hot."

Fred sat down on a rusty lounge chair next to the house wall, pushing aside a pile of garden hoses.

He sat for a moment, then said "I've got things to write about too. There is some stuff I want to put in a novel, and when I get time, I'm going to sit down and write."

"Good for you, Fred," Tom said without looking at him.

"You ain't no different than me," Fred said. "You're just another reporter. You're not different ... or special ... just because you you're a writer, dammit."

Fred took a long drink, emptying the beer can.

"Okay," Tom said, "I think the coals are about ready for the burgers."

"Did you know," Fred said,leaning forward on the rusty lounge chair, "Marge was ... married ... before? Eleven months she was married to a mechanic. Yeah."

"A mechanic," Tom said, puzzled, "what does that ...?"

"It means our first girl is his, Tom. The second baby girl is ours. That's what it means."

"Okay," Tom said,shaking his head. "Okay."

"It didn't bother me when we first got married but lately, it started bothering me."

"To-om," Virginia said throught the screen, Marge next to her, "are you ready for the burgers? We're boiling the corn on the stove. We put it in a big pot of water."

"Okay, give me the meat," he said, "and wrap the potatoes in foil with a dab of butter. He went to the door for the burgers and took them carefully, keeping the plate level. "The potatoes will roast quick over the fire." he said up to Virginia. Marge held open the door.

"Tom that air is damp," Virginia said. "You want a sweater, or something?"

"It's warm by the fire, Gin."

"Fred, help him with the burgers," Marge said.

"Yeah," Fred said. He stood up, dropped the empty beer can on the lounge. "We do a lot of Bar-B-Que in our yard," he said, placing the burgers over the grey coals.

"To-om," Virginia said through the screen door. "Change of menue, honey. No Idaho potatoes, we're going to put french fries in the microwave."

"Okay," Tom said, "the burgers won't take long." He was watching Fred turn over the patties. "Maybe you can warm the buns?"

"How did I just know you would say that?" Virginia said, folding her arms. "Br-r," she said, "the damp out there goes right through you," and turned, away from the door.

Fred stepped back from the grill smoke, "You know,Tom, I'd hate to think I'm going to be stuck in this crummy newspaper business ... with this reporting job ... for the rest of my life," he said. "You know what I mean?"

"I know what you mean, Fred."

Monday morning, the whole news room knew Tom had not caught anything Sunday, out on the boat,fishing. Fred had told everybody about his catching two kingfish, and Tom, sitting next to him could not even get a bite. Fred even made a remark that Tom would never catch up with Hemingway, some one told Tom, because he did not have any luck.

Tom went over to the press room in the Broward County building, and after checking in by telephone the city desk back at the newspaper, started downstairs to the coffee shop.

The guff Fred said about the fishing was just fun, Tom thought riding the elevator down to the coffee shop. But the cracks about Tom's novel writing, and the Hemingway life, bugged him. Now, everywhere, not only the news room, would know his secret hope of becoming a famous writer. And now that it was out in the open, all mouths would be upon it.

Bert Halpin, the blind man who operated the coffee shop, was an avid fisherman, started on Tom as soon as he heard his voice.

"Got skunked, huh?" Bert said, grinning. "You must of used up all your luck catching all those fish you said you caught up there in Canada — and Michigan. Huh, Tom?"

"Ah-h," Tom said as he stirred his coffee, "you have a bad day on the water and Fred makes a mountain out of it."

"Yeah, sure," Bert said using his hands to check the paper cup rack on the counter. "But he ain't lying, is he?"

Tom watched as Bert. smiling wide, enjoying teasing Tom and talking about fishing at the same time, dropped a stack of new cups into the rack, then checked them with hishands.

"You know," Tom said. "that was first time not Fred's first time out. What does he know, anyhow?"

Tom thought to himself, that he did not know if he was talking about fishing, or what Fred said about the novel writing and the famous writer.

"You should always go fishing in the morning," Bert said, his hands flat on the counter. "Never take the afternoon trip. Fishing is no good in the afternoon. You should know that."

"Ah, what's the difference?" Tom cracked teasing Bert for being serious. "When you're lucky, it don't matter."

Two women clerks came to the counter for coffee. Tom waited until Bert served them, talking with them and smiling. Tom knew Bert was going to ask to go fishing.

"Maybe Sunday you and me can go out from Bahia Mar? Bert asked Tom across the counter when he came back. "I'll show you how to fish," he said grinning wide. "I'll have the wife fry a chicken — you bring the beer."

"Has it got to be Sunday?" Tom asked.

"It's the only day I can get away — from here," Bert said quietly.

"I have to talk with my wife." Tom said. "I'll let you know. Okay?

A group of maintenance workers came through the door way into the coffee shop, talking and laughing.

"Okay, Tom," Bert said slightly disappointed, "I'll be waiting to hear from you."

As the maintenance men closed in around the counter, trading remarks with Bert, Tom moved away and sat down at a table near the magazine rack.

A sports magazine had the headline on the cover: FAMOUS WRITER SIZES UP NEW MATADORE.

Looking through the pages of t magazine, Tom saw photographs of the famous writer at the Madrid bullring. One photo showed him standing with his favorite torrero and a Spanish officer, who wore a small black mustache, while the author brandished a full-face white beard. In another photo, the famous writer's bare stomach was hanging out. He is aging fast, Tom thought.

Reading the news article further, Tom found out the famous writer was now living in Ketchum, Idaho, near his old haunt of Sun Valley, and not in Cuba.

Tom had talked with Virginia about taking a trip to Cuba, maybe visiting the famous writer, but she said she was afraid of Castro. So Tom gave it up for a while.

Looking at the pictures of the famous writer again, Tom sensed what it must be like to make your living by writing, and being respected, all over the world, and at first was envious, but then felt guilty.

He knew that if he ever wanted to live like the famous writer, that he had better get back to writing fiction. He was wasting his time writing for a newspaper. He should

be doing quality fiction writing, not throw-away newspaper writing.

The way he was living now, was comfortable, he had to admit, but he could not really enjoy completely with the guilt of not writing his books and stories. Nothing else but writing mattered to him, and he was not writing.

He would have to do something, he could not go on like this. Tonight, he would have a talk with Virginia; they would decide on a way for him to work at his fiction stories.

On his way out of the coffee shop, Tom paid Bert for the magazine, but did not mention anything about going fishing.

Chapter 18

"I like that O'Brien's in New Orleans, honey," Virginia said, "and those hurricane drinks in those cute glasses like a lamp." She glanced at Tom who was driving, looking straight ahead. "They were a pretty shade of pink but I don't know what those drinks had in them. And I like that town Biloxi, the name, I like to say it, even though we didn't stop there."

Tom smiled, looking forward. He was tired from driving around the Gulf Coast; they were travelling from Fort Lauderdale to Mexico City. He had not slept well last night in the motel at Victoria, Texas, and the four cups of coffee he had for breakfast were not working.

"It's getting hotter by the minute," Tom said as if talking to himself.

"I'm just chattering," Virgina said, resting her hand on his arm, "to take your mind off being tired."

"I know, babe," he said, turning to smile at her.

"Things are working out for us, arn't they, Tom?"

"You mean because of what they told us back there in Victoria?"

"Yes, about that crossing into Mexico at Loredo and heading for Monterrey ... avoiding all that mountain driving," she said looking at the side of his face. "They were nice at that motel, weren't they?"

Tom inhaled, then exhaled, nodding, "I saw it on the map. First Saltillo, then Monterrey. I probably would have headed this way anyhow. San Miguel de Allende, that art colony,is right on this same highway ... just above Mexico City."

"Well, it was nice of the people at the motel to mention it, anyhow, Tom."

"Yes, it was," Tom said, nodding, slowly.

"I'll drive, honey," Virginia said putting her hand on the side of Tom's face. "If you're tired, I can drive."

"Not in your condition, babe. Are those pills helping you any?"

"They make me a little drowsy, to tell the truth."

"Take a nap, babe. Put you head on my lap," he said taking a quick look at her. "I wish we had air conditioning."

She laid on her side on the car seat, her head resting on Tom' thigh.

"I'm not much good for you around the end of the month, am I, Tom?"

"You are always good for me, Gin. I mean it. I couldn't make it without you."

"I love when you talk like that," she said putting her hand on his knee.

He set his hand on her red hair.

"And I love anything you say, babe.

"Oh, you don't have to talk like that, Tom.

"I mean it."

"Except when I start about talking about having a baby ... you always ... get angry."

"No, I don't get angry, and I even like it when you talk about having a baby ... someday, babe."

"Oh, Tom, how can I help but not love you so much," she said, and kissed the side of his face. "I wish we could have made love last night, and I wish we could make love right now," she said kissing him again.

"Careful, Gin, before you cause an accident," he said grinning. "You're not supposed to talk to the driver, like on a bus ... at least not that way."

"Well, you know what I mean."

"I sure do, Gin," he said smiling. "Now take a nap. It's really getting hot. Take a siesta like they're doing in the rest of this Mexico. I hope the car don't melt."

"I want to be a good wife. Am I a good wife?"

"I couldn't get a better one, Gin."

She laid back down, her head on his leg.

"Tom, you're going to work hard writing your new book, aren't you?"

"You bet," he said and glanced at her head, and the side of her face. "I'll do my best, Gin." He could sense what she was thinking.

"You're going to make a pile of money, aren't you, Tom, so I can have a baby, and we can buy a house and I can feel ... complete? Right, Tom? We don't want to be a ... tramp family ... do we, Tom?"

"No, honey," Tom said, suddenly remembering the picture of a poet her father had in his office at home. The poet was writing by the light of a candle up in an attic, or garret, holding a broken umbrella over his head because the roof was leaking. Her father, Tom recalled, never liked him and his wanting to write, and must have told Virginia writers do make much money, and were risky husbands.

"Tom, cheer up, honey. I can feel you getting depressed. I can sense it in you."

"Okay, okay, Gin, you're right. But no more talk about money. We agreed I can work exclusively on my book until next spring. Can we stop talking about money, Gin, Please?"

Tom looked out the car window at the grey desert, dotted with squat mesquite bushes, that shimmered in the sun. It looked a hard place for anything to live in.

"To-om, it's just that I get scared when I think about not having any money. I'm sorry."

"Don't worry so much, Gin, it's not good for you. Just let me ... do the worrying."

"I have never had to live without money, Tom."

"Don't you have any confidence in me, Gin?"

"Of course I do, honey," she said sitting up on the car seat. "I'm ... just being ... silly."

"I won't let you down, Gin. I'll do my work. If I don't make it, well, it won't be because I didn't do my work, my writing."

"I know," she said looking at him sheepishly, "and I'm sorry for talking negative. Don't let anything I say shake your confidence. I'm not as strong as you are about these things."

"You're strong, Gin. You're plenty strong. In fact you're one of the strongest."

"I don't understand what you are saying — for sure— but it <u>sounds</u> very nice, Tom. You're talking like a writer and I'm never quite sure what you are saying." She smiled. "But I take it as a compliment."

"Yes, it was a compliment — one of the highest, Gin."

She kissed the side of his face, then sat for a moment. "Look at, the heat-waves rising off the road up ahead ... it's too hot to sleep ... unless ... you are sleeping with me."

"You — lovely red head," Tom said putting his hand to her face. "You are lovely ... for saying that, and for being a red head."

Virginia smiled. And later when she was sleeping, Tom drove thinking of what he had left behind in Florida.

He thought of Ed Bonderman, the managing editor, who was surprised when Tom said he was leaving, and how Ed asked if he was leaving because he wanted more money, and how, Tom, had to say no, and then good-bye.

He recalled to, how Fred invited him, Tom, out for farwell drinks, and when Fred got drunk, he said he wished he had the guts to quit the newspaper business, and how Fred babbled that Tom had a destiny and it was easy for him to follow destiny because destinies were like that. Tom ramembered he was going to tell Fred just how scarey it was leaving the security of a job, but changed his mind and just had another drink,

He was learning, Tom thought, to keep real feelings to himself, because he disliked it when people, like Fred, spilled out all their fears and feelings; it always made Tom uneasy when people did it, sometimes he even felt contempt for them and he could never explaine why. Maybe it was because he had the same fears, or maybe it was because people who spill everything are always looking for sympathy and are not really trying to help themselves.

Bert Griffin was different from Fred. Tom felt bad telling the blind man that the fishing trip was off. He felt more a heel when Bert said his wife had already bought a chicken and the disappointment rose on that blind face. He wished now that he had never started the whole fishing thing with Bert. It was a crummy thing to do to a fisherman, who was a real fisherman, much less a blind one. But good people like Bert cannot be damaged by disappointment the way people like Fred Terrel are. People like Bert have fishing to hold on to, and when they are fishing, the disappointment fades away.

Learning these things were really difficult, these dealings with people, but they were good for a writer.

That was probably true about the famous writer, Tom thought. He suffers like everybody else. But once he starts to write — he has that to hold on to — and even if the writing is a flop — it heals him up and he can go on, because the writing is always there for him. He writes down what he is feeling and there is a permanent record of the feeling.

When someone reads what the famous writer has written, they feel what was felt by the writer again, and that is art; there is nothing mysterious about art.

If he ever met the famous writer, he would ask him about art, Tom thought. Someday, Tom thought, smiling, when his new book is completed and published, he and Virginia would go to Sun Valley and. talk to the famous writer. It would be one writer meeting another and maybe they could go bird shooting or trout fishing together.

But now, it would be writing here in Mexico every day, Tom told himself. Finding an inexpensive place for himself and Virginia to live for a book-length stay was top priorty. This was his ticket to fame and fortune.

He hoped all he read about this place for artists, this San Miguel de Allende was true, and if it was, he had the answer for writing his book and at the same time a place for Virginia to enjoy herself.

Tom inhaled, then exhaled, moving his legs, attempting to stretch while driving.

Virginia woke when Tom moved his legs.

"Where are we?" she asked sitting up, turning her head to Tom.

"Coming to the border," he said smiling.

"Oh-h, good," she said stretching her arms.

When filling out the paperwork at the border station, Tom saw a sign that said the temperature was one hundred and four degrees.

After spending the night in Satillo, the next day when the sun was directly overhead, Tom stopped the car in front of a sign: San Miguel de Allende.

From the roadside,overlooking the valley, Virginia looked down and slowly said, "So that's it."

They looked down onto bright red tile roofs of what appeared a deserted Mexican village. They drove down the road into the town, Tom heading for the church tower, guessing that must be where the town square — the plaza— was located.

"It's kind of nice here, Tom, but where is everybody?" Virginia looked up each street they passed. "It seems awful quiet for such a big place."

"That crossed my mind, too," he said as they drove into the plaza, then he began looking for a parking place.

He parked at a corner, and they stepped out of the car in front of what looked like a souvenir shop. Tom said quietly, "Well, this looks like a good a place as any to start —— see if we can find some people."

"Just look at this stuff," Virginia said smiling.

Outside the shop were different sizes of straw sombreros and baskets, and even a monkey woven from straw, all hanging on lines over the doorway. On another line, hung lanterns shaped like stars, made from tin and glass, and among them, tin masks, that glowered with metallic uglyness.

Inside the shop doorway, Tom could see bright colored rugs draped over chairs, red, white, yellow and green stripes. And farther back, inside, were tables and chairs and a counter stacked with whiskey bottles.

"You want to go back there?" Tom said. "Maybe a drink would make you feel better."

"Let's walk a little," Virginia said, "we've been riding a lot in the car — get the kinks out of our legs." She looked into the shop. "Ther's nobody back there."

"A walk sounds good," Tom said, locking the car doors.

"Let's go this way," Virginia said pointing to a string of archways over the sidewalk in front of a row of shops. "It looks so — foreign."

"Look there," Tom said pointing to a television antenna with a tall metal frame and guy wires holding it up. "Cripes."

"Some art colony; television," Virginia said to Tom as he came around the car, then took her hand.

When they were under the arcade, walking, Tom said, "Feel that damp? " running his hand on the thick stone wall. "We're deep in the heart of Mexico, babe, that's for sure."

"It's like walking back in history, isn't it, honey."

"It's more like history that stopped, or something," Tom said.

They walked under the arcade for more than a block in the shade and at the end came to a bar. The sign over the door read: La Cucaracha.

"Hey," Tom said pointing, "we found Poncho Villa's watering hole."

"If you want a drink, Tom, we can go in. Something cool would help — something with ice."

"Gin, maybe we should find a doctor to take a look at you. Maybe you got something ..."

"I'm not going to go running to a doctor every time I get a tummy ache, besides I'm not going to doctor down here."

"Okay, okay, gin. Let's get something cool — wet our whistles."

When the walked into the bar, they saw a high ceiling with thick wood beams. High on the back wall was a narrow window, the only other opening in the room besides the door. A stairway ran along the right wall to the upstairs.

"It reminds me of a cell," Virginia whispered.

"Yeah, but look at the brand names on those whiskey bottles," Tom said pointing. "They even have Cutty Sark."

"But where is everybody?" Virginia asked.

"Hello," Tom shouted toward the steps. "Anybody here?"

Tom heard someone walk across the wood floor overhead, then a young man in faded brown corduroy pants and a faded work shirt, spattered with paint on the front, came down the steps.

"What can I get you?" he asked crossing to the bar, and Tom saw be wore thick-soled sandals.

"Ah, you're American," Tom said looking at Virginia, who was smiling.

"We would like something cold to drink," she said to the young man who stood now behind the bar, resting on his hands, his thin fingers spread. "Something with ice."

"Where are you from?" Tom asked.

"Michigan."

"Where in Michigan?" Tom said, raising his eyebrows.

"Birmingham."

"I'm from Birmingham," Virginia said smiling.

"Ah, we don't have any ice, today ... yet," the young man. said. Then to Virginia, "I went to Cranbrook."

"No ice for the mixed drinks, heh," Tom said. "What do you have that is cold?"

"We had Cokes in the refrigerator, they're cold," the young man said pulling back a curtain, "but I don't know if there are any left," he said before going through a door way that had been hidden by the curtain.

"I didn't know there was a doorway there," Tom said in a low voice to Virginia. "What do you think about ...?"

"Exactly," Virginia said quietly, "this place is creepy ... and so is this guy."

The young man came back, and said flatly, "There are no Cokes."

"Well," Tom said looking at Virginia, "if the beer is cold, we'll have two."

The young man went out and came back with two bottles of Mexican Double-X beer. He opened the bottles with an opener on a string that was attached to the bar, then poured the beer, half filling the tall glasses.

While he was picking up the change from his twenty Paso bill, Tom asked the young bartender, "Where is everybody?"

"It's siesta time," he said. "It gets very hot here during the day."

Tom took a drink of beer, then asked casually, "Are there a lot of artists here? American artists?"

"Yes. Quite a few,"

"Are there a lot of places to rent?" Virginia asked. "You know, places that are not too expensive?"

"There is an art school here for ... painting," the young man said, being non-committal, "and the students rent places all over town. I guess you just ... have to look around."

"You live here, upstairs?" Tom asked. "Are there any more rooms — here maybe, to rent?

"No," the young man shook his head. "I use most of the upstairs for my studio. It's the only room."

"Is there anyone over at that souviner store that might know about places to rent?" Virginia asked.

"Could be," the young man said turning to her, "they're locals. Natives."

"Thanks," Virginia said, turning away and rolling her eyes up. She took a few sips of beer, looking at Tom.

"I'll be in the back," the young man said, " I have to stock the cooler. If you need me, just call," he turned and went through the doorway. Then there was the sound of bottles rattling.

"Friendly cuss," Tom said to Virginia as he emptied what was left in his beer bottle into his glass.

"He certainly doesn't put himself out any to be hospitable," she said quietly. "Tom, I can't drink this," she said and quickly set her glass on the bar. You ... finish it, honey."

"Let's take a walk over to that straw shop, babe," Tom said, taking her beer and pouring into his glass.

When they were crossing the plaza to the souvenir shop, Virginia said, "This place is beautiful, but there is some- missing. I can't put my finger on what it is."

"Well, let's check it out a little more — while we are here — before we make another move, okay, Gin?"

"That kid-bartender back there," Virginia said, "his father is probably an auto executive back in Detroit."

"Probably; he went to Cranbrook," Tom said. "That's the kind of school only automotive big-wigs can afford to send their kids."

"And now he's down here," Virginia said as they came up to the souvenir shop, "trying to be a Vincent Van Gogh. That doesn't make sense, Tom."

"I know, babe," Tom said smiling.

"Maybe I'm just dyspeptic," Virginia said, "and it's affecting my judgement; that sort of thing."

"I doubt it," Tom said as he stepped aside the door of the souvenir shop to let Virginia go first. "You don't understand, the kid-bartender can afford to do anything he wants."

Chapter 19

"But where did you hear about San Miguel?" the man with grey streaks in his beard asked, looking up at Tom. "I mean, how did you come to pick this place?"

He was sitting with two young men at a table in the bar of the souvenir shop. Tom had come back to the bar, leaving Virginia to look at the wares in the store, and. introduced himself as a writer who was looking for an inexpensive place to rent.

"I read about San Miguel in one of those writer's magazines," Tom said looking down. He was standing at the bar, near the tables, a beer bottle in his hand. "I think the article was by Roman Ford. He said it was an art colony here, and not expensive; I remember reading it, maybe, two years ago."

"Ro-man Ford," the bearded man said. "I doubt, if he has ever been here. I've heard of him. What does he know about San Miguel?"

The two younger men at the table were smiling. One of them, a man with heavy eyeglasses, picked his pipe off the table, and began packing tabacco, slowly, into the bowl.

When Tom saw the nine beer bottles on the table, be guessed the three had spent the afternoon siesta time here in the bar, so he was making allowences for the way the bearded man talked.

"Well, this looks like an interesting place," Tom said, "I mean, I can see why artists would like San Miguel. Me and my wife were planning to stay long enough for me to finish my second book. But, we don't have much dough."

The bearded man waved his arm, and said, "Ever since they closed Maria's whore house last month, San Miguel has been on the decline. They say; they say they making San Miguel fit for the tourist trade."

The two young men smiled, and the one with the pipe, took it out of his mouth, looked into the bowl, and poked it with his finger.

"It's the general's doing," the pipe smoker said.

"General Victor Morales," the other young man said, and all three smiled.

"Did you see," the bearded man said, "that God-awful television ariel that is currently gracing our town plaza?"

"Yeah," Tom said. "I saw it when I came into town; how could you miss it. I wondered who it belonged to."

"The damn General," the bearded man said. "He's got to watch his damn soccor matches, so we have look at that eyesore — that hideous ariel."

Glancing back to the store, Tom saw Virginia talking with a woman in Mexican clothes, holding a bright-colored rug over her arm.

At the same time, Tom held up his beer bottle, so the woman in Mexican peasant dress, who was polishing the bar mirror, would bring him another,

"Yeah," Tom said down to the bearded man, "that ariel sticks out like a sore thumb in the plaza: aesthetically.

"And did you see the damn super market up on the hill when you drove in?" the bearded man asked.

"No," Tom said, reaching for the fresh bottle of beer from the woman behind the bar.

"How could you miss it?"

"Maybe he drove in on the north road," the pipe smoker said.

"The road I came in on was like a donkey trail," Tom said.

"That's the north road into town, all right," the bearded man said, waving his arm. "It's a wonder you got here at all."

They all laughed.

"Well, the super market belongs to the general to," the bearded man said. "We've got everything here but a drive-in restaurant."

"The prices at that market are ridiculous," the young man sitting next to the pipe smoker, who had not spoke before, said quietly.

"When the general retires next year," the bearded man said, "he'll have all these businesses set-up for himself. He's got a gas station to ... and I think a laundromat is coming in."

Tom was paying the woman bartender for his beers; she had stood there all the time he was talking, waiting.

"Can I buy you guys a round of beer?" he asked.

"No thanks," the bearded man said, "I'm going to a party tonight. It's one of those buffet things, where everybody brings a dish of something. My wife wants to make potatoe salad. I promised I'd help her make it, so I'm leaing."

Tom, smiling, nodded.

The man with the pipe said, "I've got to go to the super-market," to the young man who barely who was now rolling up his shirt sleeve to cover where the elbow was worn through. "I hear they have a special on corned beef. You should get some."

"How much is it?" the young man said, checking his other elbow.

"I'm not sure."

"I'll go with you, then."

The three of them stood up from the table; the bearded man had been listening to the two others talking.

Tom said, "If you guys hear of anyplace decent to rent, will you let me know? I'll be around town."

"Sure," the bearded man said. "If I hear of anything." Then he smiled. "You might ask over at the La Cucaracha Bar..."

"I was over there," Tom said setting his beer bottle on the bar. "I didn't get very far."

They all laughed.

"It's a town joke," the bearded man said. "Charlie, the bartender, doesn't have much to say. We give him hell when we're dinking over there."

"But if anybody would know about a place for rent," the pipe smoker said, "Charlie would, that's for sure.

"The Cucaracha is sort of the night hangout for the art students up at the school," the pipe smoker said, and after looking at his watch, added, "I've got to go."

He went to the door quickly, the man with the worn shirt following him.

"If you like soup, vegetable soup," the bearded man said, "they have very good soup here at the bar. It's a meal by itself."

"Thanks," Tom said smiling.

"I'll see you around," the bearded man said, "if you decide to stay. But, this place is visual, this town… that's why all the painters come here. But, I don't see much here ... for a writer. Okay?

He turned and went through the doorway.

Tom drank down the remaining beer, slowly, put a tip amounting to the cost of one beer on the bar, then went through the door to meet Virginia.

"You don't look happy, honey," she said as he walked up to her. "What did you find out from those guys?"

"Well," Tom said looking at the bright striped blanket and two wicker-woven monkeys she bought, "this place, I think, is a little too expensive for my wallet. And. we got here just as the town is changing from an artist haven to a tourist trap."

"Do you want to stay, or drive down to Mexico City, Tom?"

"I'm deciding," he said slowly. "Hey, they make a vegetable soup in the bar "that's a meal in itself' so say those guys I talked to. Would you like a bowl of soup?"

"I can't hold anything down, honey, but, if you want to try it, I'll sit with you."

"Gin, maybe we should talk to a doctor about that stomach problem you are having ..."

"Tom, don't start that again. You know how I feel about <u>foreign</u> doctors. I'll just wait..." she started to say "until we get back home," but caught herself, and instead said, "because I don't think it's anything serious."

"If that's what you want, babe," Tom said, and pointed to the rug and monkeys. "We can carry this stuff to the car. We've got to find a hotel for tonight."

"You're going to skip the soup, honey?"

"Yes." Picking up the two monkeys, he said, "The famous writer had Paris when it was cheap, to do his early writing. I got to hole-up in a tourist trap to work on my book."

"Honey," Virginia said, "don't feel bad," and while picking up the rolled blanket, added "your famous writer was just lucky... in things like that."

"These are paid for?" Tom asked. "These things you bought?"

Virginia nodded.

As they walked to the car, Tom said, "You're right about the famous writer being lucky, babe. He was lucky all the way around, I'm just beginning to learn every day now.

Tom chose the Romfels Hotel in Mexico City from the tourist book he bought, not only for the low expense, but because it was on a sidestreet near the plush Prado Hotel.

After taking a shower, Tom sat down on the bed and read through all the tourist brochures he had taken from the racks in the hotel lobby.

Virginia was in the bathroom, the third time since they had arrived this evening. When she came out, she said, "I'm so-o sick," to Tom. "I've never been so sick in my life, like this. I'm sick at both ends."

"I know it's bad, babe, but it only lasts a day, or so," Tom said taking hold both of her hands while she stood in front of him. "There is some medication that stops it. I can go get it at a pharmacy," he said shaking her hands. "I feel for you, babe."

"What time is it?" she asked.

"Almost ten," he said looking up at her. "Gin, you really look pale, maybe I should call the hotel doctor to have a look at you."

"No, no," she said going over to her side of the bed. "I feel so weak and tired, Tom; all I want is to sleep — for a week, maybe. Then I'll be okay. I don't need a doctor, Tom, honest.

"Well, tomorrow if you're not improved any, I'm going to call one, Gin. I can't stand seeing you suffer like this."

He watched her lay down on the bed, then resting her hands on her stomach.

"I'll read for a while, Gin. Will that bother you?"

"Honey, all I want is to rest — sleep for a while.

And if I have to get up for the john, you being here, well, it makes me self-conscious. Could you go get the medication? Take you time, have a drink — or go even to a movie —— just let me sleep. Ple-ase?"

"I don't want to leave you alone, Gin."

"Please?" she said, getting up slowly and going to the bathroom. "I'll be okay, Tom," she said from the bathroom.

Tom went over to his shaving kit and took out a small bottle of aspirins and put them on the night stand on her side of the bed.

Pulling on his cotton sports coat, he said to her in the bathroom, put some aspirins by your bed. I'm going out."

"This is so humiliating," Virginia said in a low voice. Then in a louder voice, "I might telephone home — to Michigan — tell my parents — what we're doing."

"If you feel up to it," Tom said. "Maybe it will help you…"

"To-om, stop it."

"Okay, I'm going out."

"Take your time."

The night clerk at the desk in the hotel lobby told Tom there was an all night pharmacy on the Avenue Juarez, near the Prado hotel. The clerk wrote the name of the medication and the address of the pharmacy on the back of a hotel card. This was all done in a business manner, there was no grinning, and. when Tom offered a tip to the clerk, he refused.

Outside it was colder then Tom expected. Mexico City is at a high altitude in the mountains, like Denver, and the night air is always cold. He knew that, and when he stopped on the curb at Avenue Revillagigedo, he thought of going back to the hotel and getting a sweater, but then he decided not to disturb Virginia.

Walking, his hands in his coat pockets, shoulders hunched against the night cold, he passed an all night ambulance station. Often, up in the hotel room, he heard the sirens and they sounded close, now he knew why. Over the doorway of the station hung a white globe with a red cross on it, and it made him think of Virginia being sick.

"Her end of the month cycle, and the turistas, ganged up on her, poor kid," he said outloud to himself.

Ahead, up the street, Tom could see the bright lights and the people walking,and cars passing, on Avenue Juarez, a showplace street for the city.

When he turned the corner, Tom felt the strong wind blowing cold down the wide avenue. Shaking with cold, he walked briskly toward the brightly lighted Prado hotel, looking for a pharmacy sign.

"It's okay for me to bum around in all kinds of places," he muttered, "but Ginny is different. She has no reason to go trapsing around the world, she's not a writer. She should be in a place where everything is — orderly. You can see what it's doing to her, all this travel, you bum."

Standing across the street from the Prado, he decided to go inside and ask directions to a pharmacy, and get warm at the same time.

"But, what the hell," he said to himself, "this is the life I have chosen — what can I do?" he said walking quick across the wide avenue, "She even wants me to stay away from her. I guess — you can't blame her."

He passed a thin man in a loose-fitting grey suit, who was leaning on the fender of a car, arms folded.

"Can I help you, senor?"

Tom stopped and turned around, and as the man stood up straight, Tom saw the car was a Buick. There was a string of three or four cars parked behind, and each one had a man leaning on the fender, wearing a suit; Tom thought they might be chauffers.

"Yes," Tom said fumbling for the hotel card from the clerk, "I'm looking — for a pharmacy."

"You want a nice girl?" the man asked.

"I'm looking for a pharmacy."

"Yes."

"Farmacia?"

"No girls at farmacia.

"Medicine for my wife," Tom said grinning, handing the man the card.

After the man read the card in the light from the hotel portico, he pointed off to the right, up the street.

"Gracias," Tom said, taking the card back, then pulling his coat collar up around his neck.

"Senor, do you want a taxi? I am a taxi."

"You don't have a meter," Tom said. "And no sign."

"I am not that kind of taxi, senor. I take you to the farmacia.

"How much?"

"A few American dollars."

"I will give you two American dollars if you take me to the pharmacy, then back to the Ronfels Hotel, and no tip."

"Yea. I will do this," the man said motioning with his hand for Tom to get into the car.

In the back seat, Tom could see in the glow from the overhead streetlights, the inside of the car was kept very clean. The ash trays were empty, the floor mats swept, and he noticed on both door posts a vile, like a test tube, with purple plastic flowers that gave out a lilac scent.

Tom smiled, looking around the car, thinking this must be used for weddings, or something, it was fancy by any standards. And it was warmer than outside.

"I am called Sylvester, senor."

"Yeah," Tom said looking outside at the people on the street; couples were window shopping just like in the daytime. There seemed to be just as many people out at night as during the day.

"Ah, Sylvester," Tom said, "there are a lot of people up at this hour. How come?"

"In Mexico, it is not late, senor," he said driving, looking into the rear view mirror.

Tom nodding, said, "I shouldn't of asked."

They stopped at a pharmacy, and when Tom came back and got in the car, Sylvester turned in the front seat to face Tom.

"You have the medicine?"

"Yes," Tom said and watched him closely.

"Now, senor, I will show you a place for a drink, a club where there are girls also. Not country girls. Girls from the city who dress well. And very clean."

"Just take me back to the Ronfels Hotel," Tom said looking at Sylvester's face which was thin, and a thin nose that was too long. "Wy sick wife is waiting."

"It will not take much time," Sylevester said turning forward to the steering wheel and. starting the car. "It is on the way back to your hotel, senor," he said as the car drove away from the curb, "and I will not charge for just the showing. If you take a girl, then I ask for money."

Tom was grinning.

"What the hell," he said, "as a writer, I should go see what the place is like," remembering a story by the famous writer where the main character fights a British sailor in Istanbul over a Turkish girl dancer. Tom liked the part where the main character hits the sailor in the jaw, then says to himself that the punch had everything he, the main character, had, and it did not floor the sailor, and that it was going to be a long fight. Tom thought about those lines for a long time; then he realized there was no fear in the statement and that was why be liked it.

"Senor is a writer?"

"I'm trying to be one," Tom said smiling at the question.

"There is a world known writer, here senor, in Mexico City. He lives over on the avenue called Rio Mississippi. They made a film out in the Sierra Madre mountains from his book of men seeking gold. The actor, Bogart,was the star. Maybe, you would like to visit him? As a writer."

"I know the movie, but the writer," Tom said quietly trying to recall if he ever heard the name, "I've never heard anything about the guy. I have no idea who he is."

"He is widely known, senor, and has many visitors."

Tom shook his head, and saw outside, they were passing the Prado Hotel, and then they turned off Avenue Juarez, suddenly.

They climbed out of the car in front of a stone house with a high wall, Tom following Sylvester through an iron gate and up a walkway. A man in a shiney dark-blue suit, who looked like a wrestler, held open the door. Tom, smiling, followed Sylvester, and the bull-neck man up a stairway carpeted in black.

Upstairs, they came into a living room with overstuffed chairs and couches, lighted with dim blue light, with music playing low. Girls in tight dresses were dancing with fat, older men, and some of the girls were sitting with the older men on the couches. The floor was carpeted, except near a short bar, where they were dancing on the bare wood.

Tom and Sylvester sat down on a couch near the bar.

"They do not like," Sylvester whispered to Tom, "that you do not wear a suit, senor. I told them you are a rich norte American writer, and you are here to look."

Tom whispered back, "Okay, I think I've seen enough." Then looking around, said, "This place must really be expensive."

"It is one of the best in the city, senor," Sylvester whispered. "These are men of importance. Many are officials of the government. Some are even generals."

Smiling, Tom whispered, "Why does Mexico have so many generals?"

"The country, senor, is made with military districts," Sylvester whispered. "Each district has a general in charge — in command."

"Very interesting," Tom whispered, "but I think we should go."

"You should have a drink, senor," Sylvester said looking around quickly. "They have the scotch-whiskey."

A man in military uniform came out a hallway opening, buttoning his tunic over his belly. Tom watched as the uniformed man walked to the bar, after glancing in his direction.

"Let's get out of here," Tom whispered hoarsely.

"Senor, there may be trouble if you buy no drinks. They may not believe you are a rich American writer — or they may think you are — an informer."

"All right," Tom whispered, "but just one drink and. then we go. I want my scotch on ice."

"I will need money, senor. One-hundred pesos."

"Damn," Tom said and handed Sylvester the money, and watching him go to the bar, shook his head.

A girl with long legs and high heels came out of the hallway opening, looked around, then came over and sat down next to Tom.

"Hello," she said quietly, "my name is Amber." She was wearing a dress that looked like flannel, and she smoothed the brown cloth over her thighs, slowly, with her hands.

"You want to go with a girl in there?" she asked pointing to the hallway opening. "I go with you."

"I don't have much money," Tom said smiling.

"Maybe, you don't want me?" she said and leaned against Tom. "I treat you nice, if you go with me."

Tom saw a thin scar on the side of her chin, that pulled her lip down when she smiled.

"I like you," Tom said smiling, "but I don't have…"

She leaned against him to cover her hand between his legs.

"You and me," she said nodding toward the doorway.

"I don't have enough ... dinero," Tom said, thinking that would discourage her and end the soliciting.

"You have how much?" she asked, moving her body against his, the scent of her rising in his nose, exciting him.

"Twelve ... American," he said, figuring she was much more expensive than that. Her slim body moved across his legs, covering her hand, that took his, and slowly rubbed her it over breasts that were bare under the dress.

When she felt Tom getting aroused, she got up, "I will ask regarding the twelve dollars," she whispered, and went into the hallway opening.

Tom looked for Sylvester at the bar, but he was gone. Tom stood up and started for the stairway down, when the girl came out of the hallway.

"Yes," she whispered, taking Tom's arm, "twelve dollars."

"But I have a wife," Tom whispered to her.

"Come with me. They will beat me, and send me off to work the hotels out in the country. I will be an animal to them."

Pulling his arm, she lead Tom into a high-ceilinged bedroom with a large double bed, a large round mirror over a dresser, and a bed table with a lamp that shone red. The drapes were red also, and a leather hassock by the door, was a dark red.

The girl, smiling, held out her hand for the money and Tom gave it to her. She went out the door, then came back, closed the door softly, and pushed the hassock with her foot against the door.

Tom stood watching as 8he took off the dress and laid it carefully over the chair in front of the dresser.

Then she stepped up on the hassock, holding her arms out to Tom to undress what left she had on. When he did, standing naked, she motioned for him to undress, which he did.

"I know," Tom said when he picked her up off the cassock, "that I'm going to be punished for this," and carrying her to the bed and gently setting her down, added "but I can't help it."

She put her arms around his neck when they lay next to one another, then said, "Kiss me."

"God, you're beautiful," he whispered after kissing her, his face next to here. "You're so long ... and beautiful ... I can't stop myself.

She was smiling.

Later, in the car outside the Ronfels Hotel, Tom handed Sylvester two American dollars over the front seat.

"It is customary to give five dollars when you go with a girl, senor."

Tom opened the car back door, and had one leg out, when he said, "That's all I have left, besides, you kept the money I gave you for drinks."

When he was out of the car, Tom heard Sylvester shouting in Spanish just before he slammed the door.

Walking into the hotel lobby, Tom check for the medicine check bottle in his sport jacket pocket,by pressing his hand against it, outside the pocket.

"At least I did one thing right today," feeling the guilt of going to that house descending on him.

The night clerk, who gave him the room key, was not the one who wrote the name of the medicine and the pharmacy address on the hotel card.

Upstairs, Tom entered the room quietly. The bed lamp on the stand next to Virginia, made her red hair shine on the pillow where she was sleeping.

"I must be crazy," Tom said to himself, looking down on her. He shook his head, slowly, "Forgive me Ginny."

When he set the bottle of medicine on the nightstand, he saw the clock; It was just after twelve.

He undressed quietly, then took a shower before getting into bed.

Chapter 20

Tom came out of the bathroom, the next morning, after showering and shaving, and saw Virginia sitting up in bed.

"How's it going, Gin? You feeling any better?" he asked sitting down on the bed next to her.

"Terrible," she said making a sour face. "And I'm as weak as a kitten."

Tom kissed her forehead.

"I called home last night, Tom," she said putting her hand on his arm, "and there's some bad news."

"What, Gin? Is it something about our families?"

"Tom, Karl Rolfson had an accident, and he's dead," she said,putting both arms around his neck.

"No-o, not Karl. No-o," Tom said and sat up straight. "He's got so much to give to the world," Tom said, and then remembered what he said in that house last night; that he would be punished for what he did with that girl. "It not true. I can't believe Karl is dead, Not Kar-l."

"My father went to the funeral. He talked to Niels, Karl's oldest son. He said Karl went to the Griswold Sporting Goods store downtown, and outside, standing on the curb, was hit by a bus mirror that sticks out so the driver can see back along the bus. Karl had massive head injuries and died in the hospital in less than an hour."

"Gin, when did all this happen?"

"A week, then three days," she said slowly, "eleven, twelve days ago," she said quietly. Tom sat with his elbows on his knees, looking at the floor. "That was about the time we left Fort Lauderdale, when I quit my job on the newspaper."

"The son said he was going to have Karl cremated and bury the ashes up at the cabin," Virginia said. "Karl's wife wanted to bury him in Detroit, but gave in."

"Anybody, anybody but Karl. Why him?" Tom said, still looking at the floor.

"The son said Karl had bought a gas lamp, a Coleman lamp, at Griswold's,and was carrying it when he was struck. It was for the cabin, the son said; the police found it and gave it to the son. It was still in the box."

"No more, Gin. Don't tell me any more," Tom said, sat up, then laid back across the bed, Virginia pulling her feet up. "I can't take any more. What a shock."

"I'm going to miss him too, Tom. He was always so nice to me, and he was so-o distinguished. Father is going the legal work for the family, and I think they are going to sue the city about the bus."

"Things like this are not supposed to happen, Gin," Tom said arching his right arm over his eyes. "Today I was going down to the restaurant and write a few pages. You know, like the famous writer did in Paris,when the apartment got too cold? I thought that was all a writer had to do — just write — not worry about friends and relatives."

"I'm sorry about Karl, Tom. And I'm sorry I'm not much company," Virginia said quietly. "I know here we are in Mexico City and you want to go to a bullfight, and I'd like to see the floating gardens; I know you'll like the musicians on a boat in the gardens."

"I was going to write today because it's raining steadily outside," Tom said taking his arm away from his eyes, rolling up on his elbow to face Virginia.

"It's not much fun here for you, is it Tom?"

"You could say that, yes, Ginny. I really feel bad about you being so sick, babe; you're my right arm. But, I'm sure you'll be better — in a day or two. You'll see," he said and squeezed her leg under the blanket.

"You can still go down to the hotel restaurant and write — if you want, Tom. I can't eat; I can't hold anything down."

"Give me a kiss, Gin."

She leaned down and. kissed him slowly, then said, "But that's <u>all</u> I can do, honey."

Tom did not smile, but said in a professional tone, "I've decided to scrap the book about Germany, the army, and all that. Instead, I want to write a novel — a love story — about a young man and woman, who are not married, and who travel to Mexico, and vow to seperate if they ever stop loving one another."

He laid back down on the bed looking up at the ceiling, as if there were a message written up there.

"That sounds delightful, Tom; honest. Don't tell me any more, honey ... I want to wait and read it." She slid her feet toward him under the blanket. "To tell you the truth, I didn't like the story about Germany and the army too depressing."

"Now you tell me, yikes," Tom said, throwing up his arms. "Oh well, better late then never. But next time I ask your opinion, please tell me truthfully what you think, okay? I really need to know what your opinion is."

"I will, Tom, honest," Virginia said putting her hand on his arm. "I just didn't want to — upset you — you were so involved in the writing work." When she took her hand away, he could still feel her feet on his shoulder, under the blanket.

"You couldn't help it, babe," he said and waved his right hand at the ceiling. "You just did what you thought was right."

"Tom, honey, while we're being so truthful, with one another today, I have something serious to talk to you a-bout. You won't like it."

"What is it, Gin?" he said,rolling up on his side to face her, taking hold of her leg under the blanket.

"Yesterday," she said and put her hand on the side of his face, "when I was so sick — I felt — afraid. For some reason,it just came over me when I was laying here. I became so afraid ... it was as if something bad happened.

"Afraid ... of what, honey?"

"After you went out, I slept for a while, then I woke up, and I had this terrible feeling that you were gone — and I was alone. I was afraid you wouldn't come back, or something, and it really frightened me."

"Well, I did. come back," Tom said,flushing red when he thought of last night in the house where Sylvester took him. "You're being silly, Gin. You were just feeling low because of your medical problems. You were depressed."

"Yes," Virginia said, "taking her hand away from his face, "it was a mental feeling. Something as if you didn't understand me any more... something pushed between us ."

"Stop it, Gin," Tom said shaking his head.

"Tom, your face is burning. My hands are hot from your face."

"Maybe I caught that disease you had.."

"I hope not, honey." She put a hand on his shoulder. "Tom, I know how important your fiction writing is to you. And, I know a writer has to go places, and do things, and see a lot of things ... "she said raising her hands to her face. "But, there doesn't seem to be much room for me."

"Gin, we hashed all this out before we left Fort Lauderdale. We agreed I could leave the newspaper and have a novel-length stay in Mexico. Now, all we got to do is find a place — a fishing village, or something, and you can make friends, and ..."

"I know, Tom, I agreed. But when I was scared, I telephoned home. Honey, I want to go home."

Tom sat up straight.

"But we just arrived here. Don't you want to see those floating gardens? If you don't like the city here, we can go to Acapulco, or…"

"No, Tom. I would feel better — if I were closer to home." When she saw Tom's shoulders drop she knew he was disappointed. "Honey, you like this kind of life, this wandering all over the place, but I'm not like that. I have to have a home. And Tom, you can write at our home as long as you want. I promise."

"In a few days, you'll feel better, Gin. Maybe then, you would like to take a look around this country, and …"

"Tom, ple-ase.

He stood up and walked over to the dresser and picked up his camera, looking close at the lens settings.

"When do you want — to go?" he asked.

"Tomorrow, honey.

He inhaled, then exhaled, and set the camera back on the dresser.

"Okay, Gin. Tomorrow it is then," he said turning around.

"Don't be sad, Tom," she said getting up from the bed, putting her arms around his waist. "It'll all work honey. You'll see."

Brownsville, Texas, was up ahead in the dark, as they drove the next day.

"Tom, you've been quiet all day, ever since we left Mexico City. I could hear the gears grinding in your head, so I left you alone."

Tom looked over a Virginia for a quick moment, when the lights of an oncoming car shone on her.

"I know," he said. "I've been doing a lot of thinking. About the book I want to begin ... and some of the things I want to do when I get home,"

"Tom, you mean when <u>we</u> get home, don't you?"

"Yes, babe. That's what I meant, You know that."

"Have you decided on what type of work you want to do?"

"Yes. A novel about ..." he said, adjusting the car side mirror,so the truck headlights behind would be deflected.

"Tom, I mean work that gives a paycheck at the end of the week."

"I thought we agreed that I could go on writing my new book. I mean, that's what I understood in Mexico City before we left this morning; I would be free to write for as long as I want."

"You can't change my mind, Tom. You have to be practical. I thought I explained it a breakfast. We must have a steady income, and if you writing does that, you can write as much as you want."

"I'm glad your stomach is better, Gin. I'm glad you feel better, and can eat." He kept looking ahead at the dark road. "But, I can't sell a novel unless I write a novel, then send it to a publisher who will buy it."

"Tom, where are we going to live when we get home?"

He looked at her for a moment in the headlights of an oncoming car. Her face was set, looking forward.

"Well, Gin,pheasant season will open next month. Then, after comes duck shooting season..."

"What are you saying, Tom?' You're not working, but hunting?"

"I'd like to live on Harsen's Island, Gin. It's almost on the great international flyway for migrating waterfowl.

"No, Gin. I'll write in the morning; that's the work part, then shoot ducks when they move to feed in the evening before dark. Or, visa versa."

"And,Thomas Cohill, how do you plan to pay the rent, and buy incidentals? Groceries, for one, and not to mention such luxuries as furniture, for another?"

"By selling what I write, babe."

"Well, your first book keeps coming back. Just what do you plan to live on — until you finish this new one?" She put her hands over her eyes. "What kind of a future are we going to have — if we waste these young years? And how are we going to live later — in our golden years?

"Gin, you're looking at it from just <u>one</u> side — one point of view failure. You should try to look at the positive side."

"How can I do that, Tom?"

"Just look at the situation through <u>my</u> eyes, babe."

"I don't understand what you are saying, Tom."

"Well, Gin, what is a man if he doesn't do what he wants to do? Life is short, and it doesn't give much latitude."

"You sound like that senator, that politician running for president. The Catholic one who will never get elected."

"Kennedy."

"Yes, he's the one. He says stuff like that. Courage in the face of disaster, and all that. But, Tom, that is just rhetoric. When Monday morning comes, how are you going to pay the bills?"

"I think he has a good chance of being elected; Kennedy," Tom said. "He understands stuff like a man who chickens-out, puts aside what he really wants to do, just to be secure, is failing himself. He even wrote a book about courage."

"You're being totally unrealistic, Tom."

"When a guy reaches thirty ... forty ... and he looks back over his life and sees what he <u>could</u> have been ... an artist, a painter ... instead of a shoe salesman, he knows he wasted his whole life. He feels he could have made a better contribution ... to humanity. You see my drift, Gin?"

"Okay, Tom, but what about a man's wife, and children, if he has any? Don't you think this man is selfish?"

"You might say that about either side of the arguement," Tom said, taking a quick look at her. "It's a matter of choice. '

He saw her shaking her head in the light from the oncoming cars.

"We keep going around and around., Tom, and we don't settle a thing. We are both pulling our seperate ways, and my whole happiness is falling apart in front of my eyes, and I can't do anything. I can't stop it."

"Gin, you're being too dramatic. No wonder you feel sick."

"We've got to do something, Tom, I can't go on like this. I can't live like this."

"We're on our way back home, honey," Tom said feeling the desperation in her voice, and it scared him. "When we get home we'll think straighter. We'll work things out. You'll see. Even if it means me going back to newspaper writing."

Chapter 21

Sunday morning, Tom was up at first light, hurrying to start fixing the steering on his boat. In the kitchen he filled the coffee maker to twelve cups, and while it perculated, he took a cantalope from the refrigerator, halved it, scooped out the seeds, then sliced it, and put it back.

He and Virginia bought this house on Harsen's Island, and had a baby girl they named Nancy, all during the past three years he worked a reporting job for the Suburban Bureau of The Detroit News He used the forty thousand dollars his parents gave him and Virginia, as a wedding present, for the down payment on the house, and paid the mortgage with the earnings from the newspaper job.

The house was a sprawling three-bedroom ranch style structure with a wide fireplace in the living room, and oversize windows all around. He could sit, writing at his desk, looking at long freighter ships gliding past outside in the North Channel, the empties upbound to Lake Huron, the loaded ones, downbound, heading south to Lake Saint Clair,

Then Virginia inherited almost a third of a million dollars from her father's estate. He had a second heart attack and died four days before last Christmas.

Virginia's mother was given the lion's share of the funds, her husband, Calvin Handley, accumulated, along with the house in Birmingham. But, the mother had chronic arthritis in her knees and ankles, and was barely able to walk. It was a family agreement, that Virginia would over see any needs the mother had since the oldest daughter was away studying at the Sorbonne. The lawyer rather knew it would be difficult for Virginia, married, and now with the child, to run her mother's household affairs, and gave her the money as sort of an incentive to do a good job.

This past spring, with the new money, Tom quit the reporting job when the house mortgage was paid off, and bought a used boat from a neighbor. He still had a part-time writing job; his local fishing report, stringer writing, turned into feature writing for the same outdoor magazine.

The only time Tom could write fiction was on the week ends while he worked for the newspaper. Now, the Handley money freed him to write fiction full time.

He begun to work on a new book recently, an adventure story about a smuggler with a boat, similar to the famous writer's novel set in Key West with the Harry Morgan

character.

Now, walking outside of the house through the kitchen screen door, Tom looked over at the morning sun.

"It's going to be another one like yesterday, a real scorch-one today," he said, and took a sip of coffee from the mug he brought, then looked down at the tops of his boat shoes getting soaked from the dew on the long grass.

At the boathouse, the door made a loud rust-crunch noise when he pulled it open. Inside, Tom stepped aboard his twenty-seven foot Bertram, then reached down and pulled open the motor hatch. He drank down the coffee, set the mug on the gunnel, and climbed down next to the engines. Since buying the boat this spring, he had been over every inch of it. The craft was not quite six years old.

He had planned to go drift-fishing for pickrel this morning, to catch today's dinner for the bar-b-que. Virginia bought sweet corn on the cob and Idaho potatoes and wanted to bake them with the pickrel.

But the boat steering arm was sheared off back under the stern deck, and Tom had to install a new length of pipe to the rudder post to make it work before going out.

The pipe broke last night down on the lake near the Grosse Pointe Yacht Club, where there was a fireworks display for the up coming July Fourth holiday. On the way home in the dark, some boat-drunk crossed Tom's bow, Virginia screamed, holding the baby, and he jammed the rudder so hard, the pipe arm on the rudder broke as they lurched starboard. Tom heard the snap and knew what happened; to get home, be used the two engines, right and left, to steer. No more boat rides, Virginia said, ever, for her and Nancy.

Taking a flashlight from the toolbox, he held the beam on the broken pipe as he crawled in the dark bilge with a new length of pipe and a pipe wrench.

After installing the new pipe, he was connecting the cable-clamp to the end of the pipe pulling the cable tight when he heard Ginny, "Tom-m!"

"Just finishing up," he shouted,his face moved back toward the motor hatch opening.

"Tom," she said in an even tone, "Hemingway is dead. It's on the television news, He shot himself out there in ... Montana, early this morning. Suicide."

"Idaho," Tom said chocking, as if punched in the stomach, unable to breath. "His house is in Ketchum, Idaho."

"What does it matter <u>where</u> he shot himself," she said quietly, like an aside in a play, and then paused before she said "Honey, I knew you would want to know."

"Okay, " he said quietly. "Thanks for telling."

He crawled backward into the light of the open hatch.

Sitting up, he switched off the flashlight, and looked up.

"I know you feel bad," she said from the doorway of the boathouse. She was still in her bathrobe. "I know what he meant to you as a writer. Honey, maybe if you ate something, you'd feel better ... ah, I am making pancakes."

" I don't think so, Gin. I'm not hungry," Tom said, climbing up from the open hatch, hooking his finger through the coffee mug handle, then looking into the empty container. "I need something strong to drink. Something that will make me numb."

"You look terrible, honey," Virginia said putting her hand on his arm. "I've got to run ... the baby."

Tom handed her the mug as she started out, and turned to the sink, where they always cleaned the fish they caught, and began washing up.

"She's a gem," he said. "She understands everything," he said soaping his arm, "and she has a hell of a lot on her plate, these days, with this family."

The sun was hotter now, he could feel the heat against his face,as he walked up to the house and opened the screen door.

Nancy had more syrup in her bowl than pancake, he saw bending over to kiss her on top of the head,and make a noise. She smiled, looking at him, and he made another noise.

"Tom," Virginia said "I found a dozen frozen perch in the freezer. We have enough," she said flipping pan cakes on the griddle, "if you don't want to go fishing today. We've got plenty for a bar-b-que."

"Are you sure, babe?"Tom said as he straightened up, looking at her. "I know you prefer pickrel."

"It's <u>all</u> fish," she said and turned back to the griddle.

"Okay," he said, " I'll go out in a day or so and relfill the freezer."

"You sure you don't want to sit down and eat something? Virginia asked again.

"I'm really not hungry," he said, "and I want to check the news. Thanks,Gin."

He stepped out of the kitchen and into the brightness of the sitting room on the sunny side of the house facing east. He snapped on the television set and dropped back on the leather couch.

The news spokesman was saying that President Kennedy was inspiried by Hemingway to write a book about "Grace Under Pressure," Hemingway's definition of courage in time of crisis. Tom smiled., thinking Grace was, also Hemingway's mother's name, whom Hemingway claimed strenously to hate.

"To-om," Virginia said coming into the sitting room wiping her hands with a towel , "Why don't you go have a drink someplace honey, It'll make you feel better."

"Is there anything here?" he asked still looking at television as if waiting to hear it was all a mistake in regards to the death report.

"I looked," she said, "there's only half a bottle of Burgundy. Oh, I hate to see you crushed like this,Tom. I wish there was something I could ..."

"I'll go down to the Idle Hour and have a few," he said without looking at her. "But I want to watch the newscast first. For a minute."

"If you want anything ..." she started, but stopped, then waved the towel realizing she could not help Tom,and went back to the kitchen.

When the news changed to a different subject than the Hemingway death, Tom turned the television set off and went to the sliding glass door, out of the sitting room onto the grass back to the garage.

Reaching for the Jeep keys, that hung over the work bench, piled with garden tools, Tomsaw the bota bag hanging on its string from the edge of a shelf. It was the wine bag most American skiiers used when they want to act European. Tom had seen a lot of pictures of Hemingway drinking from a wine bag, and he had an idea.

"No better way to salute Hemingway than with a wine bag," Tom said quietly. "'Inhaling the red'" Hemingway called it ,Tom read somewhere Tom read somewhere in a magazine showing a picture of the famous writer arching the wine stream to his mouth from a bag held out at arms length.

Tom took the bag and the Jeep keys and climbed into the vehicle. As he was backing out, passing the kitchen window, he sounded the horn twice, so Gin would know he was going.

" 'It's all fish,' " Tom said to himself, and laughed, driving on the road that followed the shoreline. "All is fish."

He always liked driving here on this stretch of road, passing the closed-down Coast Guard station that faced the narrow shipping channel, called the North Channel. Across the road, to the west, were the Flats, which in reality were simply a mile wide shallow bay filled with high reeds. The bay opened out onto Lake Saint Clair. The Indian name was Muskamoot Bay for this prime fishing and waterfowl swamp. The bay was not part of the Ojibwa reservation across the North Channel over in Canada.

Tom remembered an incident last fall, when duck hunting out in the reeds,that he did not even tell Virginia about; an incident, he thought, involved Hemingway. It was sort of a mystical, or religious, incident, involving the famous writer, who ended it all this Sunday morning.

The day before going duck hunting, reading a news magazine at home, Tom remembered seeing a photograph of the famous writer, showing an old man with white hair and beard, gaunt, and smiling with almost a childish expression on his face. The article said the famous writer was admitted to the Mayo Clinic in Minneapolis for treatment of hypertension.

Tearing the page out of the magizine, Tom had crumpled it into a ball and threw it into the fireplace blaze. That was not the famous writer he knew in the photograph.

The next morning, Tom remembered sitting in a duck blind out in the bay, listening to the rustle of the dry cattail reeds, watching for ducks in the high blue sky. High winds made it a bright day. There was skim ice at dawn, and Tom rembered he waded slowly, careful not to puncture his hip boots on the sharp edges of broken ice.

It was not a good day for duck hunting, the clear November blue sky made the ducks fly high out of shotgun range. Cloudy, even rainey weather,made the ducks fly lower, making better shooting.

It was just the opposite weather for pheasant hunting. In wet weather the pheasants roost, stay put, and are hard to find. Tom had bagged nine this season, near the limit. A he had to smile, thinking of the red fox he shot for the farmer in Richmond, Michigan, who said the fox was eating his chickens, and was suspected of eating the family cat on the back porch, and in payment for being allowed to hunt his farm, if the fox was spotted, shoot it.

When he was walking in those corn fields in Richmond, Tom began thinking, remembering, that he thought about a hunting story written by the famous writer that involved ice.

Rain and sleet had frozen everything in the famous writer's short story, and the main character, the famous writer himself, and a young red dog, where out partridge hunting, the young dog slipping and falling on the ice coating covering the ground; the bushes and trees were covered with ice and hanging down. But what stuck in Tom's mind was the one word the famous writer used to describe the ice coating; 'varnished.'

Tom remembered wishing out there near Richmond walking the field, that he could write, just the right word like that.

He wished it again now, shifting his weight, sitting in the duck blind, trying to rest his back.

There came a dull wump, wump sound of a shotgun being fired in the distance, out over the water and high cattails in front of Tom's blind.

Suddenly, two black ducks appeared, coming toward Tom. When he stood up to shoot, they flaired., almost stopping midair, the sun glinting on them, turning them golden for an instant, as they turned.

Tom fired and the lead duck crumpled. He saw it falling as he racked the ejector of his Remington 870, then taking aim at the second duck. Following, then leading the flying bird in his sight, he fired, and the second duck's right wing dropped,as it rolled over to that side, falling.

"Good shooting," a voice shouted across the water.

"You bet," Tom said, looking, but not able to see anyone out in the reeds. Then he smiled, "Maybe it was Hemingway," he said shaking his head. "You never know."

Tom remembered he pictured the famous writer up in Minnesota, under this same high blue sky, only further north, looking out the window of the Mayo Clinic at the fall colors of the countryside.

"You can bet," Tom said out loud, "he is wishing he could be outdoors hunting.

Wading in the reeds, Tom found the first duck, and while pushing it into his rubber-lined haversack, continued searching for the second. He stepped up on a patch of high ground, the was the end of a dyke, and spotted the second duck.

When he was wading back to the high ground with the duck, a coldness hit the back of his head, like a punch, and the cold sunk down his spine, giving him a shivver.

"What the hell was that?" he said touching the back of his head. "Felt like someone hit me. What the hell?"

He shook his head and stepped up on the dyke. Looking up, there was only the open blue sky.

"It had to be Hemingway," he said quietly, " and I better keep my mouth shut about it." He remembered thinking for a minute, and saying, "No one would believe me anyhow."

The Idle Hour bar loomed ahead when Tom turned onto the gravel road. It was built to look like an old castle, and was right at the edge of the North Channel. In the

Prohibition Era of the nineteen thirties it was a blind pig, the bootleg booze brought from Canada across the narrow channel, Wealthy people came to the old castle back then to drink, and. there was gambling too. The building had bedrooms and a swimming pool, but only the bar was used now, and the rest of the old castle was slowly falling apart.

Tom entered the bar carrying the wine bag by the string. When the door closed behind him, the bright of the parking lot outside was gone, and he stood for a moment in the dark barroom. The only light was at the far end of the room from the windows that looked out on the channel. There were tables along the windows,where people sat with their drinks, and watched the long freighters go by. There was a group sitting there now.

"Hey, Tom," Ralph, the bartender said, "what's with the wine bag?"

As Tom's eyes adjusted to the dark, he saw a man and woman sitting three stools away at the bar, and over by the windows, the group was all women at the table.

"It's a souvenir from Spain," Tom said and held up the bag. "My wife bought it over there on a student trip."

"What are you going to do with it?" Ralph asked, wiping a glass then holding it up to the light from the window, looking for spots.

"Well, I was going to use it to make a tribute to Hemingway," Tom said sitting down on a barstool in front of Ralph. "He died today, out there in Sun Valley."

"O-oh, that's right George," the woman three stools away from Tom said to her companion at the bar, "I heard it on the news on television. Hemingway, the famous writer, shot himself this morning."

"Suicide? Ralph asked looking at Tom.

"Yeah," Tom said, "With a shotgun."

"I'll be darn," Ralph said and turned to set the glass on the back bar. "What can I get you to drink?" he asked facing Tom again.

"A Papa Double Daiquiri," Tom said said smiling, setting the wine bag on the bar. "That's the rum drink Hemingway always drinks at La Floridita bar in Havana."

"You know we ain't got no drink like that," Ralph said. "This is the United States, not no Havana."

"Okay," Tom said smiling, "make it scotch on the rocks. A double."

He watched as Ralph poured a generous J & B scotch portion into a wide glass and set it in front of him. He saw Ralph look at the bag. It was bothering Ralph, but Tom

sat, silent, sipping the scotch., trying not to laugh.

Finally, Ralph asked, "What you planning to do with the winebag?

"Drink wine from it as a tribute to Hemingway's life,"

Tom said picking the bag up by the nozzle. "You got any bottles of wine, Ralph?"

"We sell wine by the glass only," he said holding up a bottle by the neck from the back bar, then setting it back. "and it's a dollar and a quater a glass."

"I need a bottle of wine at least," Tom said taking a five dollar bill out of his pants pocket and sliding it to Ralph across the bar. "The bag won't work with just a little wine," Tom said,and took a long drink from the scotch glass.

"Look," Ralph said, "I don't have no license to sell by the bottle," He walked to the cash register, and when came back and set Tom's change on the bar, said, "I'm strictly a by-the-glass business."

Tom finished the scotch in his glass, and motioned for a refill.

"What kind of wine you got back there?" Tom said watching his glass on the bar being filled by Ralph.

"It's white wine," Ralph said.

"Let me see," Tom said, twirling his empty glass.

Ralph handed him the bottle, and said, "I don't want no tricks, Tom."

"Liebfraumilch," Tom said reading the label. "That's a German wine, and it's kind of sour," he said as Ralph took the bottle back. "You got any Burgundy?"

"Strickly by the glass," Ralph said, putting the bottle on the back bar counter.

"I was in Sun Valley last summer," the elderly woman down the bar from Tom said. "I saw Hemingway's house out by the river there in Ketchum. I was there in the summer, not the winter ski season." She turned to her elderly man companion, "The house was plane, nothing fancy."

"That's where Hemingway shot himself," Tom said, looking down the bar at her. "Right in that house — in the foyer."

"Where?" Ralph asked.

"He shot himself in the foyer," Tom repeated.

"Keep it clean, okay Tom."

"By the front door, Ralph. In the foyer, by the front door, Hemingway shot himself with a double barrel shotgun."

"That's so sad," the woman said. "And he was so famous." She took a drink, slowly, her glass, thinking. "And they made movies from his books, I remember the movies, back before World War two. Everything he did was so much publicized. He'll be so much missed by people who read his books. And he lived in all the famous places. People all over the world read his books. It's so sad."

Her companion, George,asked her, "How old was he?"

"He was sixty—one," Tom blurted out, the scotch on his empty stomach taking effect. "I think, sixty—one."

"Such a shame," the woman said. "He lived such a wonderful life. I wonder what was wrong that he did something so tragic?"

"Maybe," Tomsaid quietly, "he felt he was no longer in control — of his destiny. It must of been something like that."

"Sixty—one isn't very old," George said thoughtfully.

"It's the end of a literary era Tom said. "We should celebrate the man who wrote the walnut prose we all like to read. We should drink a salute to the fallen author."

Tom held up the wine bag.

"You better calm down, Tom," Ralph said quietly. He was standing opposite Tom across the bar. "If you don't— you're out of here. I mean it."

"Ralph, sell me a bottle of wine," Tom said. "Any kind."

"Only by the glass, pal."

"I'll pay," the woman from down the bar, she waved her arm. "Bartender, what ever you ask for a bottle of wine, I'll pay it."

"Now Doris we don't want to get invol..."

"You mean that?" Ralph said,not wanting to miss the opportunity to make extra money, now, with more customers asking.

"Of course I do," she said. "It's symbolic of the Hemingway life in Spain. Wine in a bota bag is a trib..."

"Doris," her companion George said, leaning to talk into her ear, "maybe we drank too much this afternoon, and..."

"Nonsense, George," she said leaning away from him, "I'll purchase the wine as a tribute to an exceptional life. A literary life, a literary talent consummated."

"Doris," he said, "I—I've never heard you talk like this before."

"Do you <u>like</u> it? My dead husband liked it."

"Yeah, I do-o like it," George said. "Yes. I never saw this side of you, Doris. This Hemingway character really struck a cord in you. You're so — lively." He waved his arm. "Hell, I'll buy the wine. A bottle of wine bartender,"

"That's very nice of you, George," she said and put her hand on his arm. "Very nice."

Ralph brought a bottle of Burgundy from the shelf behind the bar and set it in front of Tom.

"I'll only charge them twenty bucks for this full bottle," he said to Tom who was smiling. "I'm giving them a break on the price."

"The red wine makes the whole thing perfect," Tom said as he was unscrewing the part of the cap that opened for filling the bag.

Ralph turned the corkscrew into the cork, then holding the bottle by the neck, pulled on the corkscrew, the cork made a <u>pop</u> when it came out.

"Here's the money," George said putting a twenty dollar bill on the bar. He was excited and his hand slapped down, like a card player. He slid the money toward Ralph and put his wallet away.

"Good for you George," Doris said smiling at him. "This is very heart warming," she said sweetly. "We are all working to make our tribute — or wake — a fitting one,"

After Tom finished pouring most of the wine from the bottle into the bag, he replaced the cap screwing it tight, then pulled the nozzle cap off that swung down on a short red string.

"To Ernest Hemingway, an artist in both writing and living," Tom said holding up the wine bag. "Salute."

Holding up the bag at arms length he squeezed it slightly. A spurt of red hit the side of his chin, then moved in a stream into his open mouth as he held his head back.

"Bravo," Doris said. "Hemingway, he showed them all how it was done." Then she took a dainty sip of her drink.

George was standing now since he put the money on the bar, and his eyes were locked on Doris.

Tom, his head back, saw the customers at the window tables watching, so he continued with the wine bag a little longer.

When he finally brought the bag down, he winced at the the strong flavor of the newly tanned leather of the inside of the bag, and quickly took two swallows of the melted ice from the scotch glass to kill the bitter taste.

"This bag is in a class by itself," he said and took another swallow of the scotch—water.

"Hey," Ralph said to Tom, "either drink one drink or the other. Not both. You're going to fall off the stool you keep that up."

Tom, grinning, picked up that bag, "To all <u>aficionados</u> of Hemingway the world over," and took another drink.

"Wonderful," Doris said clapping. "Such <u>elan</u>."

George began clapping too.

"You show them kiddo," he said. "You show them."

Four women at a window table were laughing now at Tom with the wine bag. One started clapping. "Give him another bottle of wine," one of the women said. "What an imaginative gesture for Hemingway's passing."

"You serious?" Ralph said ,and when the lady held up a hand like at a auction, he said, "okay, it's twenty a bottle."

He uncorked another bottle of Burgundy wine. When Tom refilled the wine bag with it, he held the bag out toward his new audience.

"Anyone want to try it?" he said in aloud voice. "It'll curl your hair. It's not for the feint hearted. Only the big and two hearted."

"I would," Doris said softly. "I always wanted to, but wasn't able — to bring myself to do it."

"Here you go," Tom,standing up and handing her the bag ,stumbled when his foot hit the leg of her barstool.

George flinched, but did not speak.

Doris held the bag up for a short taste. “O-oh,” she wrinkled her nose, “thats sour. Too bitter for me” she said and gave the bag back to Tom.”I prefer Tom Collins.”

When Tom offered George the bag, he said, “Not me,I’m more conventional. I prefer drinking from a glass.”

“I’ll try it,” the woman at the window table said in a loud voice. She was the one who paid. “I loved reading Hemingway. And I love his style — in everything.”

All four of the women at the table were laughing, they had been drinking margaritas.

“Nancy Pelkys’ reached her limit on margaritas,’ Tom heard one of the women say.

“Librarians are all like that,” another woman said.

Tom, looking at the red-haired Nancy Pelky, tripped over the extended legs of one woman sitting sideways at the table.

The wine bag hit the floor, wine squirting rapidly.

Tom reached for the bag saying quietly, “Don’t want to waste good wine.” He was still on his knee when he offered the bag up to Nancy. “There’s not much left, but Hemingway will understand.”

The women were not laughing now, Tom’s fall had intimidated them.

Taking the bag, Nancy said, “I feel obligated to have a drink.“ Holding out the saging bag in front of her face she said in a steady and firm voice, “Here’s a farewell arm to the sun that also riseth and tolls for thee and the old man and the sea. And may your Kilimanjaro snows always be up in Michigan.” The wine squirted directly into her mouth, but she abruptly lowered the bag.

“That was terrific,” Tom said. He was climbing into a chair at the table next to the group of women. “A better tribute couldn’t ... be ... made.

“Wow,” Nancy said putting the wine bag on the table. “That wine’s got a real sour taste.”

The women all laughed when she made a face and a gesture that she would like to spit the wine out.

“The whole world agrees,” Tom said with his head, down, his shoulders dropped, “sour is the loss. Hemingway gone.”

The women were avoiding looking at him at the next table.

“You’re going to be gone too,” Ralph said mopping the spilled wine behind Tom’s chair. “I called your wife and told her to come and get you. You’re causing too much ruckus.“

“Want to drink to Hemingway from the winebag, Ralph?”

“No, and neither should you.”

“A literary star is gone,” Tom said. “Forever.”

“That ain’t got nothing to do with me,” Ralph said. “And I don’t like this mess.”

Chapter 22

In August, 1966, Tom took his family in a new air-condition Chevrolet station wagon to Yellowstone National Park, and while he was photographing the "Old Faithful" geyser, Virginia said, "We are getting closer and closer to Sun Valley, aren't we Tom? I've been west before."

She was holding the newest daughter, Caroline, while Nancy, held on to her mother's leg.

Tom looked away from his camera, "Honey, what are you accusing me of now?" he said quietly.

"All right," Virginia said shifting the baby from one arm to the other, " I'll just come out and say it; we are on our way to see where the famous writer is buried. Aren't we Tom?"

"Well," Tom said smiling," since we were going to visit your mother, I thought we might as well ..."

"Tom, my mother is down in Tucson, Arizona. That's a long way from here."

"It's not as far as you think," Tom said closing the camera case. "We'll be there in no time, Gin, you'll see."

He picked up two-year old Nancy and gave her a double bounce to make her smile.

"You're un-believable, Tom, totally." Shaking her head Virginia said, "I'm only a wife and mother, I don't what to do about your Hemingway obsession, about how to make you change ..."

"There's no need to change anything," Tom said as they walked toward the car. Nancy squirmed, and he put her down to walk, holding her hand.

"I give up," Virginia said, but did not smile. "Nancy's ready for a nap, Tom, she's tired, and it's Caroline's feeding time ..."

"Right, babe," Tom said, "that's why I parked our new wagon near the picnic bench under the tree, right there. Ain't I smart? How's that for planning ahead? He patted Nancy's hand, grinning.

After eating a lunch of peanut butter and crackers, with sliced oranges for dessert, Virginia sat watching Tom, who was studying a road map he spread out on the wooden picnic table.

"Honey," she said, "did the famous writer have anything to do with us driving through Billings, Montana, and that Cooke City and Red Lodge place?"

"Well, sort of, Gin. I wanted to photograph that Baretooth Pass ... and those mountain peaks, Pilot and Index.

"How much 'sort of' does the famous writer have to do with us coming here to Wyoming — on this tour — instead of heading down to Arizona?"

"A lot, Gin."

"You're still not over your — infatuation — with the life of the famous writer, are you honey?"

Tom shook his head while folding up the map.

"I guess not," he said.

"Well, at least you can admit it, honey." Virginia put her hand to the side of her face. "That's something."

Tom drove directly to the cemetery when they arrived in Ketchum, Idaho.

"Not much of a place to look at, is it?" Tom said to Virginia, standing next to the car door while she put a pink corduroy miniture baseball cap on Nancy's head. "I mean for such a prominent person as Hemingway — being here."

"I know what you mean," Virginia said as Tom helped her get out of the car with the baby. "You're not seeing what you expected."

"Right," Tom said, picking up Nancy in his arms.

Overhead, the sun was white-hot, and it was silent except for the grasshoppers buzzing their flat sound, as Tom shaded his eyes with his hand, looking at the cemetery,

that was a bare patch of grass on a slope, surrounded by a low wire fence. Off in the distance, Tom could see the Sawtooth mountains.

He led the way,under the grillwork metal letters arching over the entrance, that read; KETCHUM CEMETERY. He could see a small tool shed off to the right, where a rusty pick—up truck was parked. When he walked further, he saw an old man in overalls pushing a lawn mower, cutting the grass over a grave; his view had been blocked by the truck.

"I hope you're not in for a bigger disappointment, honey," Virginia said, shading the baby with the floppy straw hat. "This doesn't look very promising."

"Well, let's go find where he's buried," Tom said picking up Nancy, holding her on his hip. As they walked toward the old man, Tom held up his camera to Virginia and said, "I want to take some good photographs. Maybe you'll take one of me, Gin, you know, touching the grave? Okay?"

"You're getting excited, honey," Virginia said shifting the baby to her other arm. "I've never seen you so — tense."

"I can't help it, Gin."

The old man was now unrolling a length of sod-grass on the tailgate of the truck, when Tom asked for directions to the famous writer's grave.

"Right over there, the last time I saw him," the old man said pointing, a smile on his thin race. "Between those two young evergreens."

Tom and Virginia walked on the grass to a long, grey stone slab, marked only with a thin white cross at the head. Lettering was cut into the stone; the name, date of birth, and date of death.

Tom stood silent, looking down, and when Nancy squirmed, he set her down. The grave next to this one had a shock of daiseys growing, and Nancy reached for the flowers.

"Famous writer," Virginia said from behind Tom,at the same time watching Nancy pick the daiseys, "meet Tom Cohill ... one of your staunchest admirers. Maybe the <u>staunchest</u> of them all."

Tom said to the grave, "Well, I've finally met you. It's taken a long tine, covered a lot of miles, but now, I'm finally here. Hello."

There were grass clippings on the side of the granite slab, and Tom bent down on one knee and brushed them off.

"Maybe you want me to take your picture, Tom? Doing that brushing?" Then Virginia looked at Nancy, "Honey, come to mommy. Leave the flowers alone."

Tom handed Virginia the camera. "Just look through it, and pre the button on top,"he said slowly. And after the first photograph, Tom reached up, took the camera, cocked it, and gave it back for a second photo to make sure he had the picture.

Tom stood up when he saw the old caretaker walking toward him and Virginia. Nancy, holding her mother's leg, still held on to three daiseys, one with most the petals off, lost when she pulled the flowers by the head.

"My daughter likes your daiseys," Tom said to the old man as a half-apology for her picking.

"Hope she don't eat 'em," the old man said. He wiped his forehead, smiling, took off his western-style straw hat, then put it back on.

"She's been riding in the car for nearly a week," Virginia said, as a half-excuse.

People comes from all over the world to see this place where we planted Hemingway," the old man said, watching as Nancy headed for the daiseys again.

"See, Gin, I'm not the only <u>aficionado</u> who visits here — like this — there are others," Tom said looking at Nancy pulling a daisey.

Virginia smiled, shading one child, watching the other.

"Just the other day," the old man said swiping at a bug near his face, "two old ladies come here, when I was digging a new grave over where that wheelbarrow is, and they asked where the Hemingway grave was, I showed them where, and they said they was school teachers all the way from New Zealand Australia."

"Tom, nodding, grinning, said, "Yeah, people all over the world read his stories."

"Everybody was taking handfuls of the white stones from the top there," the old. man said pointing at the grave, "so much we couldn't keep anything for a cover. "Then, his Missus says the hell with it, and she orders this granite plate and has it put right on top."

"Hemingway spent a lot of his boyhood in northern Michigan," Tom said. "We're from Michigan. We drove here just to see the grave. Right, Ginny?"

"That's right," Virginia said, then added, "Tom, get Nancy. Look at her."

The child had sat down and was picking daiseys with both hands.

"Shoot," the old man said, "I'm from Michigan myself. When I was a youngster, I did some loggin' in the Upper Peninsula, and when it petered out, I come out here with my brother. We did some loggin here, until it petered out to."

Tom picked up Nancy, daiseys in both hands, and started her walking back to where the old man stood.

"Did you know the famous writer?" Virgina asked, intrested, now that she was here,and understood the mystique about the famous writer better, and also did not mind holding the baby and the shade-hat, while learning about him.

"I seen him around here when he came before the war," the old. man said slowly. "He was a big guy, big shoulders and arms. He could be a prize—fighter if he wanted."

Tom came walking with Nancy, and when he heard the last remark by the old man, he made a sour face of protest to Virgina.

"Where did he live when he was here?" Virginia asked, looking down when Nancy clutched at her leg, touching the child's head.

"The last place he lived was right over there," the old man said pointing was across the valley, "behind that clump of cottonwood trees. And that's where he died." Then he added, "The Topping family built the house; they was millionaires. They sold the house to Hemingway." -

Tom looked in that direction.

"Can you get close to the house?" he asked,still looking across the valley. "I mean, close, so you can look at the house."

"Yeah," the old man said, "but it's across the Big Wood river, kinda on the side of a hill. But you can see it all right, from a little ways, this side of the river."

"Thanks for all the information," Tom said looking down at Nancy, who had dropped all the daiseys now. He bent down and picked her up.

"Is anyone living in the house, now? Virginia asked, shifting the weight of the baby, slowly.

"Naw," the old man said, wiping his forehead with his hand. "The Hemingway Missus stays in New York city. She comes here in late September sometimes, but just for a week or so. Mostly now, the house is empty."

"Well, thanks again," Tom said turning Nancy's face away from the sun. "We've got to go, get the children out of this hot sun."

"So long," the old man said, walking away, swiping at the bugs in front of his face.

Walking down the slope to the cemetery entrance, Tom, carrying Nancy, spoke over the top of her head, "Gin, did you know his middle name was Miller? I saw it on the stone."

"What does it matter, honey," Virginia said as they walked under the archway and turned to their parked station wagon, "what his middle name is?"

"It just struck me," Tom said unlocking the car door, then pulling it open, "that it's a common name — ordinary."

"Why does that bother you, Tom?" Virginia said,seated in the car, reaching for Nancy, looking close at his face.

"It's just not Hemingway — ordinary — that's all," Tom said, helping Virginia put the child in her car seat.

Nancy travelled in her children's seat between her mother and Tom driving. "It don't fit him at all."

"Tom, honey," Virginia said before he closed the car door, "maybe being here is too much for you. You're too close to the flame. You need a rest. This Hemingway stuff is overwhelming you."

He closed the door, and went around and climbed in the car from the other side, behind the steering wheel, closing the door, gently.

"Gin, your right — in a way. There's just so much to see here, and absorb, that my mind is working double-time just to soak everything up. If I seem excited, well, it's just — I don't want to miss anything."

"Tom, we <u>all</u> love you, honey. We don't understand you, but we still love you. Okay?"

"You always know what to say, Gin. You're my right arm. You always will be."

"Does that mean no more talk like 'ordinary' talk?"

"Right."

"Where are we going now?"

"I just want to take a quick peek at the famous writer's house, babe. I want to see the place where — the shot was fired,that was heard around the world."

"Your back to your 'ordinary'-type talk again, Tom."

"Sorry, Gin. I think it's the writer part of me talking."

"Well, try and stay with us ordinary people, Tom. Save the writer talk for the pages you write."

"I'll try harder, babe. Honest."

"Tom, honey, please make this a short 'peek," Okay? We have to get a motel for tonight. We are all, tired."

"Right, Gin ... look, there's his house ..."

The car veered onto the gravel on the side of the road.

"Oh, man, what the hell am I doing? Sorry, everybody."

"Watch where you are going, Tom."

"Sorry. Is everybody okay?" Tom said slowing the car.

"Yes," Virginia said, shaking her head,"we're okay. But the point is,are you okay, Tom? I mean, don't put your family in the ditch."

"I just took my eyes off the road Gin, just for an instant." He patted her leg. "I won't do it again."

"You're scaring all of us, Tom."

"'Across The River And Into The Trees,' Tom said looking up at the house where Hemingway died,through the windshield. It was a large, square structure, facing east from the side of a hill; the Big Wood river flowing just at the bottom of the hill with stands of cottonwood trees growing along the banks. "It looks like a fort, or a bunker," Tom said, stopping the car at the grassey river bank.

"It doesn't look too homey," Virginia said leaning forward to look up through the windshield.

"Look at the windows, " Tom said, " it's got big picture windows, upstairs and down."

"It looks like a double-decker log cabin," Virginia said, leaning forward over the baby's head for an instant. "Is it made of logs?"

"Wouldn't it be great to see Hemingway come walking out that front door, Gin?"

"Oh-h, Tom. Stop it now."

While looking for a motel in Ketchum, Tom saw the McDonald cabin sign; OVERNIGHT RENTALS, DAY - WEEK, and turned into the gravel driveway surrounded by six large log cabins. The price was right, and once Virginia saw the inside, and the living room size bedroom, the big bath room, and. the kitchen with all the appliances, she wanted to stay.

Tom went out to the Christiana restaurant and brought a chicken dinner home, and the family sat at the table for dinner.

He was wiping his hands in a paper napkin, when be said, "Honey, I can't sit here tonight ... I'm excited ... stirred up. Being here, after all I read about Sun Valley, and Ketchum, and how the famous writer wrote here, his book 'Bell Tolls' and all that ... I'm ready to explode."

"Go. Go get a drink, Tom," Virginia said, turning to look at the baby sleeping on the large bed near her.

"Tomorrow, Gin, we'll all tour Sun Valley ... the whole place around Ketchum here ... from top to bottom."

"Simmer down, honey. It's not good to get so worked up, Tom, the way you are. I've never see you so ..."

"I can't help it, Gin," Tom said buttoning his sport coat. "Did you know the famous writer wrote," he began unbuttoning the coat, absently, "finished writing his Spanish Civil War novel in room two hundred six, here, in the Sun Valley Lodge?"

"Tom, leave you coat buttons alone," Virginia said.

Nancy laughed at what her mother said. She was sitting in her car seat at the table, the seat tied to the back of a heavy wood chair.

"Siding with your mother ... against me ... already," Tom said, and kissed the top of Nancy's head. "I forgive you," he said, smiling, "I have to."

He lifted Nancy out of the chair seat and set her on the floor near her mother.

"In that same room at the Lodge, the famous writer, while shaving one morning, heard two geese out in the pond outside the windows," Tom said to Virginia getting up from her chair.

"Don't tell me he shot them?"

"Yep," Tom said smiling. "He went out on the porch of his room at the Lodge there and cut loose at the geese ... with his 'old stopper,' the name he gave his model Twelve, Winchester pump shotgun."

"I bet the Lodge manager,and other guests, were happy about all that racket, right?" Virginia said,as she set Nancy on the edge of the bed,and began untie-ing her shoe laces.

"Aw, there weren't too many other guests, Gin. It was back in nineteen-thirty-seven, when they were still building the place."

"Honey," Virginia said standing up in front of him, patting the side of his face, "you go for a walk, and let off some of that steam inside you. I'm taking a quick shower and want to get some sleep."

"Okay, okay," Tom said quietly, "I just thought you would like to hear some of the stuff about the famous writer — that went on here in Sun Valley."

"I do, Tom. But please save it for tomorrow. We're all worn out. Tomorrow, we'll be an appreciative audience."

"Okay, Gin."

He kissed her, and turned, stepping quickly to the door without speaking.

Loud rock music came out the open door of the brightly lighted Savage's Bar in downtown Ketchum. The bar was at the corner of Trail Creek road, where the turn off main street Ketchum is made to go out to the Sun Valley resort, a quarter mile away.

Looking in the bar door, Tom could see young, long hair people, some barefoot, some sitting on the floor, and he decided not to go in.

Looking across the street, he saw the sign Alpine House Bar on the outside of a bar built like a log cabin, and smiling,said, “That’s more like it.”

Walking in the front door, Tom saw the inside was all wood panels with a dormer built over the bar that had small shingles made of split wood. Four men in cowboy hats were playing pool at a t along the left wall. Above them hung a bear skin, a mountain goat hide, and the mounted head of a giant elk. On the right wall, under the dormer over the bar, above a painting, were all types of old rifles.

Tom sat down looking at the painting behind the bar that covered the entire back bar wall. The title over the painting: THE HAPPY HUNTER. It showed a be-whiskered old hunter leading a mule into town; the mule loaded with a dead deer three rabbits and a half dozen partridges. The old hunter was carry a jug of whiskey, and all the town people were looking at the game he had shot, smiling.

“What are you drinking?” a tail bartender wearing thick eyeglasses, asked Tom.

“Scotch on the rocks,” Tom said and pointed to the painting. “Who did the picture?”

“I don’t know,” the bartender said pouring the scotch. “It’s been here twenty years or so.”

Tom put money on the bar, the bartender took it down to the end of the bar where the cash register was, and when he came back said, “You just passing through?”

“Yeah.”

The bartender put Tom’s change on the bar, nodded, then went down the bar again and sat down on the end stool.

Sipping the scotch, Tom realized he was the only customer sitting at the bar.

Suddenly, the bar door flung open and a fleshy-faced man wearing a baseball cap came in, and when he stepped between two stools, almost fell, tripping on a stool leg. He sat down two seats away from Tom.

“Give me a stinger, Earl,” he said to the bartender coming up the bar. Then turning to Tom, said, “Hi.”

“Hi,” Tom said back, grinning.

While the man in the red baseball cap was drinking, the bar door opened again, and two girls and a boy, all barefoot, followed by a small black and white terrier dog, came in and stood behind him.

“Dad, we want to go home,” the oldest girl said to the man in the red baseball cap. “We want to watch television.”

Turning around, the man in the red hat took a key from his shirt pocket, “Okay, but don’t lose it. He handed the girl the single key.

“I won’t,” she said looking at it.

“Can I have a coke, dad?” the boy asked, scratching at the back of his leg.

“No,” he said turning back to the bar. “It’s getting late,” he said his back to them, “so go straight home.”

The two girls went to the door, the boy and the dog following.

"You want me to put the stinger on the tab?" the bartender asked. "Yes, and make me another one, Earl."

The bartender went to the cash register down the bar, took a white card out of a box, and wrote on it.

"I'm baby sitting tonight," the man in the red cap said to Tom. "My wife's working over at that madhouse called Savage's Bar."

"I passed that place," Tom said. "Things are really lively from what I could see."

"They only have music once a week over there," the man in the red cap said, and started on his second stinger when the bartender set it in front of him. "When I managed that bar,it was packed like that every night. I had pizza to. I had the first pizza in Idaho, I think. Nobody around here knew what the hell it was, until I showed them."

"You're not from Ketchum then?"

"Naw. New Hampshire. My wife is to. We came out here, ten, almost eleven years ago," he said and. took a slow drink from his stinger. "Where are you from?"

"Michigan."

"What do you do?

"Write fiction stories. Work on a newspaper when I have to."

"Like the famous writer?" he said, smiling.

Tom just shook his head, aware he was in Hemingway's yard.

"I haven't had anything published — yet. That's why I have to do newspaper work from time to time."

"I'm a painter. Portraits. But during the summer I'm a landscaper ... until It gets cold. I only have time to paint in the winter. I have to make some money in the summer."

He finished his drink and rattled the ice cubes in the glass, then held it up for the bartender to see.

"Did you see the famous writer around town?" Tom asked.

"Yeah," the red hat man said, giving his glass to the bartender for a refill. "He drank more than me. Him Gary, the cowboy actor, would come in to Savage's, get a snootful, and sometimes want to make pizza, their own pizza. They would stop at the bar after pheasant hunting.

What the hell could I do? They put everything I had in kitchen on their pizza, even some leftover steak. And lots of onions. I used to charge them twenty bucks apiece for being let loose in the kitchen."

Tom shook his head, grinning, "I wish I was there."

The bartender set a fresh drink in front of the man with the red hat.

"Them two was always doing something crazy like that," the man in the red hat said smiling. "They just loved going hunting. Hell, they'd hunt for anything, as long as it was hunting."

"Yeah," Tom said,"I read about that, somewhere."

"You seen the painting of them two in the back room, there?"

"I didn't know there was a back room."

"C'mon, I'll show you."

Carrying their glasses, they walked to a small dining room with tables and chairs, and a fireplace, behind a wall at the end of the bar. Above the fireplace, was a long, narrow painting, showing the famous writer, and the star of the movie, "High Noon," both sleeping, their backs resting against a big tree, dressed in hunting clothes, their rifles across their knees.

Surrounding the two sleeping hunters were all sorts of game; elk, deer, rabbits, squirrels, and birds; pheasants, partridge, doves, all standing, looking curiously at the sleeping hunters. A small card at the bottom of the painting read, in red pencil, "The famous writer's dream of heaven. Price, two thousand and three hundred dollars."

Tom was looking closely at the painting, when he saw what looked like a dent, the size of a quarter.

"What's that a hole?" he said to the man in the red hat, who was sipping his drink.

"Yeah, some jerk threw a pool ball during a fight one night, when the painting used to hang out front in the bar. When the painter saw the hole," the man in the red hat said smiling,"I hear, that's when he added the three hundred bucks more for the painting. He said the hole made the painting 'authentict.'"

"That's terrific," Tom said when they were walking back to the bar. "By the way, my name's Tom Cohill."

"I'm Bob Chapman," red cap said, just before he sat down on a barstool, almost falling off.

"I guess you really did know the famous writer, Bob, I mean in an everyday sort of way," Tom said, and held up his empty glass for the bartender to see. "Another scotch," he said when the bartender came over, "and another stinger to."

"Oh hell yeah,"Bob said, "sometimes he'd call me up late at night, and ask me to open the bar and bring some booze to his house.

"That's when he was staying here in Ketchum, over at McDonald's cabins ... he didin't always stay at the Sun Valley Lodge, you know?"

Tom smiled, enjoying the stories Bob was spilling, and when the bartender came with the drinks, payed quickly, so as not to interrupt the flow of anecdotes.

"What did he drink?" Tom asked Chapman.

"Oh, rum mostly, but gin and scotch to, and a lot of wine, all kinds, but I think his favorite was red wine."

"He stayed at the McDonald cabins?" Tom said feeling his scotch. "I'm in the second off the road. He didn't stay there did he? Me and the family are camped in that one."

"No. He stayed back in the one that faces the road, the one tha's away from all the others," Chapman said and near slid off the stool. "Remember one night he called me three o'clock," he said grinning, "we live only down the street from the cabins, "he says he's havin' a party and they're runnin' low on booze. I get the car and get some booze from the bar ... and took the bottles in to him."

"Yeah, Bob, I think you mentioned that before."

Chapman took a long drink of the stinger.

"They were in the kitchen, that night. He was standing up, using the top of the refrigerator for a bar. He <u>always</u> stood up. He never sat down. Well, he was talking, to a priest, and two other ministers of some kind. Boy, they were all swacked ..."

"Did you hear what they were saying?" Tom asked smiling, probing.

"No, I don't remember," Bob said slowly. "I just remember, he paid me, and I stayed for a few drinks, and I wasn't much interested what they were talking, so I went home to bed."

"Wish I could have been there," Tom said, shaking his head back and forth. "I would have listened to every word of that discussion."

"Say," Chapman said, both elbows on the bar, turning toward Tom, trying to stay steady, "you ain't some kind, of a plant, are you?"

"What do you mean, 'plant?'" Tom asked.

"Well, his blond wife asked me not to say anything," Chapman said, nodding. "Not to say anything to newspaper writers. She asked me not to spill anything I know, the day after he died. She called me on the phone.

"I do the landscaping around the house for her. I'm around that house all the time, working, so's to keep my job, I gotta keep my yap shut."

"I'm no plant," Tom said. "I just like hearing what the famous writer was like. His writing knocked me out, and I liked the way he lived. I tried to meet him once, went to Key West, but it didn't work out."

Chapman nodded, and Tom ordered two more drinks.

"He used to come to this bar a lot," Chapman said. "After he bought the house from the Topping family, he'd walk down the hill, mostly in the afternoon, and go to the post office,that used to be in the drug store, and he'd get his mail and the newspapers. Then he'd come over here to the Alpine for a drink.

Tom took a long drink from the glass of scotch the bartender had just set down on the bar.

"Ah, Bob, I saw the house," Tom said, hesitating a moment for what he was about to ask, "but from way down by the river. Is there any chance of going up with you for a closer look?"

Chapman picked up his fresh stinger slowly, thinking.

"You can't go inside," he said. "I don't have the key. But I guess it wouldn't hurt if you just want to look in the side windows."

"Maybe the drapes are drawn shut?" Tom said. "Only on the front windows ... facing east."

"Great."

"I'm cutting the grass up at the house, this week, and weeding the garden. The famous writer's wife is supposed to show up next week. Me and my partner are really trying to spruce up the place."

"No kidding, wow?" Tom said and took a sip of scotch.

"You just want to look-see, right?"

"Yeah. Maybe I can see his library, or his writing desk," Tom said. "some of the stuff he brought when he left Cuba."

"Naw, he used to write upstairs on a bureau thing, standing, " Chapman said and rattled the ice cubes in his empty glass. "You can't see that, but you can see the living room downstairs, where there's zebra skins and antelope horns on the walls."

"Great," Tom said, finishing his drink and rattling the ice cubes for the bartender to see. "Another round."

"Meet me tomorrow morning, ten o'clock, here at the bar," Chapman said, weaving. "I got a truck ... we go up in the truck. My partner comes up in his truck."

"Right," Tom said. "Maybe I can help pull weeds."

"I've got to go check the kids ... right after this drink," Chapman said.

"Tom, you've done nothing but talk about going up to the famous writer's house since breakfast," Virginia said. Can't we let it rest for a while?"

They had just climbed out of the station wagon in the parking lot of the rustic Sun Valley resort.

"Okay, Gin. Sorry," Tom said and shifted Nancy he was carrying from his left to right arm. Virginia carried the baby, Caroline, shading the infant's face.

"I thought you would get that excitement out of your system after yesterday," Virginia said in almost a whisper as they walked toward the cluster of buildings looking like wood chalets.

"Okay, okay. Where do you want to go now, Gin?"

"I want to start over there ... walk through all those cute shops in that pavillion. And I'v got to stop at the Post Office," she said nodding at the building where the flag was flying on a pole.

“This is the world famous Sun Valley, sweetie,” Tom said to Nancy. It’s quite a place. Hope you remember it.” She began squirming, looking at the duck pond. “Okay, okay,” Tom said and set her on the ground.

“Tom,” Virginia said, following Nancy, “take a photograph of me and the girls, over here by the ducks in the pond ... for my mother.”

“Sure, Gin. Wave when you’re set.”

Tom watched them cross the grass to the pond, and when sighting the camera, saw the building behind with a sign, Opera House. Later, that day,he found out it was also the resort movie theater, meeting hall, and sometime church. As Tom was trying to get a photograph, looking into the camera, he overheard, two girls in waitress uniforms, sitting on the bench nearby, “Is that really the famous writer’s son?”

“Yes. They call him ‘Hoppy,’ or something. It’s a nickname.”

“Is that his wife?”

“Uh—huh. They have four kids, all girls.”

Tom turned, and seeing a middle-aged man with a mustache, wearing a tweed sports jacket, walking with his wife, and took a photograph of them. He quickly snapped a second photo,as insurance of having the picture, and was about to step over and introduce himself, when an elderly man stopped and shook hands with “Hoppy” and began talking.

“A pox on you old man,” Tom said to himself.

“To-om,” Virginia called from the duck pond, standing with the girls, “we are waiting.”

“Okay,” he said, waving, then taking four quick photos, he turned, but “Hoppy” was gone.

“How old is ‘Hoppy?’” the one waitress asked. I’m not sure, but I know he’s just getting over a heart attack.”

“He’s kinds, old then.”

“Yeah, he’s kinda famous because his papa was the famous writer.”

“Yeah, the second waitress said, “I heard about him, the famous writer, in a class at school.”

Virginia walked up to Tom, she was carrying Caroline in one arm, and walking slow, holding Nancy’s hand.

“You haven’t been drinking this morning,” she said, “have you, Tom? I’ve never seen you so — distracted.” When Nancy started to move back to the duck pond, she said, “No, honey. Not for a while.” Then turning to Tom, “your daughter did not want to leave the pond. She’s like her father, distracted, I guess.”

“Gin, did you see that guy with the mustache and tweed jacket behind me?” Tom said quietly, taking Nancy’s hand. “That’s Hoppy Hemingway — he lived as a kid with his not-yet famous father in Paris in the Roaring Twenties. Hoppy’s mother was the famous writer’s first wife.”

“Really?” Virginia said, looking toward the walkway.

"Yep."

"Did you take his picture?

Tom nodded.

"Sorry, honey. Honest," Virginia said. "I didn't realize …"

"I wouldn't of had time ... anyhow. I got to get going, if I want to meet Bob Chapman," Tom said picking up Nancy in his arms.

"Tom," Virginia said as they walked toward their station wagon, "after we drop you in town, we're coming back here to walk around the shops. A nice lady told me they have delicious crepes made in a shop here, while you wait. They're rolled around jelly and sprinkled with powder sugar.

"What lady?" Tom said, opening the station wagon door.

"She came by when we were at the pond, waiting for you to take the picture." Virginia smiled. "She was eating a crepe."

"You're beginning to like it here, arn't you, Gin?

She smiled at Tom while they were driving. "I'm glad we came," she said slowly. "It's so beautiful here."

Tom parked the station wagon out front the Alpine House Bar, and when Virginia came around to get in the driver's seat, he said, "I'll have Chapman drop me at our motel, and we'll spend the rest of the day ... and evening… together. Promise."

"You sure Chapman has a truck?" Virginia said, lookup at Tom, as he closed the station wagon door. "He sounds goofey."

"Not really," Tom said as she started to drive away, "but I sure hope so."

Chapman drove his pick—up truck past the PRIVATE — KEEP OUT sign on the gate of the famous writer's house.

"Up there," Chapman said, pointing as he drove, "is the Galena Summit, forty miles up the highway, near the Salmon River. You can see Galena from here,and the Sawtooth Mountains. When the sun is setting behind the mountains, they look just like the saw-teeth of a whip saw for cutting logs. The famous writer liked the view ... of the Sawtooths."

Tom nodded, looking at the house up the driveway that was paved, with blacktop like a street in the city.

"I painted that Galena valley scene for a customer, once," Chapman said. "But I liked it so much, I kept it for myself. Never sold it."

"Maybe I'll take my wife, Gin, and our kids ... for a ride up there to Galena ... if we have time."

"You want a shot of gin?" Chapman asked. "I got a pint of Fleishman's under the seat."

"Okay," Tom said, but just to set the record straight, my wife's name is Virginia. We call her Ginny, or Gin, for short. I wasn't asking for a drink. Really."

"I believe you," Chapman said, raising a bottle of gin in a paper bar from under the truck seat.

Tom was swallowing his gin drink, and watching as the truck drove along the back of the house, then stopped in front of the closed garage doors.

Chapman took the bottle and had a long drink.

Tom pointed at the house, "Look at the size of those logs they used to built that house. Where'd they get timber that size?"

"They're cement," Chapman said putting the cap on the gin bottle. "Theu're just formed like logs, and painted brown.

"No kidding," Tom said.

Chapman put the bottle under the seat, and pushed open the truck door.

"C'mon," he said, "I'll show you where you can look inside."

Standing in front of the wall of the house, facing him, Tom ran his hand over the rough surface.

"They even got phoney wood—grain, and there's a knot hole," Tom said quietly. "From a distance, you couldn't…"

Chapman waved his hand, "Hell, the lodge over at Sun Valley is the same way. None of that is wood either."

Tom shook his head. "Hard to believe," he said following Chapman, stepping on the dry weeds piled on the sidewalk from the weeding yesterday in the garden nearby.

At the kitchen window, Tom looked in seeing an ordinary electric stove, a sink, a large kitchen table, and chrome chairs with yellow plastic backs.

"Come around to the other side of the house," Chapman said. "You can see more."

Stepping around the corner of the house, Tom saw a thin man clipping the hedges that ran along the property line. Chapman whistled, the thin man waved an aknowledgement, and went back to clipping.

"That your partner?"

"Yeah, he got beat up by some gamblers down in Elko, Nevada, last week. He's still hurting. He lives just down the hill."

They were standing at the south wall of the house.

"He don't look too bad," Tom said.

"Hell, they dynamited his truck couple of months ago," Chapman said, and pointed to the window. Cupping his bands around his eyes, he leaned, "You can see the dining room here, he said, looking through the glass, his face against the window.

Cupping his hands around his eyes like Chapman, Tom peered through the glass, seeing a blond-wood dining table, surrounded by chairs with yellow-green backs and seats, crowded into the narrow room. To the left, stood a large blond cabinet filled with wide champagne glasses and tall goblets.

"Hey," Tom said, "this is fantastic, seeing what he used — actually."

"Come around this way,"Chapman said.

Tom moved to the next window where Chapman pointed.

With his hands cupped around his eyes, Tom could see the whole length of the living room, facing east, that ran the entire width of the house. On the floor in front of the couch, lay a zebra skin, on the couch itself, was what looked like a mountain lion fur. The walls were decorated with heads of animals, and a display of horns on plaques, and near the corner, thin African shields and a bundle of spears. To the left nearby,was a large gun rack, several rifles stacked upright.

Then Tom noticed the open suitcase on the far end of the couch.

"Hey, Bob, I think there's somebody in the house."

"Maybe a maid cleaning up," he said stepping up to look.

There was the sound of a telephone ringing.

Tom was looking over at the bookshelves when he saw a small blond woman come down the steps, and when she saw the two of them looking in the window, she waved, on her way into the kitchen, where she picked up the phone.

"Shit," Chapman said, leaning back from the window, "she's here — already. Missus famous writer is here and I haven't even got the grass cut. Tom, help me, go pull some weeds out of the garden — look like your working."

"Is that really her?" Tom asked smiling, excited.

"You know it is," Chapman said. "C'mon, help me pull some weeds."

They went back around the corner of the house to the garden, and Bob dropped to his knees, pulling at the weeds frantically. Tom bent down and began pulling too.

"Where did the famous writer shoot himself?" Tom asked quietly, stacking the weeds behind him.

"See that side door right there, facing the garage?"

Tom looked at the storm door, a small dormer over it.

"Just behind that door," Bob said pushing a pile of weeds to his left. "Ther's kind of a small entrance room just inside. The carpet was soaked. We had to cut it and take it to the dump."

Tom kept pulling weeds, but felt guilty. He had a strong feeling of having done something wrong.

The back kitchen door opened and the small woman with short blond hair came out. She was wearing a blue pants-suit with an alligator emblom near the left shoulder.

"Hello, Bob," said said. "How you been?"

"Pretty good," he said standing up. "Sorry I haven't got to the grass yet, but ..."

"Oh, don't worry about it," she said, waving her hand. "How's Sally and the children?"

"They're doing okay," he said, shifting his red cap to cover his eyes.

"Have you been painting?"

"Yes. I got a lot of painting done this past winter. I've got almost enough for a showing."

Tom stood up slowly behind Chapman.

"Oh," Chapman said turning, "this is a friend helping today. Tom ... Cohill."

"Hello," the blond woman said, and Tom caught her glancing at his crotch.

"Hi," Tom said, quietly, and looked at the ground; he could not look her in the eye.

The telephone in the kitchen rang.

"Well," the blond woman said, "the word's out. They all know I'm here now." She started for the kitchen door, turned to look back, "Bob, the battery is dead in the Jeep."

"I'll take car of it," he said just as she went in the kitchen door, waving.

"Jeez," Chapman said to Tom, "let's get a drink. I really need one. She wasn't supposed to be here for another week."

Tom followed him back to the truck and climbed in. Chapman took a quick drink and handed the bottle to Tom.

"No thanks," Tom said. "My head is racing so fast, I wouldn't even feel any effect from Gin. I've just seen the famous writer's house, his wife, and where he died. I can't even swallow."

Chapman took another drink, "I don't feel like working today. I'm going to tell her that I got to go home."

"I feel sick to my stomach," Tom said quietly.

"You look a lot better this morning," Virginia said, checking Nancy, sleeping in her riding car seat. The baby, Caroline, was sleeping also, Virginia holding her. "When you came back yesterday from that house … youe were pale a a ghost, Tom."

"Yeah," he said driving the station wagon, "the rest did me good. But I wish we could have driven up to Galena summit for a look. Sorry I slept the whole evening."

"Oh, don't worry about that, Tom. We really enjoyed our jaunt around the Sun Valley resort. No wonder the famous writer loved this place. We had a wonderful time when you were gone. Everything is so beautiful here. Wait until I tell my mother."

"We'll stop in Salt Lake City, babe, then down to Tucson. But I want to make a little stop down the road at Silver Creek ... take a look see."

"To-om, we'er heading for Tucson, remember?"

"The famous writer used to trout fish in Silver Creek, and he used to hunt ducks in the sloughs, but he never wrote about it ... he wanted to keep it secret."

"Tucson, Tom we're going to see my mother."

"Did you know the poet Ezra Pound was born right here in Hailey, Idaho?"

"Pound who?"

"Ezra, the poet,was born here back at the turn of the century when Hailey was a little mining town. The famous writer met him in Paris in the nineteen twenties. Ezra was sort of a mentor to the young famous writer, he read the young guy's stories, did some editing, made suggestions to improve the writing ..."

Tom's conversation had grown faint; his words barely audible.

"Tom, honey, are you all right?"

"Yeah,I'm okay. Something just struck me about Ezra."

"What, Tom? What are you thinking?"

"Oh look," he said, "see the sign pointing to Silver Creek. We'll just stop for a minute."

Tom turned the station wagon, following where the sign pointed.

"Tom, what struck you about Ezra? Tell me."

"Just that the famous writer came here for the sport— life, duck shooting, trout fishing, years after Paris and Ezra. Then the famous writer dies in the place Ezra was born … in kind of a circle, or something."

"Oh-h, Tom."

Chapter 23

A year ago, when Tom and his family returned home from the Sun Valley and Tucson trip, he found two letters to him among the other mail dropped through the front door mail slot.

One was an offer to work again as a reporter for The Detroit News. The other was a note from Tim Guier, a re porter friend down on the Fort Lauderdale News, telling that Fred Terrel had committed suicide. Guier had telephoned the Detroit News for Tom's address, and wrote a quick note saying Fred shot himself in the bathroom at home, after, what Guier said, was a "prolonged arguement over the years aboutFred's inability to make a lot more money."

Tom felt bad about Fred killing himself, but there no way he, Tom, could have helped Fred, no more than Fred could help Tom with his problem at home with Virginia's mother.

When she was in Tucson, Virginia's mother wanted to be at the large house in Birmingham, close to old friends and family. Then, when she's here in Birmingham, she misses the dry climate which makes her arthritis bearable. Her oldest daughter, Linda, married a French lawyer while attending the Sorbonne, and is living in France. So, Virginia is left to care for her mother in addition to caring for her and Tom's two young children.

Tom did not like the pressure Virginia was under, especially when her mother came out to the house on Harsen's Island, which the mother called, "a swamp house," and totally rejected the way her daughter and two children were living.

On the days the mother came to the island, Tom took the boat out on day-trips, sometimes anchoring in a cove, where he could write in peace, sitting on a chair in the stern, a clipboard on his knee.

Then, when the weather turned cool, Tom took the reporting job with the suburban bureau of the News, more or less just to get out of the house. Virginia's mother was coming to the house more often, "because her grand daughters were getting bigger."

The News, in an economy move, suddenly did away with the suburban bureau, and now after eight months, Tom was out of a job — and a place to go everyday.

There had been a bitter editorial strike at the News, lasting over a year before Tom was hired. Most of the reporters scattered, some taking other jobs, during the long strike. Tom had been offered the reporting job after the strike was determined illegal by the court, and The News was allowed to start publishing again — which meant it could hire who it wanted — leaving the striking reporters and editors out in the cold. At first, Tom stalled taking the job with the suburban bureau, where he worked hard three years, before quitting after the "swamp house" was paid off,and he was planning to do a lot of writing; he had a new book idea, then. He had not liked it when he was hired when the regulars from the editorial staff were still on strike for better wages, but he took the job simply to get out of the house.

His fiction stories, and his books, were not selling — in fact the only money he made writing was from newspaper writing. And he was running out of answers to Virginia's questions about selling his books and stories. Coming to work every day took the pressure off him about the selling. He could say nothing about this to the dozen other reporters, drinking at the Anchor Bar, who lost their livelihood with the closing of the suburban bureau, and who called The News' treatment of employees "cavalier."

After nine publishing houses returned Tom's second book, he stopped sending it out. Working at the newspaper did not leave him much time for writing fiction except on weekends. He wrote four short stories, but eventually had to retire them from being sent out when they did not sell to magazines.

He read in a news magazine that adventure books and the suspence genre was selling, so he wrote a book about Nicaragua gun smuggling and a harrowing escape from a jungle prison camp. Five publishing houses turned down the Nicaragua book. Then Tom read an advertisement in a writer's magazine by an editor who claimed to have first-hand knowledge about the book publishing business. For a fee, this editor would read your book, make recommendations, when these were made, take the book around to publishing houses, acting as a agent.

Tom sent the Nicaragua book to the editor and the two-hundred dollar fee. A post card came back saying wait three weeks.

A four-page letter came a month later saying the book had good potential and that "it was reminiscent of Hemingway in form and style." Tom was excited about the prospect of being published, and when another letter came, he thought it would be news the book was sold to a publisher. Instead, the letter explained that the editor-agent would reduce his commission fee from twenty to ten percent on the first thousand copies of the book sold. The letter hinted if the book sold over a thousand, the author stood to make a substantial amount of money. With the letter hinting the book was near to being sold, Tom sent the additional hundred and twenty dollars.

It was during this time of excitement Tom began a new book about alien smuggling from Canada, across the St. Clair River, to the U.S. The book was a new version of Hemingway's story of Harry Morgan in "To Have And Have Not." This new book and the business dealing with the agent went on away from home while Tom was working downtown at the News.

Last week, the editor-agent wrote a letter he was ill and forced to retreat to the "Ozarks" to recouperate and "possibly retire," and wished Tom the best of luck. The alien smuggling book, titled "Holcomb's Last Run," was returned from eight publishing houses. Now,Tom lost the newspaper job; today, he cleaned out his desk and drew his last paycheck. But he had no money worries.

It was sunny when he came out of the revolving doors of The News, and stood under the long brass plaque that gave the name of the newspaper and its founding date.

Glancing left up West Lafayette boulevard, he spotted the giant, light-blue-painted, bookstore. It was the John King used bookstore, all four floors of it. He had not been there in months. It was only three blocks up the boulevard.

King was a department store for people who liked old books. It had books on every subject. People browsed for hours among the shelves.

Inside, Tom passed though the lobby and pay-desk room, with creaky wood floors and worn carpet, into the stairwell. He could hear the echo of his climb up the wide steel steps up to the fourth floor. Upstairs, the shelves sagged, the floor tilted toward the outside wall, and there was an oder of decay; this was his favorite section, Biography.

A clerk sat at a table up the center aisle under a light bulb, looking like something out of a Charles Dickens setting.

In the old days there were no floor clerks.

"Can I help you?" the middle aged clerk asked, looking up from his sorting of file cards he had spred all over the table top.

"Just looking to see what you have in the Hemingway section," Tom said, trying not to act intimidated or stupid.

"Sections B through H," the clerk snapped. "Sixteen-hundred through two-thousand."

"Right," Tom said and turned into an asile between the shelves, looking for the numbers thumbtacked on the wood. He heard of a picture book, the size of life magazine, that was photographed around 1939 showing Hemingway's activities at Sun Valley. They were mostly hunting and fishing photos of Hemingway and celebrities like Gary Cooper. The book was titled "Out In The Wilds With Hemingway," or something similar to that.

At the end of the "D" shelf row, Tom came face to face with two men looking out a steel tilt-out window. He said nothing, but turned,looking out the window for an instant. Below was the Greyhound bus station. These men were cops, looking for drug deals, or maybe thieves stealing luggage.

Tom continued looking for the Hemingway section.up the next aisle, not looking back at the cops.

Among the Hs, Tom saw the Canoe Baker biography of Hemingway's life, a definitive work, a thick book, and next to it, a thin paperback. On the cover of the paperback a photo of a young man in a white shirt, sitting with a young Hemingway in some bar with wicker tables and chairs. The title read: "My Year With Hemingway, Fishing In Cuba and Key West." 1934. Arnold Samuelson.

"Wh-a-at?" Tom said, his mouth dropped open.

One of the cops looked around the corner from the end of the aisle. After a hard look, he disappeared.

Tom was stunned. Here was a guy who did the same thing Tom did, go to Key West to meet the famous writer, twenty years earlier. And wrote a book about it. Unbelievable, Tom thought. Other people were under the influence of the famous writer's lifestyle too. Incredible.

Opening the book, Tom came to the center where six pages of photographs, one showing the young man, Samuelson, standing on the stern of Hemingway's boat, the Pilar, with the famous author and a sailfish on a hoist.

Tom shook his head, saying quietly, "I've got to read this. Man, this guy's story is incredible. It's my dream, but it came true for somebody else."

Opening the thin book to the title page, Tom saw the price of six dollars written on the corner in ink. On the outside cover the printed price was two ninety-eight.

"Robbers," Tom said quietly not wanting to draw the attention of the cop again.

In his student years, Tom and others dropped the books they wanted out the window, and later,outside, picked them up. King books caught on to that trick and the one where your girlfriend hid the books you wanted under her bulging sweater. Students in those days had no money and wanted the best of everything. They thought they deserved the best.

But that was not King Books problem, what students thought, he was in the book selling business, Tom thought while he was paying for the book,back on the ground floor, just before going through the thick glass door that automatically could be locked if the need came up.

Driving north on Jefferson Avenue, passing Belle Isle out in the Detroit River, Tom could not help thinking about the Hemingway book he has been sending to publishing houses. It was a book about a young writer's attempt to meet Hemingway, then followed by a lifetime of attempting to live as the famous author did.

One publisher wrote Tom a letter with the rejection slip:

"...,'This book will not be a commercial success, but you have talent and the story is very interesting. If you do more on this book, I would like to see it.'" .

The letter was signed by The Editor-In-Chief.

Two days later on closer inspection, Tom remembered reading the letter again, and the second time, his heart not pounding so hard, how he spotted the written intials PD in small parenthesis under the Editor-In-Chief's signature.

It was then he realized that someone in the office had written the letter, and not the Chief. Tom thought about it for a few days, he remembered, and decided it was still a very encouraging letter, and the Chief must have given some sort of approval.

At the time the letter came, Tom had been a reporter at the News for almost two years. He was sore that book editors have it made; they can just pick and choose what will sell. The poor sap of a writer is out in the world, doing what he must do to make ends meet, while writing his stories. Nobody, Tom concluded, gives a darn about writers until they become famous. Writers have to be crazy.

Driving up the ferry boat ramp for the trip across the channel to Harsen's Island, Tom said out loud, "Maybe it's not that simple."

Opening the book, Tom read how Samuelson hopped a freight train back in 1934 for a ride down the Florida Keys to meet Hemingway. Samuelson had only a squashed loaf of bread and no money. He came all the way from Minnesota on freight trains.

When the car ferry bumped the dock, Tom had to put the book down on the car seat, and drive off.

After dinner with Virginia and the kids, Tom said he wanted to read the book he just bought.

"You seem so — absorbed — ,“ Virginia said to him as he stood up at the table. He had told her a little about the book. "It must be a very compelling story," she said smiling. "Am I right, honey?" She knew about his trip down the Keys to meet Hemingway, and she knew the book was about another writer who did the same thing.

"You might say, babe," Tom said pushing the chair for- against the table, smiling, "it's a kind of parallel universe type book."

She understood he was shocked about finding Samuelson had gotten there first.

"We won't bother you, honey," she said to Tom. Then to the children, "We won't bother daddy, will we?" The children, smiling, looked at him. "Daddy doesn't feel too good today."

"Thanks, Gin. I'll make it up to you. Promise.

"Sure," she said smiling, getting up from the table.

Tom sat on the couch in the living room where he could read in the light from the picture window that looked out over South Channel. An up-bound freighter glided past the window. The days were getting longer now in June, it was light well past eight o'clock.

Tom read about Samuelson's reading a Hemingway short story about smuggling Chinamen to Key West from Cuba, that was later used as part of the novel, "To Have And Have Not" and "'wanted to learn to write like that.'"

Samuelson, a journalism studen at the University of Minnesota, decided in April,1934, to go down to Key West, and ask Hemingway to teach him how to write stories that raised strong emotions like the famous writer did.

On the evening he arrived in Key West, Samuelson wrote in the book, he walked up the yard of the Hemingway house on Whitehead Street and knocked at the front door. When Samuelson told Hemingway what he wanted, the famous writer was dumbfounded, he stood there on the porch, just up from the dinner table, hesitating, but then said, "'Okay."

A few days later, Samuelson wrote in the book, Hemingway took delivery of his new thirty-eight foot boat, named the PILAR,and told his apprentice, the twenty-two year old Sam-uelson, he could sleep aboard as night watchman for a dollar a day.

Samuelson wrote in the book he had been sleeping in the city jail,after the Key West police found him sleeping on the dock one night. Hemingway did not know this until one day the author asked where Sameulson kept his stuff, and the apprentice told him the city jail and the famous writer drove him there. This was just after Samuelson got the job on the boat. The police had been watching him.

Tom looked up from his reading. The City Jail down there in Key West had been his home for fifteen days when he was on his way to visit Hemingway over in Cuba. Tom remembered he had no money either. He had been arrested in the "sweep" Key West police make after the bars close. Tom remembered a shrimp fisherman told him in jail that the usual sentence when caught in a sweep is thirty days. Tom had told the judge he, was a student of literature and was on the way to see Hemingway. The judge must have cut the sentence in half out of courtesy, Tom thought.

According to Samuelson's book, Hemingway would give writing lessons, only when not fishing, and would read the the stories Samuelson wrote, then made corrections and then made comments.

Tom looked up from reading about the help Hemingway gave Samuelson with his writing and shook his head.

"Unbelievable, Tom said out loud. "This guy is the luckiest guy in literature. This Samuelson was handed everything a young writer, any writer, could only dream about.

Samuelson said in the book he stayed with Hemingway's boat, most of the time in Havana marlin fishing, and in October, 1934, when the fishing season was over, returned to Key West with the famous writer on the Pilar. It was then Samuelson decided it was time to go home. He had written and sold four fishing articles to magazines, accompanied by numerous photographs.

The day Samuelson was leaving, Hemingway sitting at his writing desk, said to his apprentice, "Now don't get discouraged, just keep writing, and write good stuff... it won't sell, maybe, but if it's good, it will eventually. It might be two years before you sell, but keep writing."

Samuelson said in the book, Hemingway and Pauline were standing next to a palm tree, waving, after he said good-bye and walked across the yard of the Key West house and out the iron gate and closed it.

During the course of the writing lessons, Samuelson says in the book, he continuesly asked Hemingway, '"Do I have talent?'" or "'Will I be a writer?'" and even said "'I just have to be a writer. Will I be a writer'"?

Tom smiled when he read Samuelson asking questions like that. How could anyone know the answer.

Hemingway, who had been generous and fatherly to Samuelson, had to be evasive with the answer, and said, "'If have it, it will eventually show if you keep writing.'"

Tom reached up from the couch and turned on the light. The sun had set and the remaining light reflected on the channel water in long streaks. He could hear his wife with the kids in the kitchen.

"All Samuelson got from that year on the PILAR with Hemingway," Tom said in a low voice,"was, in reality, a non-answer. For allhis luck in getting close, he got no answer."

All this showed up in this book Samuelson wrote, but was not published, until his daughter found the manuscript, edited it, and had it published in 1981 shortly after her father's death.

Tom set the book down on the couch and sat with his hands behind his head.

"In nineteen-thirty-four another Hemingway apprentice was born in Detroit," he said smiling, "Me," Looking up at the ceiling, he said slowly, "And twenty years later, I headed down the Florida Keys to visit Hemingway only I wasn't as lucky as Samuelson."

Virginia came to the living room doorway.

"How you doing in here?" she asked drying her hands in a towell. "You okay, Tom?"

"Yeah,"he said, dropping his arms and sitting forward. "There's something about the job at the News you should know about. The paper did away with the Suburban Bureau and about a dozen of us were let go."

"Yes Tom, I ran into Carol Teppert at the farmer's market last week. She said Alan was mad about being let go. He's talking to lawyers about suing the News."

"He covered the downriver beat," Tom said nodding. "He can probably get a job on one of the local newspapers down that way if he wants to. You know Alan, though. Vain."

"I thought the problem with the News had gotten to you too Tom ... you came home down in the dumps."

"Naw," he said shaking his head. "It was this damn book I found at King's. It knocked the wind out of me."

"Honey," she said smiling, "I thought you were worried we would have to live on fish and beans, or something ... "

He smiled at her smiling.

"Do you need help with the kids, babe?"

"No—no, we're making fudge."

"Let me sit and brood a little longer, babe,"

"Suit yourself, honey. You know where we are." She thought a second. " And I know where you are. Right up in your writer-mind. Alone."

He nodded, then shrugged.

"Bingo," she said and turned back to the kitchen. Tom picked up the Samuelson book, swung his feet up on the arm of the leather couch, laid his head on the opposite arm, and looked up at the blank ceiling.

That fall in 1954, Tom remembered how he wanted to go to Key West and meet Hemingway, the most famous living writer in the world. Tom had read most of the prominent authors by age fifteen, he remembered being called a"book-worm." But when he read "For Whom The Bells Toll," something snapped, and the other authors began to fade away. The impact of Hemingway's style made Tom feel he was right there at the location of the story, feeling what the writer felt.

Then Tom remembered reading "The First Forty-Nine Stories," and he was never the same. To write like Hemingway, wow! He could taste the canned apricots in the tent of "The Big Two-Hearted River." And the story written about Spain, "Hills Like White Elephants", here Tom could feel the heat of the white-hot sun and the curtin of beads in the doorway.

As if that was not enough, Tom remembered "The Snows Of Kilamanjaro was a short story beyond belief. "Snows," besides the African descriptions, was packed with other stories, so much so, it resembled a giant airplane with cargo packed under it's wings, so heavy, you wondered if it ever could fly. Hemingway took the short-story form to it's extreme with"Snows;" it was jammed with information.

The short story, "The Killers" was different in that it put you on edge, and the tension climbed from there as dialogue made you want to yell out, it was so devastatingly controlled. In some places, the dialogue was only a word or two. But each word carried a ton of meaning. Uncanny.

Tom, still laying on the couch, said quietly, "No one had ever written stories the way Hemingway did. He was in a class by himself. His style was devastating. And it seemed simple, the words ordinary, yet they came like bombs. A lot of writers tried imitating Hemingway's story writing style, but they failed; othe writers caught the rhythm of the words, and their pattern, but they rang hollow. There was no magic that could grab you, pull you into the story."

Virginia's voice called from the kitchen, "To-om. Want to sample the fudge?"

"In a few minutes," he said without opening his eyes. "I need a little more time. I'm almost done."

"Okay, honey, we'll be here."

Tom first read about "Meastro'" in a collection of Esquire magazine short "letters" Hemingway wrote. The editor,who was a friend in the 1930 depression era, launched the new magazine, and asked Hemingway for help. The sarcastic reference to Samuelson's violin playing, earned him the "Meastro" tag, and because of his ineptness aboard the Pilar during the heated-action of landing marlin, the nick name was reduced further to "'Mice.'" Both these names referred to Samuelson, Tom had found out later.

Then, in 1972,a book called "Jake and Hemingway" appeared, and Tom read in one chapter about Hemingway teaching a young apprentice aboard the Pilar. Jake was a friend of Hemingway's younger brother, Leicester, both of whom were visiting the famous writer, arid both spent time marlin fishing, before setting sail further south on the younger brother's sailboat.

The young apprentice was Samuelson, and Jake eavesdropped on one of the writing lessons aboard the boat off Havana. Hemingway was reading a story Samuelson wrote.

" 'But how do you know what's good stuff?' " Samuelson asked after Hemingway repremanded him for too much verbage.

That made Hemingway roar, Jake said and concluded the young apprentice's writing lessons were soon coming to an end.

Samuelson, on the other hand, said in his 1982 book that Hemingway was kindly and fatherly in his advice during the lessons.

Tom thought a moment; you have to believe them both.

Remembering back to 1954 when he was in Key West trying to save-up the thirty-six dollars for the fare to ride the railroad ferry over to Havana, then thought if he got to the Finca Vigia home of Hemingway, he wondered now, what the reaction of the famous writer would have been with. The lessons with Samuelson must have soured Hemingway about all future writers seeking advice. Particularly those who showed up at the front door.

Maybe the dogs would have chased Tom off the Finca property if he had ever gotten that far. The "Bee-Lips" - Georgie Brooks introduction, probably would not have helped much because Hemingway did not think too highly of the Key West lawyer. All you have to do is read the book "Have Not"and the few lines about Georgie.

Tom thought for a moment, if things turned ugly over there in Havana at the Hemingway house, he might even see the inside of a Cuban jail. But dogs and jail were just gloomy speculation.

The Nobel Prize was awarded in November,1954 to Hemingway for his book, "The Old Man And The Sea," and Tom saw the crowd of well-wishers in newspaper photos, and once on the tv news. That was the end of any chance of talking to Hemingway, for a while any way, until things quieted down at the Finca.

Tom remembered he had just turned twenty that September, and now was facing being drafted because he dropped out of the university. He had read a mountain of books and had been writing stories four years, when he hit on the idea to go talk with Hemingway in Key West. He was not sure about what to ask the famous writer, except to tell him his stories were great and he wanted to write like he did.

Tom drove from Detroit to Miami in a Cadillac,he remembered, the transit company paying for the gas to deliver the car to a Miami Cadillac dealership. But Tom paid the twelve dollars to ride the Greyhound to Key West from Miami.

Grinning, Tom remembered the bus stop at Tavernier Key where he first had Key Lime pie. He was drinking coffee at the lunch counter when he saw slices of the pie on the shelf across from him. It looked the same as key lemon pie, but it was dark green. The sign, printed on a piece of cardboard read: Key Lime Pie 25 ¢ . He like lemon pie, but he was leery of that dark green, and what it tasted like,

"Key limes is real sour," the woman cook said. "They about the size of a quarter. They grow on runty trees down here."

"O-kay," Tom remembered saying. "I'll try a slice." He had two pieces of the biting-citrus pie, he recalled.

When Samuelson rode the freight train down the Keys and was found sleeping on the docks, he had to sleep each night in jail, the door unlocked, because he had no money and the cops wanted to know where he was. The book says that.

Tom had a few dollars when he first landed on the island, and stayed a few nights, he remembered at the Atkinson House, or some name like that. It was a fancy wood house painted all white. Later, Tom found a cheaper place on Eaton Street.

Tom remembered finding out the house on Whitehead Street was owned by Hemingway's second divorced wife, Pauline. The writer lived with wife number four in Havana at the Finca Vigia not here in Key West. To get over to Havana you had to ride the P&C rail ferry and that cost thirty-six bucks. That was a lot of money to earn in job scarce Key west.

After a week of asking around town for work, Tom remembered the Canadian guy from Miami, who gave him a job on his four-man Cuban tile-setting crew. One of the part-time crew, Mark, was an auxillary policeman, who later arrested Tom in a after bar hours sweep by city police. The crew set Cuban tiles in restaurants, swimming pools, patios, bathrooms, porches, and even steps. Tomes job was to mix the heavy sand and cement with a hoe in a flat tin box the shape of a small barge,and unload the boxes of tile and put it in tubs of water to soak. It was heavy work, Tom remembered, and no body gave him a helping hand.

Tom smiled when he thought about the cemetery incident and tile job. An old man was caught having sex with a dead body of a woman he took from the cemetery directly across the street from the tile company front door. The picture of the grave in the newspaper was the exact same as the one across the street. If Tom came to work early, and the door was locked, he would stand looking at the grave.

The graveyards on the island, all had the bodies "buried" above ground, the newspaper story said, because the ground was marl, dead coral, and absorbed water quickly when the sea level rose, The caskets were all placed in a cement vault that rested on the top of the "ground."

The old man, Tom remembered reading,was declared feebleminded. A jury of his relatives exonerated him of a crime.

But the story made a big splash in the tabeloids after it was disclosed the old guy was involved in the sexual exploit for more than ten years.

The tile-setting work turned out spotty, Tom remembered, because the Canadian boss, who married the Amencan woman up in Miami, had to do errands for the wife; take her to the doctor or dentist, things like that. When the boss was a no show on a Monday, four guys down in Key West lost a day's pay. Sometimes it was two days, and Tom remembered he could not pay the rent sometimes and still have money to live on.

The plan to buy the thirty-six dollar ticket on the car ferry was fading, Tom remembered. Hemingway was on hold.

Then the Miami woman's spoiled twenty-one year old son crashed his Piper Cub and was killed. The Canadian tacked a note on the tile company door after a drinking spree; He would not be around for six weeks, due to a funeral. Tom remembered it felt like <u>his</u> funeral too, regarding going to Cuba and see Hemingway. When he walked down to the ferry dock and watch the workers unpacking new typewriters, sewing machines, refrigerators and even air conditioners, then putting a scratch on the new appliances with a screwdriver and. putting them back in the boxes. The scratch qualified the appliances as used goods and not subject to Cuban import tax. Tom asked to work his passage over to Cuba, him but the rail employees told he remembered, that half of Key West would go over if they started that. You had to pay, that is business, and the only way to stay in business.

Tom thought of that Samuelson guy who caged a steady "job" as night watchman on Hemingway's boat: how lucky he was Tom felt at the time. Samuelson did not have food and rent worries, got to go deep—sea fishing every day for a year, and to boot, got writing lessons from a master. Free.

"How lucky can you get?" Tom muttered still laying on the couch, one arm over his eyes, comparing the Samuelson trip with his own. "That guy got it all, and on a platter."

"Last call for fudge," wife called from the kitchen, "and I mean it. It's going fast."

"I'll skip the fudge, babe," Tom said. "I'm in the middle of reminiscing Key West. Comparing my trip to this book. I need a little more time ... Okay babe?"

"I'll save you a morsel, Tom. The fudge came out so good ... You can have it later. When you're done, honey."

"Thank you," Tom said, his arm still covering his eyes.

"Key West," he heard his wife say softly with contempt. "Key Pest is more like it. He's polite, but can't help you."

Tom sat up when he heard what Virginia said, and looking at the book laying on the couch next to him, nodded,

"She's right," he said quietly. "There was no help for Samuelson. Hemingway could only read Samuelson's stories and make suggestions." Tom stood up holding the book. "It would have been the same for me. Hemingway had no magic formula to give me. The magic was in the reading of the stories that was unique to Hemingway alone. There's no way of passing the unique - ness on.

Tom set the book on the desk near the doorway.

"Hey!" he shouted into the kitchen, "you guys save me some fudge?"

Later, the kids in bed, Tom and Virginia were cleaning up the kitchen.

"That book you bought today, honey ..."

"Not much to compare," Tom said.

"Was it ... pain ... ful? I mean, how did your hopes end?"

"No, my Canadian boss showed up late at my room one night, drunk. He said his wife cried all the time over her dead son, and he couldn't take it anymore. He flopped down on my bed, said he wished he never married her, and that she cried the whole past week. So he drove down the Keys, stopping for drinks. When he started snoring, I went out. No shoes even.

"What else could you do?"

"Yeah, I went out and ended up at the Rose Garden bar. The bartender kept telling me about the after hours police sweep and that I should go now. But I no place to go. When I left that night, I got arrested, with by one of the guys I worked with setting tiles. An auxiliary cop showing off."

"Everything seemed to be against you, Tom.

"Right. I decided when I was in jail it was time to head home. I decided to volunteer for the draft too, get that over with."

"Well, Tom, that was one way to get to Europe!" She grinned.

"That's the way I figured it. Kill two birds with one stone. Get rid of the military obligation and tour Europe at the same time," he said. "Ain't I smart?"

"That's why I married you," she said sliding her arms around his waist. "How tired are you?"

"Not that tired babe."

"Let's go to bed, Tom," she said taking his hand. "I have something I have to ask you."

What? Ask me now, Gin?" he said following her.

"Mother ... is coming back to stay. She thinks our girls should live in her big house, make friends in Birmingham, go to a good school. I agree, Tom," she stopped walking and looked at his face. "Honey, I would have to go to and be with them. What do you think, Tom?"

After a pause, he said looking at her face, "Well, it would give me a chance see Spain ... Madrid, Valencia, and maybe even the Balearic islands."

THE END

Saint Clair Shores, Michigan

31 July, 2007

About the Author

When Donald Sinclair wrote a news story for his college newspaper regarding a campus fire, the dialogue of a hippy telling the event merited an honorable mention by the college press association "for colorful use of the language (dialogue)." Fiction writing was looming in the background.

After graduation in 1963 with a degree in journalism, and working for a newspaper in Fort Lauderdale, covering the crime beat, he began a series called, "The Gold Coast Unsolved Murders," for the Sunday edition. It outlined the murder investigations that went cold, using all the news reports covering the events over time. It was a popular read and even the police stored the clippings in their file.

Day to day journalism began to fade and Sinclair began writing short stories, then a novel. When the book was submitted to a major publishing house, a reply came from the Editor-In-Chief, "This book is closer to literature than those of the commercial market." It took five months for the reply.

Sinclair wrote genre novels, but could not penetrate the saturated market in the 1970s and 80s.

Travel while a working newsman took Sinclair throughout the United States, to Canada and Mexico, and extended to a trip to Europe where he had been in 1955 while serving two years in the army.

In 1997, Sinclair began re-writing the novel that "was closer to literature," while recovering from an illness at home with his family in Michigan overlooking Lake St. Clair.

Reading the definitive Hemingway biography by Carlos Baker, Sinclair discovered youong writers were constantly showing up on the famous writer's doorstep in Key West and Havana. This re-enforced Sinclair's idea-theme regarding the effect Hemingway's writing and celebrity had on readers.

Then a BBC documentary on television in 1999 with Michael Palin, who explored the Hemingway trail and lifetime, gave Sinclair the jolt to submit the novel again to a publisher. This time the book was sent to the new media of "electronic publishing" on-line for those who find literary subject matter interesting reading.